AMERICAN
AFTERLIFE

AMERICAN AFTERLIFE

A NOVEL

PEDRO HOFFMEISTER

CROOKED
LANE

NEW YORK

Copyright © 2022 by Peter Brown Hoffmeister

All rights reserved.

Published in the United States by Crooked Lane Books, an imprint of The Quick Brown Fox & Company LLC.

Crooked Lane Books and its logo are trademarks of The Quick Brown Fox & Company LLC.

Library of Congress Catalog-in-Publication data available upon request.

ISBN (hardcover): 978-1-63910-134-4
ISBN (ebook): 978-1-63910-135-1

Cover design by Nicole Lecht

Printed in the United States.

www.crookedlanebooks.com

Crooked Lane Books
34 West 27th St., 10th Floor
New York, NY 10001

First Edition: December 2022

10 9 8 7 6 5 4 3 2 1

To Rue,
a dragon claramente,
como Cielo

CHAPTER

1

MY ISLAND

Two days after, and I can already smell the bodies decomposing in the houses. I stand on the sidewalk outside, wondering if it's the meat of them—not the bones, but the soft tissues—and the gases building, the scents of rancid fats coming through skin. No flesh wrapped in plastic. No flesh refrigerated.

I close my eyes and tell my mind to go somewhere else.

But this is where I am. Stuck.

The houses in the neighborhood are pulled sideways off their foundations, all of their upper stories caved, and some of their lower stories too, trees through roof gaps, houses like boats broken against rocks.

I've spent the last twenty-four hours searching through the wreckage on the upper half of the block. All of the other survivors are gone now, people evacuated yesterday morning, moved out while I hid. I waited for them to leave, and now my hill is an island, the floodwater from the broken dams reaching the bottom of the block at Nine-teenth Street. All of lower Moss Street is underwater, the houses mostly covered, but a few of the taller roofs above the waterline still, the dark archipelago spaced along the straight lines of city planning.

I stay up here on the hill, move though houses, take items back to my garage where I live: bottled water, food, matches . . .

*   *   *

I organize at night by the light of three or four tea candles. If my mother comes back, I'll be here, ready—I'll be all stocked up. And she will come back, I'm sure of that. She wasn't worried about me before, but after this, after the earthquake, she has to be.

*   *   *

I do a pull-up before bed. Rest, then another pull-up. And a third. Get down on the floor for sets of ten push-ups and twenty sit-ups. I have to stay strong because only strong girls survive.

My tío taught me that the Gila monster, *Heloderma* en Sonora, doesn't have venom fangs. But it bites down and won't let go. The poison is pumped along the base of its teeth, the lizard chewing the venom into its victim. Slowly. Never releasing its jaws.

I am not always a good person.

I try to fall asleep, but instead I stare . . . into the darkness.

2

PLUTO

WHEN THE DAWN comes, and the sky begins to lighten, I fall asleep for a few hours, then wake suddenly, sweaty, the day already warm. I drink an entire bottle of water and toss the empty. Slide my shoes on. Leave the garage and cross the street, looking left, then right—still in the habit of looking for cars—and I do pass one car, but it's upside down, its passenger door hanging open; then another car on the grass, this one right-side up, its front end angled across the sidewalk as if driven home by a drunk.

At 1981 Moss Street, there's a refrigerator still closed. I open it and see whole milk, not cold but cool, still smelling like milk when I lift the cap, the outside of the gallon sweating against my hands. I pour a tall, creamy glass and gulp it down. Pour another. Never know when I'm going to have milk again. It could be a while.

I find a sealed stick of summer sausage in the cupboard, cut slices, the warm fatty meat bending and breaking apart on my knife. There's a box of crackers on the floor behind the table, and I pick them up. Stack them with slices of sausage. Eat quickly because it's still strange to be in my neighbors' kitchens, to be eating my neighbors' food. It seems like they'll come back at any moment, and I listen for them, even though I know they won't.

I wonder if I'll get used to all of this. Or how long that might take.

I put the milk carton back in the fridge and tell myself that the milk might last another day, but it's the middle of July, near a hundred degrees each afternoon, and now that the fridge has been opened, I know the milk won't stay cold anymore, not unless I think of something. So I rummage in the freezer and find juice-concentrate cans, not hard-frozen but slushy. I line six of them around the milk carton, take a Sharpie from the counter and write "MILK—1981 Moss" on the back of my left hand to remind myself to return.

I fill my backpack with water bottles and cans of refried beans, take them across the street to my garage and stack them with the food I've found so far. Then I head out into the neighborhood to scavenge some more until late evening.

When it gets dark, I stand in the middle of the street and look at the sky, the one thing that's unchanged, the steady chemistry of stars and planets, see Venus ready to set. Jupiter in opposition. No star-blink but a steady, straight, bright light, the reflected light of the sun. I imagine looking at our earth from the surface of Venus, wonder if the blazing light on this planet—our own—would appear larger than what I see now, if I would be able to tell the difference in size.

Three years ago, I stole a solar system book from the school library, stripped the magnet from its spine and walked out, memorized the facts of each planet, stared at NASA's New Horizon pictures of Pluto and its Charon sister moon, made a promise to Pluto: as long as I lived, I'd count it as a full planet. I wouldn't let people abandon it, people who didn't consider the object good enough. People who didn't understand its true value.

CHAPTER

3

THE FIRST

I CROSS THE STREET and work up the opposite block, search the odd-numbered houses on the top half. There isn't much until I get to 1999, where there's a noise as I come through the door, a movement in the living room. I duck low, hide behind a wall-bolted shoe rack, wait for whatever it is.

I don't hear anything else. I wait and listen, creep forward—into the living room—the chaos of toppled furniture.

Then I hear the noise again and stop.

Peek around a couch. See something on the floor on the far side of the room. I move closer, step over a chair, see someone lying on his back. He's gray haired, wearing a dark-colored suit, and I recognize my neighbor, Mr. Francois, a retired French professor at the University. Everyone in the neighborhood used to talk about him because he always wore a full three-piece black suit, in any weather—even summer—and he didn't like any of his neighbors—or children or dogs. He'd sit on his porch and glare at everything. Just his angry eyes.

But Mr. Francois isn't dead yet. He's flat on the floor, on his back in the living room, opening his mouth and closing it. Silently. Opening his mouth and closing it, like a fish pulled up on a rock by a bird.

Mr. Francois's eyes don't seem to be working, or whatever connects those eyes to the rest of him, because he can't see me even though I'm standing directly above him. His vision doesn't track my movements, his eyes don't shift or blink. I wave my hand in front of his face, and his expression doesn't change.

I don't wanna get stuck helping him. I don't have the energy for that. I don't have the skills.

But when I start to step away, he hears me, hears the sound of my foot creaking a floorboard, and he turns his head, says, *"Aidez-moi?"*

I stop.

There's a dresser on top of his legs, a dresser of dark hardwood, heavy built, and the blood is coming out from underneath the bulk of that furniture. The pool of blood to the side of Mr. Francois makes a map of South America. That's what I think of—strange as it is—the thick liquid in the shape of a continent, and I know this is also weird, but I think, *Shouldn't it be in the shape of France?*

Honestly, though, I don't know what France is shaped like. I look back at the blood and close my eyes, shake my head.

The continent of blood is already turning a darker color, drying on top, and I look at where my shoes are—close to the borders—and I step back. I don't want to step in it.

I also want to leave this house. I know it's not right to leave Mr. Francois where he is, but I'm not ready to *watch* as anyone dies. The problem is, he already knows I'm here. He isn't moving or breathing loudly, but he says, *"Aidez-moi"* once again, and I know I can't just walk away.

The earthquake made the floor tilt permanently, so I step to the uphill side of the dresser, away from the pool of blood. I bend down with two hands and make an attempt to lift the dresser. It's too heavy for a half effort, though, and I realize that I'm gonna have to squat down and really try to move it with all of my strength if I want to lift it.

So I try again, and this time I get low and set my hands as solidly as I can. I take a couple of breaths, strain and lift, get one end of the dresser up in the air, a few inches Mr. Francois's legs, and I hold it there—the dresser hanging above him—and I say, "Pull your legs out! Get your legs out now!"

But he doesn't move.

I stay there, straining, holding half of the heavy dresser up in the air, shaking from the weight, breathing hard, but Mr. Francois doesn't react. He has a look on his face like a person who's staring at puffy clouds in a bright sky.

I'm a strong girl, but I don't weigh much, I'm not very big, and I know I can't hold this piece of furniture for long, so I say, "Go now! Move!"

I'm shaking, straining under the weight of the hardwood dresser, trying to focus on my grip and my breathing, trying not to let it drop now that I have it lifted.

Then I notice blood—the new blood—flowing out over the top of the old, and I realize that lifting the dresser has opened something in Mr. Francois and the continent of South America swells at its top. Peninsulas jut in two different directions, on both sides, and Mr. Francois shakes a little, shivers as if he's cold, then his head tilts and he stops moving.

I look at his face and see that it's over. He was never going to pull his legs out.

I try to set the dresser down gently, but it's too heavy and I'm too tired. I drop it the last few inches and Mr. Francois's body jolts with the impact. But he doesn't say anything—doesn't make a noise—and his eyes don't change.

I step back. Stare at him. Wait a minute. His chest doesn't rise or fall, and his eyes don't blink. I'm not going to check his pulse because there's no point.

I leave the house, walk out the front door, and stand on the porch. Take a few deep breaths.

It's a hot day and the cicadas are buzzing in the trees. I've always loved the sound of them, the way they would drone above me as I biked down the hill toward the river. But the river isn't a half mile away anymore, and it has no current. The floodwater sits at the bottom of the block, backed up by the compromised dams and the wreckage below the city, and I'm stuck in this neighborhood, on this new island created by an earthquake.

I look back at the house, and Mr. Francois isn't an angry neighbor anymore. He isn't sitting on his porch in the evening in a three-piece suit, yelling about a dog that's peed on the trunk of his maple tree. Now he's a dead man in a ruined house, lying in a continent of his own blood, his open eyes like two pieces of scratched glass, and I watched him as he died.

HIDING PLACES

I SPEND THE NEXT afternoon searching people's hiding places, where my neighbors put things they didn't want discovered. I have a backpack and a duffel bag to carry items back to my garage. My goal this week is to prepare, to gather anything of value, to wait for my mother to return. Then—together—we'll find a way out of this neighborhood, out of this city, past the rubble and beyond the flood.

I search people's normal hiding places, find weed stashes at the backs of closet shelves. Two Rolex watches. Mini-baggies of coke. Snack-size Ziplocs housing acid gel tabs. Molly. Eight hundred and thirty-eight dollars in cash. I take all of that.

Find dildos and vibrators in bedside drawers. KY lubrication in a cigar box: Yours & Mine, Ultra Feel 2 in 1, Intense Pleasure. Pocket Rockets. I leave all of those where I find them.

I discover porn under mattresses: straight porn, gay porn, fetish porn. Something with horses that seems like porn but I'm not sure why. I leave all of that too.

A teenage girl's razorblade in a jar under a Justin Bieber poster. One drop of dried blood. Birth-control pills. A switchblade. I take the knife. Find two condoms—snug fit—in a pillowcase.

A flip-lock Gerber, mace spray connected to a rape whistle, and a rusty machete hidden inside a rubber boot. Those things all go into my big duffel bag.

I find naked Polaroids of a yellow-haired man with his penis in his hand. A blurry picture of two clothed people kissing. Red Solo cups and Ping-Pong balls in a Target bag rolled up in a down coat and stuffed under a bed. Twenty ounces of mixed hard liquor in a one-liter Dr. Pepper bottle wedged behind the back leg of a desk. I take a big gulp. Cough and set the bottle down. Keep searching as I buzz.

An unloaded .22-caliber pistol in a size thirteen shoe. No cartridges, but I take the gun anyway.

I find what might be heroin tar . . . I think? I'm not sure. I've never sold heroin tar but I've seen it on Netflix. I leave it.

A detailed sketch of a naked woman in her fifties or sixties, covering her breasts, an arrow pointing to her shaved vagina. A picture of a tribal tattoo. A picture of a butterfly on a young woman's lower back. Seventeen pictures of the same blond-haired grade-school girl posing in a two-piece bathing suit.

I leave those. Move on.

Find seventeen gold coins. Take them. Plus a short, sharp hatchet with an engraved handle. Throw that in my duffel bag as well. It's getting heavy.

A picture of eleven staples in the scalp of a man or woman (impossible to tell). I put the picture back in its hiking boot in the closet.

I find a metal baseball bat with a dent in the middle.

A note that reads: *That was fucked up. We can't ever do that again. Ever.*

Three bottles of Xanax, rubber-banded together. I swallow a pill. Sneak back to my garage.

But even on the Xanax, I can't relax. It feels like people are watching me. I know I can't truly be alone. I get up and check the window a few times. All of the glass is broken out, and I put my head through, stare out into the backyard next to the garage.

Wind rustles the bushes, but other than that I can't see any movements. There are no animals. I don't see any other people.

If only I could sleep when it's dark.

5

LOST TIME

I WAS SNEAKING AROUND the neighborhood again this morning—looking for food—but I got tired and started thinking about lying down. Now I don't remember where I stopped.

I wake to what seems like another earthquake, the ground shaking and everything rumbling around me. But the shaking ends quickly, doesn't last more than a few seconds, and I realize it's probably an aftershock like I've heard about in science classes. I lift my head. See green.

I'm under a maple tree that's leaning but still standing. Its branches reach out twenty feet on all sides. The sun has taken a turn around the trunk to hit my eyelids, and there's drool on my right hand. I'm sweaty. The day's warmed into the afternoon, and my mind is a slow-motion movie scene, each particle of daylight spangling the edges of the screen, a panorama of a neighborhood in midsummer swelter, the weeds beginning to overgrow, the angles of the houses not quite right.

I blink.

Look at the wheel on the nearby car, how it's bent to thirty degrees against the curb.

Blink again.

Look at that eight-foot root ball on the downed maple in front of the next house. The rest of the tree is lying out across the street, the tips of its branches on the far sidewalk.

I've lost some time. I don't remember which block I'm on, which yellow grass is beneath me as I lie on the ground. My mouth feels dry. I sit up and look around. See that I fell asleep on Villard Street, one block over from Moss, on the steep hill between Nineteenth and Fairmount.

I remember leaning back against the trunk of the tree, looking at the green above me, thinking that I'd just sit here for a moment and rest, keep searching houses after. I don't remember falling asleep. I never said, "I'll just close my eyes for five minutes and . . ."

I sit and blink, spit the sleep taste out of my mouth, rub my eyes with the heel of my hand. This is how it always is when I first wake up, from when I was little. I used to fall asleep under the palo verde behind our house and the chickens from Tío Pablo's yard would wake me, scratching next to my face.

*   *   *

I stand up because I have to go to the bathroom. I've been visiting different toilets, but none of them flush and I can't go back to any of them more than once, so I decide to dig a hole in the back corner of the yard near my garage, to build myself a latrine for future use, just like I saw men do in K-59 when I was little.

I make this my afternoon project, digging a deep, narrow hole, a trench between two rhododendron bushes. I have to chop some roots to get deep enough—but I use my new hatchet for that—and when I'm finished, I put a shovel, a bucket, and some toilet paper in a plastic bag next to the fence.

6

MY BOAT

I N THE EVENING, I walk down the block to the flood line, the water not green or blue—nothing like the normal river—but light brown and murky, covering debris, cream-colored bubbles at the edge of the water, and at one street corner, an armada of Styrofoam floating above a backed-up storm drain. Across the street, the half-buried carcass of a VW Beetle, the water up to its windows.

I remember a canoe I saw up on Fairmount, and walk up Moss Street again, around the corner and three houses east. I went into that house yesterday, but it was destroyed, the upper story crushed into the lower floor, and I couldn't get through the rubble to access any of the main house. Also, I was nervous that I might find someone fallen through. I'm nervous in every demolished house now because in one of the first houses I entered I found an arm hanging down, just a single arm, with no body connected.

*   *   *

In the space between the house and the shed, sitting there, right side up, is a metal canoe. Silver. It has three inches of water in the bottom from the heavy rains of last week, but when I roll it over and dump it out, it looks like it's in perfect condition, clean and shiny, not even dented or scratched from the quake.

There are no paddles or lifejackets next to it, and I know that at the very least I need a paddle. I try to open the shed's door, but like most closed doors in the neighborhood, it's too jammed to swing on its hinges. It's an old door though, wood that gives a little when I push it, so I kick it hard, crack the wood. Then I kick a few more times until the door splinters in the middle, splits, and I work a hole big enough to crawl through.

The shed is destroyed, the roof caved in, a beam pinning a lawnmower with its wheels snapped off. In the half-light, I see two wooden paddles sticking out from under a pile of tools. They're six or seven feet away, under a low-hanging pile of wreckage. I crawl forward, get my leg over a beam, duck down again and reach for the paddles.

That's when I feel something puncture my right leg, in the middle of my thigh. I wince and pull my leg back, see a three-inch nail, dark with rust. I rub my leg and blood fills the hole. The nail went into the muscle, not too deep, but deep enough to bleed. Strangely, the hole doesn't hurt too much—it really doesn't—not as much as it seems like it should.

I look at the paddles again. They're only a foot farther than I can reach, so I work my leg past the nail this time, careful, lean forward and reach one paddle, then the other. I pull both of them back—half paddles it turns out, both of them snapped off above their blades. I slide my leg back around the long nail, and crawl out of the opening, through the shed door, out into the open.

Back in the evening sunlight, I look at the two paddles where they're splintered mid-handle. I'll still be able to use them, but it'll be awkward. I'll have to lean over the side of the canoe, reach partway into the water. I toss the paddles into the boat.

Then I look at my thigh, where the nail punctured. The hole is dark. I press on it and a little blood burbles and drips down my leg. I wipe the blood with the hem of my shirt. Shake my head. Say out loud, "Better clean that, Cielo."

*   *   *

I pick up one end of the canoe and drag it out onto the front lawn, across the sidewalk, into the street. I rasp it along Fairmount to Moss Street, and down the hill. There's an asphalt strip in the middle of the road that covers the old trolley tracks from a hundred years ago. Dragging the canoe over that black strip makes a grating sound like a cement truck rumbling down a road. I stop and look around. I don't see anyone, but I still don't like making that much noise, so I head to the grass instead. I have to work the canoe around a few downed trees to get to the bottom of the block, but at least the dragging isn't too loud.

Once I'm at the waterline, I push the boat in and see that it's not very stable. It seems like it's going to flip over, the sides rocking wildly, so I hold it as steady as I can, wait for it to stop shifting, and climb in carefully.

I normally love water—I've always loved swimming in summer—but this water is different. The floodwater is dirty, an unnatural color, and it covers a drowned city. I look down the street to the deep water and think of all the sunken cars down there. All of the dead people in the collapsed houses beneath the waterline.

I'm spinning in a circle across the street. I reach out and paddle on the right side with the blade of my half paddle. It works all right and the canoe straightens out. I paddle past the VW, turn left, and now I'm heading down Moss Street into deeper water, allowing the canoe to slide along over the surface, the parked cars underneath me like a multicolored reef. The roofs of houses are archipelagos on my right and left, black dottings above the water.

This new world. I drift and think.

It's strange to be above it all—on this dotted sea—the silver hulk of the university's basketball arena down the street in front of me, the tops of the university dorms and apartments out to my left. Even the peaks of some of the houses are under the surface of the water at this end of the street, the canoe sliding forward and mostly in open space.

There's a white three-bedroom house at the bottom of the next block, at the corner, the only structure with a full story above the waterline, and I paddle toward its exposed hull—curious—the shipwreck of it.

I paddle toward an attic window because there's something there, a shape I can't quite make out, something that catches my eye, and I glide my canoe closer. Then I see it: a face in the window, what looks like an old woman pressing her nose and cheek against the glass, as if she leaned in right after the earthquake and got stuck.

I see her left eye bulging from the swelling—the gases and heat—that one eye the size of a baseball. Her face is a horror scene against the windowpane, fluid leaking from her open mouth, and that one giant eye, colored dark brown at the bottom. I have to paddle hard on the right side to avoid ramming the front of my canoe into the window, breaking the glass with the metal bow of the boat, and I turn just in time, clank against the wooden siding to the left of the window. I hold up my paddle so it makes contact with the house above, not the window, not to put the blade through the glass.

The old woman's face is right there now—two feet away—stretched to fifteen or sixteen inches long and lopsided, with that one incredible, bulbous eye.

I push off the house and turn around, paddle back up the street toward the edge of the floodwater. I try to blink and clear my mind. Breathe. I don't want to be out here on the water anymore. I know I won't find anything good, and I'm too exposed—too visible. My hands are shaking.

*   *   *

Last year in a history class in school, I read an article that said alligators waited under trees in the Mississippi delta right after Hurricane Katrina, that they could smell the human bodies rotting up in the branches, people thrown there by the winds, the bodies dead and decomposing, and those big alligators waiting for pieces of human meat to fall to the ground.

7

THE OTHERS

I STOW THE CANOE in a front garden two houses up the block, pull the full length of it behind a hedge, fold some branches over the top to hide the silver, and I'm about to walk back to my garage when I hear a sound, something I haven't heard in many days:

A motor.

I crouch. Look over the top of the hedge. At an angle through the trees, I can see the bottom of the block, and I lean forward to get a better view.

A boat appears, moving slowly, a big, flat, black boat. It's motoring along Nineteenth Street where I just crossed a few minutes ago. The boat glides through the tree gap in front of me, past the apple tree across the street, past the sunken VW Bug, and I see them: four men, all bearded, wearing the thick white robes of The Collection—like Romans or Greeks from the past—but carrying rifles in their hands. Two of them are tall, and two are short.

One of the shorter men turns my way, so I duck down. Stay low.

Their boat slides forward some more, and I look again. They're past me now, then they continue on and go out of sight, but the sound of their motor doesn't disappear for a couple of minutes.

These men are part of the group from up the hill—a group that calls itself The Collection of Redeemed Souls. They own a few houses throughout the city, but they have their headquarters in a white house with large grounds on Columbia Street, a half mile above me on the hill. That place has iron fences and gates, extensive lawns, private guards. I'd seen them walking the neighborhood in pairs—before the quake—and had read about their beliefs on my phone, what's known and what's rumored: Claims of animal sacrifice. Human trafficking. Mutilation of cult members.

The Collection's lawyers had denied all of these claims in court last year.

I try to remember which houses are theirs in the neighborhood, and what the quake might've done to them. I go through the possibilities in my head.

It's possible that their big, old, white house was destroyed. From what I've seen in my searches of the neighborhood, no big houses survived the four-minutes of up-and-down and side-to-side shaking. The ground around me moved fifteen feet, so only small rooms survived, small spaces, nothing with a tall ceiling, only places like my small garage, a few sheds, houses with studios, or single rooms in bigger houses.

But—then again—some houses on the hill stayed together better. Maybe the ground up there is more solid or something, because a few of those Fairmont Hill houses are still in pretty good shape.

All of this matters because I've been thinking about The Collection, wondering if they know where my mother is. She was obsessed with them. She got introduced to them at one of their meetings last year—invited by someone she'd met at a Safeway grocery store—someone who she said was undercover, not in the group's robes, and "very trustworthy." She described the man's kind eyes, his clean beard, his "Don't Tread on Me" yellow shirt. She told me how much he loved his country, how polite and well-spoken he was.

She came home and read the Bible on the floor for two hours afterward. She sat on the particleboard, slowly turning the pages, but she didn't read the Bible she normally read, not the Bible she'd brought with us from Mexico. Instead, she read a new Bible this man had given her, a Bible twice as thick as her old Bible, with sidenotes and new interpretations.

She kept saying, "Hay tantas cosas que no sabía."

When she left for work the next morning, I picked up that new Bible and looked inside. It was written by the leader of The Collection—someone named The Witness—and it was his own new translation from old texts. Also, The Witness's interpretive notes were in the margins, printed in red ink. His notes took half of each page, long explanations of each verse.

* * *

After that night, things got worse. My mother was transfixed. She went to more and more meetings. She had longer and longer sessions reading The Witness's Bible on the floor at night. She started speaking phrases that sounded like oracles in the old Greek myths that I was learning in my English class at school. Sometimes I would wake up at two or three in the morning, and she would still be reading the Bible, mumbling to herself, writing in a journal on the side.

She tried to tell me about all these new things she was learning—all of the verses she was memorizing, all of the textual interpretations that meant something important to her—but I was trying to survive the start of ninth grade. I was trying to finish my homework and look cute in front of boys or girls. I didn't want to hear about all of my mother's new revelations on what heaven would look like or what hell would smell like, or how the Bible promised that members of The Collection would be raptured pre-tribulation (The Overcomers), or how the streets of paved gold would shimmer in the cities of the new earth.

She filled up a journal.

Then a second.

And then a third.

I was living on *this* earth, and my reality took all of my focus. There was a pretty girl at school that I was talking to. I was studying for a literature test. I'd been selling stolen Ritalin. My math teacher wanted me to admit that Algebra II was important.

* * *

My mother read and reread that new Bible. She wrote her own notes in the margins. Copied phrases into her fourth journal. Then—one night, two months before the earthquake—she went to a nightly meeting and didn't come back. She wasn't home when I went to sleep. And she wasn't home when I woke up.

After school, she still wasn't home. I waited up for her that night, and the three nights after. Then I stopped expecting her to return.

8

SACRIFICE

I OPEN ONE OF her four journals. Read a page, her weird repetitions of what she was being taught at The Collection meetings:

> Things we give up when God does ask of us. "Blessings hidden," says Witness Andreas, "time will reveal."
>
> There is not a thing I would not do, uncomfortable as some are. I understand that this is the way. As Witness Andreas says, "Eternal salvation and the preservation of the everlasting soul. Individual to The Collective."
>
> I am open and I am learning.
>
> The video release last night on Revelation, The whore of Babylon, instructive to each person I feel. We lock ourselves in the room before the video. Witness Andreas walking up through the middle of us,

touching our ears as he is walking by, blessing our ears to be truly listening to the voice of God.

After the viewing, in a side room, Witness Andreas says to me, "We all must share, and your body can save us. Our bodies. We are greatly out-numbered in this land, but we may proliferate and become a great nation of God, even in these final times." Proliferate is the word I look up after.

He is unhooking the clasps of my robe. I have experienced this before, but never for the blessings of God or this gentle. I whisper, "Dios, guárdame. Me limpias siempre." Everything else I write down. I close my eyes. "Wash over me."

9

THE SMELLS WE HOPE FOR

S OMETIMES I THINK about killing people. I could have gone to a meeting with my mother, taped a razor blade to my wrist. Snuck a gun in my waistband.

* * *

My father was an American, a gringo from the United States. He came with a mission crew from San Diego, or so I was told. I've seen pictures of him, tall, in a Panama hat, button-up shirts, middle-aged even before he met my mother, who was sixteen when he invited her to ride in his yellow Cadillac Escalade to survey the locations and plans for local improvements. She told me how the air conditioning in the vehicle ran over her skin, how goose bumps rose on her legs, only to be settled by his hand on her thigh. His blue eyes when he canvased her body. His German last name—Wagner—how strange it sounded in anyone's mouth.

My father came to K-59 on a series of building projects—three years in a row, each spring—framing houses on cement pads, helping people to move out of sheet-metal and chicken-wire structures next to the dump, and relocating the families into simple, insulated boxes, no running water, but clean, dark spaces that could be kept cool even in the summer. He funded these building projects with his own money.

Before then, my mother had lived in an abandoned car missing its doors, cardboard over the openings. She and her brothers would sweat their way to sleep on the back seat of the vehicle at night.

There is a picture of my father standing next to a lettuce field, between K-56 and K-59, on the third year of his mission work—the spring before I was born, the last year he appeared—his hands on his hips, a strange look on his face. And I've stood at the same spot, seen an odd sight as well. I remember walking along that lettuce field one day when I was four or five years old—one of my earliest memories—not long before we left K-59. The field hands were gathered in a semicircle around something on the ground. I was always a curious girl, so I walked up to see what they were looking at, pushed through the circle.

It was a man on his back. His shoes had been stolen and his socks didn't match—one brown sock, one blue. His pants had holes in the knees and a red patch on his right thigh. His eyes were open, but he did not blink. A globe of blood was imprinted on his white T-shirt.

*   *   *

I go into 1981 Moss again, where I drank the milk a few days ago. I open the fridge, but the milk looks like yellow cottage cheese now. I put the gallon back on the shelf and close the door. In the gap behind the fridge, I see a rat chewing on something. It glances at me, but then keeps eating.

Already—next to my foot—there's a line of ants marching across the middle of the kitchen floor.

There's a tube of triple-antibiotic ointment in an open junk drawer. I take the cap off, squeeze a big glob of Neosporin onto my finger, and mash it into the nail hole on my thigh. The puncture has been bothering me the last few hours. It's sore. I fill the hole with ointment, then pocket the tube to use later.

I go back outside and walk past houses disassembled, broken-axled cars, gap-toothed sidewalks, small trees down across devil strips. Above the flood line, the water is fetid, not lapping or moving, just sitting still in the July heat. I'm two blocks from Moss Street, and that's when I smell an overpowering stink, a smell so strong that I stop. I look around. Try to figure out where that smell is coming from. But I can't see it.

I look for a body, for someone half-crushed, a person who's crawled out of wreckage onto the grass or a driveway. This is the smell of infection turned septic. Of wet rot. Of carcass.

I turn in a circle, look up between two houses. See a yellow strip of dandelion heads, a cement walkway that leads to a backyard, the fence gate spilled open and the posts off-angled. I walk back there. Look around. Still smell that overwhelming smell, but I can't see anything. I don't know where it's coming from.

I turn again. Go out to the front yard. Look down toward the flood.

But there's nothing.

Just the smell of death in the air. That's all. No source that I can see.

I return to my garage and wonder if I'm being foolish staying here, if I should've left this neighborhood with the rescuers who came through the day after the quake with their bright red litters, loading injured people, or walking with those who were healthy enough to move on their own.

I wonder now if anyone would've really cared that I didn't have papers or personal identification, if they would've cared that I didn't have a birth certificate or a driver's license. I wonder if that would've mattered in all of this mess, and I think—now—maybe not. I also wonder if my mother went with them, if she left with the rescuers, so I'm here for no reason at all.

On that first day, I assumed she would stay. I assumed she would be coming back for me, that she would show up at my garage someday soon after the earthquake, that I'd wake up and she'd be there, injured maybe, but there with me, at my garage, planning for us to leave together.

*   *   *

I try to count the days since the quake . . .

Count on my fingers. Focus on the task and attempt to put it straight. I know there's a right and wrong answer, a true number, and I realize that I should've scratched marks on the wall to keep a record, one tick for each sunrise or sunset. But I didn't. I've already lost track of time and I'm not sure if this is the fifth or the sixth day after. I decide on five days—five days since the earthquake—and I tick five slashes on the wall, hoping that I'm right. It would be nice to keep track.

After that, I read for the first time since the quake. I pick up one of my favorite books—a dark book set in the South—a mystery thriller where two little girls disappear and are murdered, and everyone thinks they know the man who did it, but they can never prove it. I know it sounds crazy, but I've always loved reading stories where people have worse lives than mine, existences more painful than mine. There's something about reading a book that's more horrifying than anything I've ever experienced, going deep into those unsettling stories and letting my mind work through everything a person can experience.

I read the scary book for an hour, and it helps me relax. I get tired, so I close my eyes. Take a nap on the floor, hear the front door creaking in the wind in my sleep, my mind scuttling across the torn ground, the sound of a metal gutter rasping against a downed tree . . . the sound of green branches rubbing against a glass window pane . . . metal scraping . . . the sounds of jaws closing . . . venom sacks releasing . . .

CHAPTER

10

THE WOMAN

I WAKE UP. SIT and rub my eyes. Eat from a packet of beef jerky and finish a bottle of water. Go outside and look at the sky. It's a bright, clear day—no clouds—the sun a disk of hard metal.

I walk down the block again, try to picture what this neighborhood will look like in the fall—when the rains come—or in the winter after that, under a thin layer of snow. I try to figure out how many towns and cities look like this city here, how many places on the West Coast were affected by this earthquake, how far the destruction reached up and down the Northwest Coast.

I'm walking slowly, listening, and before I get to the bottom of the block, I hear something, duck down, hide beneath a holly tree, its lowest leaves pricking my skin.

In the shallow floodwater, a woman in one of The Collection's robes pushes a raft with a long pole. She's going the opposite direction of the men I saw before, and her raft is nothing like their flatboat. Her raft is made of shipping pallets laid over long wooden planks on top of inflated black inner tubes. No motor.

The raft looks solid though, at least ten feet long, nailed or screwed together—something keeping it tight—but it's not pretty. It's a jumble. There's a wooden chest on one corner of the raft, the weight of it pushing that corner down all the way to the waterline. In the other corner of the raft is a metal cage holding three bright-colored birds. Parrots? Parakeets? I don't know most birds. But next to their cage, two housecats, a tabby and a calico, sit on their haunches, flicking their tails, watching the birds inside the cage.

The woman is tall and strong, her matted hair hanging down around her shoulders. The sound I heard before was her talking to herself, telling a story or a long joke, then laughing out loud. Her robe is dirty—not clean like the other Collection members'—and darkly stained in places, more light brown than white, looking like something she hasn't taken off in days.

The woman has gallon jugs of water, plus growlers full of what looks like beer. She keeps talking to herself—pushing the raft along with her pole—and laughing. She reaches down, picks up a growler, uncaps it, and takes a long drink. The beer spills down her chin onto her robe. Stains it even more. She puts the cap back on and sets it next to the parakeet cage.

The water she's crossing is shallow enough that she's choked up on her pole, most of the stick going way over her head. She moves toward Agate Street—where it meets Nineteenth—the businesses and restaurants on the corners.

I follow her. I can't follow directly because I don't want her to see me and because she's in the water—but I sneak, run through yards, make my way west along Nineteenth Street to Columbia. That's where the water reaches higher on the street, the crossroad submerged at the bottom, and I pause at a large tree, waiting up by the house and watching the woman on the raft as she pushes along Nineteenth in front of me.

The tops of the yards across Columbia are just above the waterline, and I'm curious enough to go over. So I wade the shallows, move to the far side, walk up on the grass, slipping a little in my wet shoes as I get to the top of a yard.

The woman on the raft is way out in front of me now, poling herself to the next block at Agate. When I look at her, she's stopped under the streetlight that no longer works—staring—as if she's waiting for the light to turn green before she continues on. I sneak from porch to porch on the high side of the street. After the last house, there's a neighborhood Italian restaurant. I crawl up on the restaurant's front deck, behind the low wall surrounding the outdoor dining area, slithering past the tables and chairs to the corner. Bring my head up slowly and peek once again.

Sun Automotive is the next building over. The woman is poling her raft toward the front of the auto garage. I watch her push the raft right up to the bay windows, bang the corner of her raft against the aluminum garage door, then look in past the shattered glass. I don't know what she's looking for in the auto shop, but she stares for a long time, easing her raft from window to window, putting her head through each shattered window. Then she turns the raft, spins it around, and poles it across Agate Street to Tom's Market.

The water is a little deeper there. The woman ducks her head to look inside the store, and I don't know what she sees. I wonder if looters came in before the water rose, or after, but it's impossible to know that too. Everyone had twenty minutes before the dams broke and the floods came. It was chaos.

The woman climbs down into Tom's Market and disappears for a few minutes.

I wait, watching the store.

When she comes back, her robe is soaked to her chest and she's holding a large white bottle of something. The bottle has a bright red cap. There's a smaller thing in her other hand, but I can't tell what it is. The woman sets the big white bottle down, and the smaller thing next to it on the edge of the raft, then scrambles up, gets to her knees and stands, takes up her pole again, and pushes away from the market.

The cats flick their tails near the parakeets' cage. The raft moves across the street.

The woman poles to the roof of Prince Puckler's Ice Cream Shop, a flat roof, ties her bowline to a split in the gutter. There's a huge metal trash can—at least five feet tall and four feet wide—floating next to the roof, next to the raft, attached to the building by a chain. The woman unhooks the can from the chain, tilts and dumps all of the trash into the water next to her, kicks at a milk carton that lands on the edge of her raft, then slides the empty trash can up onto the roof where it rolls a few feet away. She tosses the white bottle and the smaller item up onto the roof as well, then goes to the other corner of the raft, where there's a heavy-looking chest.

She opens the lid, bends down, wrangles and struggles with whatever it is for a moment, then lifts it, and I see a face—a man with a beard, his face first, then his body. The woman has her arms underneath this man's armpits. She pulls him up, dragging him out of the chest. He's naked and stark white, too white. She hefts him to the edge of the ice cream parlor's roof, struggles and gets his upper body past the gutter, then lifts and shoves the rest of him onto the surface. His body is stiff.

His head folds back, unnaturally, the only explanation being that his neck had to be broken already. It is too loose. I crawl to the other corner of the deck to see better and—from there—it looks like the man's throat is open, maybe cut or torn, but there's no blood anymore. Whatever blood there might have been is gone now. His body was either cleaned or it sat in water at some point.

The woman reaches down into the chest again and pulls out a few blocks of wood, chunks of splintered two-by-fours. She tosses those up onto the roof next to the trash can, six or seven pieces. Then she climbs up onto the roof, tilts the can to upright, and puts all of the wood blocks inside. She reaches down, takes ahold of the man's two wrists, and drags his body to the middle of the roof. After that, she goes back for the huge metal trash can. Drags it over. Then she retrieves the white bottle with the red cap, and the small item, walks back to the middle of the roof.

It's difficult for her to get the man into the garbage can. She tries to lift him and put him over the lip of the can, but she knocks it over and it rolls a few feet away. One of the blocks of wood falls out. She tosses the wood back in, pulls the can back next to the body, and tries again. It still doesn't work. The man's body is too stiff. The can wobbles and tilts, almost goes over a second time. She sets the man down. Then she lays the open can on its side next to the body, kicks at his legs, breaking and folding him. She slowly works him into the trash can. Not all of him fits. One leg sticks out. But she reaches down, gets leverage, and slowly tilts the can back to upright.

I stare at the one foot sticking up in the air. A white foot. A thick calf.

The woman picks up the bottle, pops the red cap, flips it upside down, and squeezes a stream down into the can. Then I realize what it is: lighter fluid.

The woman stops, looks at the bottle, picks at the lid for a minute, then sets the bottle down, reaches under her robe, and pulls out a sheath knife. She picks up the white bottle again and punctures it in the middle. She twists the knife to open the hole, then flips the bottle and empties all of its liquid into the garbage can. She drizzles the final few drops over the top of the foot sticking out, then tosses the bottle to the side.

The woman steps back, wipes her hands on her dirty robe, then blows on them. She leans down and picks up the small item, puts her thumb on top, holds it out and flicks it. I see the lighter spark. She flicks it again, and it makes a flame. She holds it steady, then steps forward, leans over the can, and reaches in with the lighter.

There's a loud whoosh as the woman jumps back—a bright orange flame exploding—the fire lifting three or four feet off the top of the can.

The woman wipes her face, crosses her arms, and steps forward again, looks inside the can. She says something to herself out loud and laughs, bends over and leans on her knees, keeps laughing for a minute. Then she stands straight again, stares at the can, and watches it as it burns.

The man's one white foot turns black and begins to smoke.

The woman stands there for five minutes, watching the fire as I watch her from across the street. She doesn't laugh again, and she doesn't look away.

Then she turns and walks over to the edge of the roof, tosses the knife and the lighter onto her raft, and scrambles down after them. One of her cats—a Siamese—is now perched on top of the parakeet cage. The other cat—gray and fluffy—is flicking its tail, standing on the surface of the raft, looking up at the woman. She reaches down and pets it.

She unties her bowline from the gutter, picks up her pole, and pushes away from the building. She rafts across Agate toward the apartment buildings, turns the corner there, and heads toward deeper water.

I wait until she's gone—out of sight—before I stand up.

Across the street, the trash can is still burning bright orange. Thick black smoke is coming up through the color, that one foot folded over the lip of the can, charred black now, the heel pointing up, the toes pointing down.

11

THE LAST TWO YEARS

WHAT'S FUNNY IS that we were in high school, and we seemed to know more than the adults. Notice more. Young people were ahead. Right off, I tried to tell my mother what was really going on. But she'd say, "¡Basta ya m'hija!" Close her eyes and wave me away.

She kept trying to show me edited videos on Facebook. I got sick of her talking. Got sick of my teachers talking. Teenagers, we just wanted it all to go away, for things to go back to normal, but they never did. Things kept getting worse.

People were angry and got more angry. More divided. The algorithms reinforcing what they already believed. Pastors preaching politics. Boys posting pictures online with handguns, AR-15s, multiple thirty-round clips. More school shootings. Then it became normal for female politicians on one side to pose with guns. Normal for politicians on the other side to complain on Twitter.

We were kids in a country where adults acted like children. And we all knew it. TikTok was more mature than the adults around us.

It didn't surprise me that people joined cults. Everywhere I turned, people were desperate and foolish. Looking for their group.

It didn't surprise me.

I'd just hoped it wouldn't be my mother.

FROG HOUSE

THE PUNCTURE MARK in my thigh is pink around the edges. Raised a little. Tight. But it doesn't hurt too much. I put more ointment on it, paint around the edge with my finger, then use a Q-Tip to mash a blob of triple antibiotic as far inside as it will go.

I look at it and hope it's not getting infected.

I think of a house I've never been inside, two houses down from mine, the 1964 house that everyone in the neighborhood used to call "Frog House." It was the home of a university professor who specialized in frogs—something to do with them—and his whole house had a frog motif:

- An aluminum mailbox in the shape of a frog
- Frogs like yard gnomes at the front corners of the grass and along the walk
- A cement statue of a frog on the porch

- A brass frog knocker on the front door
- A welcome mat in the shape of a frog
- Stained-glass window hangings, a purple and yellow frog on one side, a green and blue one on the other.

The door of Frog House is open a couple inches. Angled in. I push on it, and it squeaks wildly. I wait to see if anyone calls out, if anyone comes to the door. I'm still not used to an abandoned neighborhood, and I lean into the opening and call out, "Hello?"—the same as at every house.

When nobody comes to the door, I push it harder, open it a little bit more, then step inside.

In the front room, there are four toppled pedestals that used to hold glassed-in frog specimens. I'm not sure what they're called, but they're like globes of glass cut in half—clear glass—with frogs preserved inside. I've seen the same thing with scorpions or tarantulas, displays like that in antique stores. The four of them are on the floor, one of them upside down. I flip it, see a bright red frog with blue legs, small, less than an inch in size.

I'm staring at the frog when I hear a sound, something strange, different, a muffled scrambling.

I stand and listen. Try to figure out where it's coming from.

The noise is like a rustling, something moving too quickly, a soft item touching something else. I take a few steps toward the kitchen. Stop and listen again.

The sound is louder now. Not loud, but louder than it was before. I take a few more steps. The sound is coming from somewhere in the back of the house, and when I step into the kitchen, I can hear more of that noise. The door to the next room is closed, a door to a laundry room or pantry or mudroom, whatever it is that's back there.

There's something happening in that room—something thrashing around—and I'm not sure if I should open the door. I hesitate. Listen through the wood. The scuffling noises are just on the other side of the door. Scuffling and a sound that's almost like growling.

I know I shouldn't open the door but I lean on it anyway. Turn the handle and lean—hoping it doesn't make too much of a creaking noise. But it wouldn't have mattered. What's going on in there is so frantic, so chaotic, that the sound doesn't register for them.

There are dogs—three of them—big dogs, and their heads are down. They're eating, and what they're eating is not frogs.

I shut the door quietly, making sure it clicks, making sure they're shut in. Then I back out of the house, move quickly through the living room, out onto the front lawn.

I look around and wait. But there's nothing going on outside, and a light breeze comes down the hill. The leaves of the maples above me rustle in the wind. Everything is peaceful.

I look at the wreckage all around, the upside-down car in front of the big house, a black Mercedes with its doors splayed open as it sits on its roof, waiting for rain and rust, the coming of fall and the turn of the weather, for breakdown.

My science teacher taught us last year that we have always been living in a world of decay, the evidence of the second law of thermodynamics. He said, "Everything breaks down, everything tends toward chaos. And remember this: entropy always increases."

I often think about the things he said to us. It seems like everything was applicable, all of his science was relevant. I always took good notes in his class.

He said, "We can't see everything breaking down, but that's sometimes because we don't know what to look for." He said, "Geologic time is slow compared to the lives of humans. And survival of the fittest means that nature will weed things out, will cull each herd to make it the healthiest."

I wonder which part of the herd I am: the part that will be culled or the part that will survive?

*   *   *

I sit on the roof of my garage in the evening and imagine the heat of the sun as something visible before my eyes. Blue and yellow streaks of light, pulses of radiation raining down. At the same time, I imagine the future decay of the houses all around me. Of this world already loosened by the quake. I run the film in fast-forward, imagine everything in front of me as it bends and leans, warps and fails.

I imagine myself warping and failing as well, my shadow growing longer. The ground opening up in front of me.

Is the opening a rift or an abyss?

And is a grave any different?

*   *   *

I will do anything to survive. That's who I've always been.

13

THE SCIENCE OF INSOMNIA

I'VE NEVER SLEPT well at night, for as long as I can remember. When I was little, before we came to the United States, I would lie in bed, and it was like I'd just had two or three bottles of Coke. I would close my eyes, but my brain would buzz, and I'd see movies of the day that just happened under my eyelids. We still lived in K-59 then—fifty-nine kilometers south of the U.S. border—in a scrap-wood house behind my abuelos' mission-built block house. I used to scavenge the dump for Fanta bottles rich people had thrown out, return them for centavos, maybe a Coke bottle here or there, give the money to my mother to buy black beans or cornmeal for the comal.

When I'd sold Adderall in the halls of my high school earlier this year, kids had told me it was the best pill ever because they could stay up all night long. One kid even said, "It's like my mind is its own animal, alive and thrashing around inside my skull."

I told him I'd pay him for the opposite: "Something to quiet it all down, to make it all go away." I held out my hands. "Imagine a peaceful substance like eating wisps of fog out of a bowl."

He just shook his head at me.

* * *

The daylight comes now with waking dreams. Sleep unexpected. Dreams again even while moving, and I find myself in random places like some kind of post-sleep zombie. Wonder at the reality all around me.

I'm in that half-conscious state as I'm picking radishes in the garden on Walnut Street, feeling drowsy, heavy-eyed. Everything around me is beginning to overgrow, to look more like a jungle (the old rain added to the new sun). I fill a basket with a pile of fresh food, and I don't realize what I'm hearing at first because the sound is so low, so quiet and strange.

But it's singing, somebody singing, a clear, human voice, and it's not in my head.

I walk toward the house, toward the window that's broken, toward the source of that singing, a sound I haven't heard since the earthquake. At the window, I step carefully to avoid all the broken glass on the ground. I get up close to the house, near the windowsill—some glass still in place there—shards of clear, jagged teeth, and I lean in.

It's a woman's voice. She sings raspy and low. I listen, her words slow and clear, with pauses, hitches, unsung words breaking the lines sometimes, then the line picking up into a song again:

Where do bad folks go when they die?
They don't go to heaven where the angels fly

They go to the lake of fire and fry
Won't see them again 'til the fourth of July

This is what I needed, something like this, a voice, someone else's voice, lyrics and in person. I lean in until my head is almost inside the window, hanging over the teeth of broken glass.

I knew a lady who came from Duluth
She got bit by a dog with a rabid tooth
She went to her grave just a little too soon
And she flew away howling on the yellow moon

I didn't know how badly I needed this, a voice singing in tune. Someone else here with me. I lean my head against the side of the windowsill, on the vertical wood where there is no glass. I lean against the house and listen, close my eyes and nod with the singing.

Now the people cry and the people moan
And they look for a dry place to call their home
And try to find some place to rest their bones
While the angels and the devils try to make them their own

The oversweet smell of the strawberries in the basket at my feet—strawberries too ripe in the sun—and the dry earth on the sides of the radishes, those smells mix with the lyrics, the sounds of the song inside my head, and I see the daylight coming the first morning after the earthquake, when I was huddled in the backyard with everything around me destroyed, roofs caved, two-story houses at M. C. Escher angles, the wide tops of broken oak trees, smashed gaps in houses, and pine trees tilting like toothpicks. That morning there was so much

silence that it was unbelievable. Until a neighbor started
to scream.

*   *   *

The singing stops and I open my eyes.

I see that I'm resting my forehead against the window frame. I lift my head. Realize that the voice could've
been a dream. I wonder if I slept here standing up—that's
always a possibility with me—and I wipe my eyes with the
back of my hand.

I was crying and hadn't realized.

I'm sure it was a dream.

But then someone coughs.

I lean in the open window, look into the low light,
smell the odor of the house, the wet and the wax, the body:
the sweat and urine and feces. In the shadows I can see
that there's something wrapped in a blanket—someone—
and I'm not dreaming. None of this was a dream, not the
song or the cough, or now the blanket.

I walk around to the back door. That door is twisted
on its hinges, jammed three inches open, and I have to lean
hard to get it open further. I throw my shoulder into it and
clear a space big enough for me to get through.

Inside the house, the entry room is in chaos, a washing machine tipped over onto its front, water from its
broken hose filling the pan, and the dryer lifted and
wedged behind. Mud boots scattered. Some kind of rack
that used to hang from the wall. Raincoats tangled on
the ground.

I step over everything. Walk through the kitchen: cupboards open; flour, sugar, and oatmeal spilled across the
floor. Broken white plates and bowls. Clear glass cups shattered on the counter, on the floor, shards in the sink.

Next is the living room, the furniture thrown around like someone large and angry went through the house. There's also a smell like a public restroom with the heat turned up. That smell is overwhelming, and I gag, put my hand over my nose and mouth. Wish I had a bandana with me.

I see the woman's form, her head out of the top of the blanket but her face turned away. She's just started to sing another song, but when she hears me in the room, she stops singing, turns her head toward me.

I'm still covering my face with my hand because of the smell. I talk through my fingers: "Hey."

The woman's eyes look unfocused, but she says, "I've seen you before." A black fly lands on her lip, rubs its legs together, then lifts back into the air. She licks her lips. Delayed. She says, "The girl on the bicycle."

I nod and realize that I'm crying again. It's nice to hear someone talking to me. I close my eyes, embarrassed that I'm so weak. I tell myself that I don't need this, that I could walk out of this house right now, leave this woman behind. But when I try that possibility in my mind, I know I won't. There's the singing. I want to hear that again. And this person's face, someone nice, talking to me.

The woman says, "I always saw you." She smiles and her lower lip cracks, a spot of blood filling the split. "You flew downhill."

I nod again. Wipe at my eyes. I don't say anything because I know I'll sob.

I look away from her face, can't look her in the eye. I can see that the blanket is the source of the smell, the blanket soiled—leaking through—the mess wrapped inside the roll. She notices where I'm looking. Says, "This isn't pretty, is it? It's blood mixed with . . ." She presses her lips together. Closes her eyes. "It has to be so infected."

I shake my head. But even shaking my head is a lie, and I wouldn't want anyone to lie to me.

She licks her lips again. "It won't be long for me now, right?"

"Won't be long . . ."

She looks at me, that one spot of blood blooming on her lip. "Not long until it's over. All of this."

I take my hand away from my face and the smell of the room overwhelms me. I shake my head. "Maybe I can help you?"

She smiles and a little blood runs toward her chin. She sucks at it, licks and smears the red. The fly lands and dips to drink.

I feel light-headed. Wavering in that overwhelming smell. Tilted. Feel as if I might pass out. The odor is so strong it seems like something I could touch in the air, and I lean against an overturned table, lower myself to the floor.

The woman says, "My name's Teresa." She smiles again.

"Cielo," I say, "like the sky."

I lie flat on the floor a few feet away from her. Turn my head in her direction.

Teresa looks back at the ceiling. Says, "Cielo." She shifts her body just the tiniest bit, and her face goes white. Sweat breaks out on her forehead.

I move closer to try to comfort her. I close my eyes and will the smell away. Attempt to turn off my sense of smell, imagine particles floating in the air all around me like wet beads, and I push through them, swim into an open space, a gap, where nothing exists except clean air. I imagine that the air is cool—winter cool—like the neighborhood after a January rain. It's no longer summer in my mind, and the evening ticks below freezing. The moisture on the road turns to black ice.

I'm in this room, and I want a person with me who is whole, a person uninjured, someone like me. I think how lucky I was to have those two pine trees holding each other up above my garage, how lucky I was that they tangled together, got stuck making an upside-down "V," how lucky I was to be unhurt, uncrushed. But I wish the same had happened for this woman.

Teresa is sleeping now, snoring a ragged pattern. Sleeping or passed out. What's the difference?

I'm in that middle place, wanting to slip deeper, to pass out or sleep. Dream. I'm so overwhelmed, and there's a couch pillow on the floor next to a broken lamp, so I pull that pillow over to me, settle my head, close my eyes.

When I open them again, it's close to dark, not late-night dark but early dark—everything gray—a little while past sunset, the start of nighttime, and I sit up, smell the horrible smell again, so close to me now that I gag once. Gag again. There's no way to turn off the smell this time, no mind tricks that work. I pinch my nose closed, look at the rolled blanket, less clear in the darkness, but still holding a body. Teresa is exactly where she was before, unmoved, breathing in and out, deep and slow and loud, the rolled blanket lifting and lowering, the stain in the middle of the blanket dark as the corners of the room.

The night is coming down deep now as it always does and I've slept the light away, slept into the hours where I won't be able to close my eyes again, and I know I'll stay awake as usual. I want to shake Teresa lightly, ask if she's okay, ask what she needs, but I also know I shouldn't wake her, probably shouldn't bother her since she's able to rest.

I'm thirsty.

I stand and walk into the kitchen, look for bottled water but find none. Walk back out into the living room and see two gallon jugs, both nearly empty next to the couch, not far from Teresa's head, where she must've dragged them at some point to drink.

I lean and reach for one, then stop and think about it, wonder if sharing water with this woman is a good idea, wonder if her infection can spread to me or if there's something else in her water that could make me sick. I don't know anything about sickness or infection, but I do know that the smell in the room isn't healthy, and I don't want any part of that.

So I go back into the kitchen, search everywhere again, more carefully this time, the backs of the cupboards, under the table, behind the shelves that pitched forward, behind the tilted refrigerator. But I don't find any other water bottles. I'm feeling around next to a cupboard when something crawls over my hand. I jump back, bump the table, and let out a little scream. I stand up and try to see what it was, but the animal—whatever it was—is already gone.

I go back to the living room to see if I woke Teresa, but I didn't. I watch her sleep for a minute more, then go through the kitchen to leave. I know if I stay, Teresa will sleep and I won't. I'll lie here all night—sleepless—watching her blanket rise and fall, wondering if she's dying or not, breathing the horrible smell in the living room.

So I leave the house.

Outside, the night isn't as dark as it seemed from inside. The stars plus a half-moon create enough light to walk home easily, duck under trees, move past ghost cars, balance over the planks of fences that have fallen across the sidewalk.

I think about the heavy summer rain that made this whole thing what it was, made the earthquake more catastrophic. The rain was unlucky in timing—random—but one of those heavy July rains that comes with thunderstorms, raindrops heavy as pea gravel, so big they made slashing sounds as they cut through the bright summer leaves of the maple trees.

Two days of those monsoon rains loosened everything, tree roots, foundations, backyards and borders, the ground soggy on the hillsides. Everything below the hills, a swamp. Trees turned in heavy wind gusts for two days, then the quake came in and finished everything, toppling what it could.

In the river flats for five blocks, houses came apart even before all the dams broke. I saw them—their forms buckling on the soggy ground, slipping from their foundations, caving—a new wreckage before the water, waiting for baptism.

I didn't need the internet to know what happened after. It wasn't difficult to figure out. The evidence was everywhere all around me as I searched houses and looked down the street:

The water came when the dams broke.

* * *

Lying in bed, I wonder about the continued flooding. It's been at least a week now, and the water isn't going down. It sits, backed up, stagnant, the city a low-lying lake and nothing draining, but I'm not sure why. I don't have a good map in my head. I try to picture the bottom of our flat valley, between the two mountain ranges, try to picture the water going away, pushing toward Portland and the Columbia River Gorge. I try to calculate whatever it is that's holding the water up—something—but I don't know what. There's an obstruction, but I'm not downriver to see it, and I realize there's so much I don't know.

My head is on my pillow now, and I picture the valley holding the water the same way that it sometimes holds fog for weeks in winter. I picture myself up on Spencer's Butte, looking down, facing north, the city's hills sitting as islands in a great lake or a new ocean, something like the pictures I've seen online of old floods, how Eugene used to look in late winter or spring.

I also wonder what other cities in the Northwest look like. The earthquake must have destroyed those places too, but who knows?

Just before I close my eyes, there's another aftershock, a strong one that rumbles twice, two big jolts sounding like furniture scraping across a wooden floor. My desk lamp falls again, and another part of the shade dents. I think about replacing the broken bulb, but then I remember that it doesn't matter. There won't be electricity again. For months? Years?

The trees shift above me, but nothing changes in my garage. I close my eyes and try to relax, but I stay awake.

NIGHT STALKING

I THINK ABOUT HOW I used to sneak around the neighborhood at night. My mother had been gone for two weeks, and I couldn't sleep. I wandered the streets first, then alleyways, looked in back windows, tried to catch a glimpse of other people's lives, their families—or couples, some of them parents or college students. I tried to imagine normal existences, different from mine. I leaned against back fences or trees, stared through plate-glass windows, sliding doors, screens, watching anything and everything I could see.

This is not something I'm supposed to do, or admit, that I watched people from the dark. But I don't always worry about right and wrong. I mostly do what I need to do. I always have.

And there was something I needed in my watching.

I remember the rays from the incandescent lights coming out, the texture they had as they reached through glass into the shadows where I stood. I waited in the waves of yellow light, watching people eat meals, pass through rooms, carry phones and tablets and books and laptops and glasses of wine. Dirty dishes. Clothes that needed to be washed or clothes that were already folded.

Sometimes the people lingered in the frames, staying in the windows, and I'd sit in the cover of darkness, sit back against a tree trunk or a fence, or the post of a bird feeder. I'd watch these other people act out their lives, do the little tasks or have conversations with each other, words I couldn't hear.

Loneliness was something edible, something I could taste, something that I'd swallowed whole. And I reached toward these yellow-lit scenes in the houses all around me.

I remember the single woman who lived at the top of the block, the one I watched as she talked to her cat for fifteen minutes at a time. She sat on her couch, rubbed her fingers together while bending down, waited for the cat to come to her. Then she held it on her lap, and I watched her mouth moving, her head nodding yes and no, the two of them having a full conversation.

Then there was the husband and wife one block over from me, the couple that would walk around their dining room before bed with their pants off. I don't know why. He'd be wearing a button-up shirt, with a tie, socks on his feet, nothing on his legs, and she'd be wearing a long T-shirt that hung over her pale, white legs. The couple always looked like they were arguing—their faces serious and their hand motions quick—but then I'd see one of them smile, and the other would respond with a second smile. They'd both laugh, and I'd wonder if they'd been joking all along. I'd wonder if this is what sarcasm looks like through a big glass window illuminated in the dark.

I also watched the two college boys down in the flats, two blocks away. They were in love, but I didn't know that at first. I watched them in their kitchen. They'd cook microwave meals together, Safeway brand pot pies or Schwan's, or Marie Callender's—anything easy—and the boys' quick brushing against each other wasn't something I noticed at first. Later though, I would see the slide of a finger against a forearm. Hips touching near the microwave. Small things.

There was something about them that I returned to. Kept watching.

And one night—while I was sitting in their backyard, leaning against a tree, watching them eat—I saw the two of them stand up, mid-meal, and start kissing. They were next to the table. Their food was still steaming on the tabletop. Neither had finished eating. I'm not sure what caused the two of them to stand like that, so suddenly, to get up and leave their food. Maybe something one of them said?

I leaned forward. It was so unexpected. They were older than me by a few years, but still young, with clean-shaven faces, and they kissed next to their table, next to their dinners as if they were in a hurry, but also as if they were trying out kissing, as if they were still learning how to demonstrate physical love. Then the thinner of the two led the heavier one out of the room, pulling that boy's hand, and they never came back to their food or their table. I just watched the food sitting there for a while. Waiting.

After that—other nights—I'd see the way they looked at each other, but they never had that sudden moment of the first time, that impulsive standing up, those quick movements that looked like they might knock over a chair, and the kissing as if they were learning how to be together.

There were so many other nights—so many other backyards—watching neighbors, watching strangers, as the stars slid above me, as the earth spun at an incredible rate of speed, as the sun took the solar system on its whirled orbit through the Milky Way.

15

TRYING TO HELP HER

I KNOW IT'S AFTERNOON by the heat in my garage. I never meant to sleep this late. I sit up and almost hit my head on my ceiling, the roof only three feet above my mattress at its highest point. The heat thickens up here, just under the slant of the ceiling, and my body is wet with sweat. Mouth dry. I lick my lips, even my tongue feeling desiccated.

I reach for a bottle of water, but it's empty. The bottle is light and uncapped, and I chuck it onto the floor below, where it bounces. I roll off my mattress and climb down the ladder, take a new bottle of water from the kitchen fridge that no longer works as a refrigerator—just a storage space. The water is warm, but wet and quenching and good. I drink it all. Get another bottle.

I brush my teeth, then drip a little water on my toothbrush and tap it on the edge of the sink. Set it there to dry. I rake my hair with my fingers, pull it all back into a ponytail. Run the rubber band around the pony four times. I take my shirt off to switch to a dry one—my old shirt wet from sweat—and I look at myself for a moment in the mirror, an old habit, looking at myself standing there in my bra. I remember how badly I wanted this particular bra, black with a fringe of lace along the top edge, how cute I thought it would be when I stole it from Victoria's Secret, how important it used to be to me to look cute.

There are dark pudges under my eyes, my sleep issues showing like gray eyeliner in the soft space. When my sleep used to get bad, I wore heavy concealer to school, spread it under my eyes to cover up the gray. But now . . .

I still look pretty good in this bra, my chest wet with sweat, and I let myself think about boys and girls for a moment, people my age I used to like or wanted to make jealous. But those thoughts make me feel so lonely that I stop myself. Take a deep breath. Stuff the thought of everyone else being gone, hide those thoughts like a note in the back of a drawer.

This is now, I tell myself. *Focus on right now.*

I have to go check on that woman, maybe hear her sing again. I pull on a T-shirt that I find crumpled on the floor by my desk, then leave the garage. Looking out for The Collection men, rescue workers—anyone—I walk the two blocks over to Orchard Street.

The house is the same as yesterday, no changes, and this surprises me, but I don't know why. I hop up onto the front porch, try the front door. But there's something very wrong with that door, some kind of compression issue, and I see that the wall looks buckled above it, bending in an egg shape, so I walk around back again.

I enter through the laundry room, like I did yesterday, two rats scurrying out in front of me. The smell in the next room, the living room, is the same overwhelming smell, the smell of an open sewage line. I gag and turn, put my hand over my mouth, pinch my nose shut. I'm thankful that I haven't eaten any food yet today.

I walk up to Teresa in her soiled blanket, still rolled up. Her face is tucked underneath the top of the roll, and I can't see her eyes. Flies duck in and out of the opening by her face.

"Hey," I say, "How are you?" I try not to smell anything. Breathe through my open mouth, under my hand.

Teresa doesn't say anything.

I say, "Are you awake?" Pull back the top edge of the blanket. See Teresa's eyes fluttering as she dreams. I brush two flies off her face. Let go of the blanket. Sit down and think.

I don't know much about health, but I do know that sitting in your own waste is bad for you. I also know that the smell might be some kind of infection. This house is hot, at least ninety-five degrees in the late afternoon, all of that heat baking whatever it is that's inside the blanket.

I say, "I'm gonna unroll you, see what's going on."

Teresa doesn't wake up.

"I'm just gonna . . ." I reach for the flap of the blanket, grab it at the top, not wanting to touch anywhere near the middle, where the brown soil mark looks dry but smells wet. I pull at the blanket and Teresa's face comes free.

She's not the age of most of the other people in the neighborhood. She's not elderly. She's youngish, maybe thirty or so. Maybe even younger than that. I think I've seen her working in her garden when I biked past, or maybe it was down at one of the shops on Agate Street, at Tom's Market or the Eugene City Bakery. I'm not sure where, but I know I've seen her before.

She's pretty too. Pretty even with her face white and colorless, sweaty, even with her hair greasy. For some reason her prettiness makes this even more overwhelming to me, even more sad. I don't want to see a pretty young woman rolled in a blanket of her own waste.

I try to pull the blanket back the rest of the way, to see what her injuries are, but the blanket's stuck, tucked in around her legs, and I realize that I'm going to have to pull hard and unroll her all the way to get the blanket off. That means I'll have to turn her over two or three times.

She's not awake, but I say, "This might hurt," before I pull. Then I do it. I pull quickly, pull hard.

Teresa rolls facedown and groans.

I pull again and she trundles, rolls twice, comes free of the blanket. Then she screams as her eyes come wide open.

"I'm so sorry!" I say.

Teresa sucks in breath and begins to cry—shaking—closing her eyes again.

I don't know if I should touch her now, if that would actually calm her down, and I say again, "I'm so sorry," but this time quieter.

Teresa is lying on her back, free of the blanket. The smell in the room is like one of those public bathrooms where poop is smeared on the walls and the mirrors are shattered. I lean back and pinch my nose shut with my fingers again. Breathe in and out of my mouth.

Teresa has her eyes squeezed shut, and she's breathing really fast. I hope that if she opens her eyes and sees me, she won't be as scared. She'll see that I'm trying to help her. I say, "It's okay. You're okay," even though I'm sure that she's not.

She doesn't scream again, but she starts to moan with each breath. She breathes in . . . moans . . . and breathes out. It's sort of a whining rhythm, and tears run out of the corners of her closed eyes. I think of her singing voice just yesterday, how it sounded in the garden by the window, how beautiful it was, and I wish she'd sing now.

I look down at her body and there's something not right, but I'm not sure what it is. It's almost as if there are two of her, the upper half of her body going one way, and the lower half of her body set in opposition. But that's not exactly right either. Her body is facing one way—all of it—yet there's a twist to her somehow.

I touch her shoulder. "Can you hear me?"

She opens her eyes, blinks, looks at the ceiling.

I say, "Are you all right?" But even as I ask her, I know it's a stupid question.

She opens her mouth, and I think she's going to say something but she doesn't. She closes her eyes again. More tears come out of the corners of her eyes.

"Okay," I say. "It's okay. What can I do? What exactly is wrong?"

She breathes some more—doesn't say anything—and I can't imagine her singing now, not anymore. Her singing seems impossible.

I say, "What happened to you?"

She opens her eyes and looks at me. I can see that she's fully awake and in pain. Her voice croaks as she says, "I think it's my pelvis, or my back. Or both."

I look down at her body, examine it, and finally see what's wrong. At the bottom of her torso, her body changes directions, but on the inside. There's some sort of twist of everything near her waist.

I look at her face. Her jaw opens. Her tongue taps her top row of teeth. She's sweating hard, and she says, "I got crushed." She begins to cry again, but it's not sobbing. Tears run off the side of her face.

I look around the room, everything toppled: a table, multiple chairs, one leg broken off the couch, and the china cabinet pitched onto its face. Then I see the tall bookshelf laid out forward, heavy, maybe eight feet tall and at least that wide—solid oak, and all of the hardback books piled where they fell, rising and falling, some under the shelf and some out on the open floor.

There's a blood smear from underneath the left side of the bookshelf. I see the blood trail where it goes up next to the couch, then back, then into the kitchen, and back here into the living room.

I follow that blood trail to Teresa. Say, "Did you drag yourself around?"

"At first."

"Can you still do that?"

She opens her eyes and doesn't cry. Closes them again. Her lips are chapped, her face wet from sweat. "I'm too messed up now. Too sick." she says.

"Sick?"

"Too infected."

I think about how before the quake I would've called 911 in this situation. If it were just a week ago, an ambulance would've appeared within fifteen minutes. Teresa would've seen a paramedic, then a doctor, then surgeons. But there's no hope for that now. All of that's gone. I realize it's like that world never existed.

Teresa seems to be waiting for me to do something. She's breathing a little slower. Her eyes are closing again.

I say, "Do you want me to try to see what's wrong?"

She nods. "I can't look down there. I can't sit up or twist."

A fly lands on her cheek and I brush it away.

Since I don't have any medical training, since I can't fix her, there's no point in looking her over, but for some reason I want to anyway. I want to help her if I can. So I examine Teresa without touching her. I don't want to hurt her any more than I already have. Also, there's the wet mess near her middle, where she wasn't able to make it to the bathroom for the last few days, and her pelvis, the strange lumps there—where her body doesn't look right, how the tops of her legs seem to come out lower than they should, pushed down and back.

I run my eyes down her thighs to her knees—which look normal, normal kneecaps, normal connections to her lower legs—then down, and I see finally that her lower legs also take one final twist above her feet. She's wearing shorts, and her lower legs are bare. I'm not sure what's going on with them, but I know that they're not right, the yellow and purple bruises showing on the fronts of her shins. I look at those, then put my face low, next to the floor, see the small bones coming out through the skin in the back of her legs, both leg bones sticking out six inches above her ankles.

"Your legs are . . ." I start to tell her, but I stop. There's something else. Movement down by the bones. I get close and peer underneath, lean in closer still, to see whatever it is, and discover maggots, crawling and writhing, wriggling over each other as if friction keeps them alive, and I breathe deeply, close my eyes, then open them again and look, see the dull color of the bones and the pale, creamy maggots in the space between the bones and flesh.

I gag and sit back. Look away.

When I finally glance at Teresa's face again, I see that she's passed out once more. She keeps coming in and out, and she's unconscious now, breathing and sweating.

I'm sweating too. I wipe my forehead with the back of my wrist.

Cleaning her up won't help. Even if I had warm water and soap, alcohol, medicine, some kind of strong antibiotics, she'd still need surgeries to put everything back into the right places, to clean everything out.

She's going to die. I realize there's no way around that.

I shake my head and close my eyes. Start to cry.

But then I think about Teresa's pain, and I wonder if I could maybe help her with that, just with that one thing. What if I could find Vicodin or Percocet, or Oxycontin, and make the end a little more comfortable for her? Those drugs would probably be in bathrooms somewhere, left behind by people who are gone now. I haven't really searched bathrooms since the earthquake, which is funny since bathrooms were always my go-to places back when I was dealing pills during the school year. But since the quake, I've mostly just searched kitchens, stockpiled water and food.

I get to my feet. Say out loud, "I'm gonna go find something to help."

But Teresa isn't conscious and she doesn't wake up.

I go through the kitchen, outside to the next house over, hop up onto the steps, climb through the shattered front window into the living room. The nearest bathroom is hard to get to because of all of the downed furniture— the front room must've been cluttered even before the quake—and I find nothing in that bathroom, nothing but deodorant and hand soap fallen out of the medicine cabinet, nothing in the drawers except floss, toothpaste, aspirin, and Vicks VapoRub. Underneath the sink, there are three new rolls of toilet paper. A dirty plunger.

I try to get to other parts of the house, but everything else is blocked by wreckage. Even the kitchen is impossible to access because the refrigerator jumped and wedged into the doorjamb at a thirty-degree angle, caught at its corner, and I'm worried that if I duck under that fridge—and accidentally brush against it—the whole thing might fall on top of me. So I move on.

The next house has a front door that's ajar eight inches, barely big enough for me to squeeze through, but when I get through the door into the living room, the house is so full of a smell—something terrible—that I have to leave immediately. I can't even breathe in there, and I struggle to get back outside, the door gap feeling like it narrowed from just a second ago. I scramble to get through that tight space while holding my breath.

Outside on the porch again, I lean against the railing and gasp huge gulps of fresh air.

The third house doesn't have any painkillers either, but in the front bathroom—in a concealed slot that looks like an old metal tampon box—I find a gun and two loaded clips. The gun is a pistol, black and short, not too heavy, but solid, and it reads "TAURUS POLICE" on one side, and in progressively smaller type on the other side:

PT 609 PRO
CAL 9 mm PARA
MADE IN BRAZIL

I hold the pistol in my hand, lift it, sight myself in the mirror, tuck my hair out of my eyes. Take aim.

I don't know much about guns. I've seen them in a lot of movies and TV shows. I know that some pistols cock with a hammer in the back and some do that slidey, clicky thing on top. This pistol doesn't have a hammer in the back though, so I try the slide thing. When I pull it, a bullet comes out of the side of the gun and clanks against the tipped-over metal trash can on the bathroom floor.

I pick up the bullet and put it in my pocket. Lift the gun and point at myself again.

I wish I could YouTube this: type "Taurus pistol" into the search bar and watch how it works, how to load the pistol, how to cock it, how to shoot it. But YouTube is not an option anymore.

I click the black lever on the side, thinking it must be the safety since it's where my right thumb could get to it, and a dot of red shows. I click it back up right away. I don't want the gun to go off by accident. Nervous, I point at the wood floor, close my eyes and cringe, trying to pull the trigger to see if the lever actually was the safety. But the gun doesn't fire, and I open my eyes again. Tuck the pistol into the waistband of my pants, put the extra clips in my pocket. Leave the house.

It feels different to be carrying a gun, more danger-ous and more safe at the same time, as if the world is now explosive but also everyone is after me. Everything on the street is too quiet now as I look for an enemy, for Collec-tion members or looters ducking house to house, somebody I might need to point a gun at, but this is the same quiet world of five minutes ago, the lonely world of wrecked houses and downed trees, cars slid to odd places or tipped onto their sides. This is the same, too-warm late-afternoon world, and the cicadas are droning again in the maple trees.

I keep searching house to house for a long time, go around the bottom of the block, getting into every bath-room that I can access, checking them carefully, hoping to find the painkillers to help Teresa.

I have to enter five more houses before I find what I'm looking for, way down along the bottom of the block near the water, in a gray house. I find a half-full bottle of painkillers—maybe half remaining of a ninety-count prescription of Vicodin—in a desk drawer. I slip the pill bottle into my right pocket and walk back to Teresa's house.

When I get there, I start to enter the house quietly, not wanting to wake her if she's sleeping. But there's something changed about the front door of the house. I pause. Look at it. It seems to be at a different angle from when I left an hour ago. I'd been going out the back door, but now the front door is pushed in, wedged open, wide enough for me to fit.

I pull out the pistol as if I know how to use it. Click the safety off. Point the barrel inside the open door, into the house, then step inside, following my gun.

Even though it's still afternoon, the shadows seemed to have lengthened in the living room. A piece of furniture is thrown down in front of me—and I'm sure it wasn't there when I left. I stop and listen. Wait.

But I don't hear anything.

I step around the chair, walk up to Teresa . . . and then I see it. Her left arm is pulled out to the side. The angle of her arm is wrong, and I realize that her shoulder has been dislocated. Her hand is open—palm down, fingers spread—and there's blood on the floor. Her pinky on that open left hand is missing. There's a small spray of blood beginning to darken.

I kneel down next to her, look closely for breathing, for the rise and fall of her chest. But there's nothing. She's dead now, her face turned away from her dislocated arm, and the thick, red bruises on her throat. Two black flies settle on her face, and her skin doesn't twitch.

Suddenly I'm breathing so hard that it feels like I'm going to pass out. I stand up and get black spots around my eyes. I lean against the couch for support, try to calm my breathing. I hold my gun out, move around the house, point my shaky pistol in front of me, aim into every corner, behind each piece of furniture, behind every appliance. But I don't find anything. Don't see anyone.

They've left—disappeared again—and taken what they came for.

I look out the front window, look up and down the street, wait and stare, scanning for any movements, but I don't see anyone or anything in the neighborhood. It's like ghosts visited this house in the hour that I was gone.

I hold my gun in one hand, the bottle of pain pills in the other. I open the cap and shake two pills into my mouth. Swallow them dry, then look back one last time at Teresa's face, her mouth open, a fly landing on her tongue.

* * *

Out on the front porch, I balance the gun on the railing and pull the triple-antibiotic ointment out of my pocket, daub some on my finger, stick it into the nail hole on my thigh. There's a red ring around the hole, and the skin is warm.

The sun is shining brightly in the west—still hanging above the trees—but it's dropping at an angle, heading toward night, toward darkness, and I wonder who's still in the neighborhood, where they are, and if they could be watching me now. I pick up my pistol. The safety's on, but I'm ready.

I look all around me. See nothing.

On the street, the leaves of the maple trees shiver in a light wind.

16

WILLINGNESS

*T*HERE IS NOTHING *to fear but God. Not armies or catastrophes.*

Witness Andreas says, "The anger of the omnipotent is fearsome. So we must stay in obedience. Never darken the doorway of another church. Never worship the high priests of science."

I write his words. My ears open and I am willing.

"Cultivate the heart of a servant. Serve me to show your willingness to serve God."

I am willing.

"Or prove that you walk in the way of the evil one, the nefarious leader, and through him your sins are multiplied. Your thought-actions become evident, weak-minded, led astray by the lies of mankind."

Hear me: I am willing.

"Men of science are not of God. They are the opposite of God. They desire your full attention, your full worship. Do not follow any of their commandments."

I will not follow them.

I am willing. I am willing. I am willing.

Come to me. Clean me.

17

DEEPER WATER

I HEAR THE BOMBS go off in the middle of the evening. It's still light out, nowhere close to dark, so I don't see the flashes. The sky is a bright, deep blue—zero clouds—and the soundwaves break through the open sky. I don't have a good sense of where the explosions are coming from. The concussions seem to come from everywhere.

The first bomb is a heavy sonic boom, a concussive bass note so low that it feels like something of enormous density—incredible weight—has been sucked into a new hole ripped through the surface of the earth. Then another bomb goes off. Then a third. Three detonations in less than a minute, and the earth seems to have split into two at each concussion.

There is no doubt that the explosions are bombs, with their evenly timed spacing and incredible magnitude. It seems that nothing else but a rupture in the earth's crust could make sounds as significant as those. But when the

shockwaves die out, I hear another sound start up, or multiple sounds all at once: car alarms on dozens of vehicles
above the water line—all the cars that didn't go off during
the quake, cars on University Hill, College Hill, Hendrix,
all the alarms set off by the concussions of the bombs, and
all tripping at nearly the same time, none on the same beat.

It's the worst grouping of sounds I've ever heard, something so frustrating that I consider breaking into the cars
that I can, the ones nearby, smashing windshields and
steering columns, trying to get the alarms to stop beeping.
But I wouldn't know how to do it, and I'm not sure anything I try would work. I also think about the impossibility
of finding keys to every car—that hopeless mission—and I
know I'll have to wait it out.

After an hour where I feel crazy, I search the basement
of a neighbor's house and find bright orange plastic ear-
muffs made for construction workers. I put those on, and
that's the only way I can handle being outside in that awful
chorus of sounds.

The car alarms go off for three days straight, until each
of the car batteries die.

*　*　*

Also, there's this: After the bombs go off, the water rises.

The flood gets deeper.

18

THIS WORLD OF CARNIVORES

I NEVER KNEW WHERE El Jefecito gathered his snakes. People said he went up into the mountains, but the mountains were a long way from the flats and the lettuce fields of K-59 and I couldn't picture him there. Since he had no vehicle, it was more likely that he caught the snakes on the edges of the dump, but I was young and I believed the stories older people told.

I was so small that his snakes were almost mythical: five or six feet long, diamondback rattlesnakes held like yard pets in a pen. The boards were dug into the ground, and false burrows built by Jefecito himself so the snakes wouldn't try to find a way underneath and out of the enclosure.

There were a dozen of them—slow most of the time— except when they ate.

All of the children of the village would gather at the pen when Jefecito had caught rats. He kept those rats in the bottom of a well-oiled bucket—the rats' scrabbling and fighting audibly against the bucket's plastic walls. And that weird shriek sound they made when they were afraid.

But the rats would become silent once they were dropped into the pen. They would smell the earth, the skin marks and drags of the rattlesnakes. Jefecito's pen was the worst-smelling animal enclosure in the village. There was always something about the odor of snakeskins, as if their deadliness leaked from the skin onto the ground.

The rats stayed near each other at first, then slowly spread out, seemed to nibble the earth and become more brave as they searched for a way to escape. They went along the fence. Stopped to smell, continued on with their futile searches.

The rattlesnakes—spaced across the pen—were completely still, none of their bodies moving. When I looked closely, though, I could see the quick flicks of their tongues, the subtle turns of their heads, how their pit vipers' sensors were open, pointing in the direction of the rats, feeling for the heat, waiting for any rat to come close enough.

*   *   *

For three days, I sleep while wearing my ear guards. On the fourth day, I wake up and it's bright outside. I slide my ear guards off and hear the world gone quiet once again, the last of the car alarms finally stopped.

Late morning, I look at the blank face of my digital clock: no more red numbers. I drink a bottle of water and open a small bag of granola, eating a handful. I chew and swallow. Eat some more.

I put on my sunglasses before going out, the ones with the yellow tint, the ones that make the world seem happier. I've saved the charge on my cell phone, only allowing myself to use it every once in a while since the quake, never for more than five minutes. I check for reception first—an old habit—but of course there isn't any. Same as yesterday. Same as every other day. I haven't received a single notification since the quake, and I wonder what all the downed cell towers look like. I imagine a pile of phone antennas, Star Wars–like metal scraps jutting out at odd angles from the earthquaked jumble.

I think: *This is the movie of real life, and I'm finally the main character.* I know it's a weird way to think about reality, but sometimes I switch to that. I think, *I'm walking through my own movie.* I tell myself, *This is the simulation where I'm the star.* So I put on my happiest sunglasses, press the "Power" button on my phone, nod my head at the idea that this could be an important day.

But I also know I'm lying to myself. I have this heavy feeling—like I've wrapped my body in a lead blanket, the metal pulling me down by my shoulders. I know I might have to do something different one of these days, not just search houses, not just find mangled or dead bodies. I'm so scared if I think about it, so lonely, and I don't know if I can keep searching houses. I don't know if I can keep drinking water, keep making daily plans, keep hoping for something better.

So I listen to a song on my phone. Just one.

I listen to "Panda" by Desiigner, for the sound of it, for the beat and rhythm that used to make me happy when I was young, the base and the flow, and I wait a few seconds after I start, for that gritty Menace drop. Then—with the beat in my ears—I tell myself that I have to leave the garage. I have to walk across the top of the block to a place I can get something other than canned food, so I do.

Desiigner starts to rap about his broads in Atlanta, twistin' dope, lean, and the Fanta, Panda, and the world around me feels bright and yellow with my sunglasses on, as if there are razor blades cutting every angle of light.

And the song does its job. It clears my mind. When the music ends, I check the phone's power, see it's at forty-three percent still since I've saved it every day, and then I power it off until the next time.

I walk the rest of the way to a garden on Walnut Street, rapping lyrics to myself, repeating lines, then look over the half fence from the sidewalk. I remember the man who used to always be here, pulling weeds or watering from a hose. I remember his tie-dye shirts, swirls of purples and blues and oranges, a basket at his hip, hose in the other hand.

But he's not here now. There's nobody. The garden is abandoned, bean rows empty and corn standing alone. The drone of the cicadas has already begun above me, and I walk through the garden, looking to see what I can eat. Tomatoes are my favorite, and they're doing fine in this heat, under this strong sun and no water, so I eat three tomatoes like they're apples, the juices spilling out of my mouth and over my hands. Then I pick cucumbers and carrots, things I can take back to the garage; the cucumbers a little shriveled but still good. I wash the vegetables in a little bucket of water by the house. There's a scum on the surface, but the water underneath is fine. I wash the dirt off and I dry the vegetables on the hem of my T-shirt.

Then I pee near the corner of the house, pull my shorts and underwear down and squat behind a clump of hazelnut saplings. As I'm peeing, I see a house cat hunched over, looking at something. I'm not sure what it is. I finish peeing and stand up, go closer, see the cat has a garter snake pinned. The snake is small, no more than two feet long, thin and black with one bright orange stripe going down the length of its body. The head is writhing back and forth, whipping around, and it strikes at the face of the cat, who doesn't seem to mind, even when the snake latches onto the cat's fur and stays there for a few seconds before pulling back and striking again.

In the middle of the snake's back, there's an opening where the cat has already bitten, and the snake's blood is dripping from the skin onto the grass. The bite is deep, the snake's body opened, spine severed, the tail end of the snake not moving at all, the tail making a straight line in the grass behind.

I close my eyes and shake my head. There are too many things in this world.

The cat dips its head to continue eating as I walk away.

PARASITES AND ISOLATION

DIRTY WATER. WORMS crawling in my abdomen. Vomiting and diarrhea. Dysentery. I've seen survival shows on TV and watched science videos in my high school health class. So I think about all of these various future possibilities if I run out of bottled water.

I've had enough so far, plenty for a while still, full bottles I've scrounged from kitchens and pantries and basements, sixteen-ouncers and liters and gallons, also a large tan jug from the basement three houses up, and a turquoise, seven-gallon camping container full of water from the house around the corner.

I know that water is a time issue, a math problem, and in one of my worst subjects—algebra—the teacher was always saying, "Algebra is important for solving to discover the unknown."

I was never good at finding the solutions because specific numbers weren't important to me. I didn't care about decimals or X or Y. I didn't know why I should bother with exponents, equations, or factoring. But now I see that there's an importance in finding the unknown, or in this case, the unknown being total days, total ounces of water needed. So I ask myself these questions:

- How long will I be here (and because of that, how long will I be alone)?
- How many total days of water will I need to survive?

Or a different question:

- How many days will I be here until I'm brave enough to go up the hill and try to find her?

Maybe that's the more important question because the other questions are linked to it. I know I won't leave this neighborhood until I'm sure, or at least until I try to find out, attempt to be sure. So I have to look.

* * *

In my life, I've spent a lot of time alone—alone even when I was in crowds—but this is a different kind of alone. There are no people to watch. No conversations to overhear. No one to judge or ignore.

I sometimes allow myself five minutes to cry at night. In bed. All alone. I say, "Five minutes. You can cry for five minutes, then you have to stop," and I have to guess how long five minutes is since I don't want to use the last juice on my cell phone for that. I try to keep it to a time limit, because crying for too long could take me somewhere dark. I'm afraid of what that might be.

There were a few nights earlier this year—before all of this—when I just let myself cry as long as I felt like, sometimes even for an hour or two. But that wasn't good, being alone in my garage loft, crying and crying like a basement full of shattered lightbulbs.

So since the quake, I don't allow myself to cry like that anymore, not in this new reality where there are actual bodies and real dangers. So I have the rule: five minutes only, an allotted time to cry, and that's all. Afterward, I always feel a little better, wiping tears and snot on my sleeve, then looking around in the candlelight, nothing changed.

20

NIGHTTIME VISITOR

Sometime past midnight in the fish entrails of my insomnia, my eyes open in the dark. I wasn't sleeping anyway, but something caught my attention. I'd been listening to the rustling of the trees, the ticking of unsecured shutters in a nighttime wind, flaps of torn materials loose on the houses nearby. I'd been thinking about summer storms, worrying about fires.

But there was a new noise, something I hadn't heard before, and I held my breath to listen.

There's a noise now on the roof, light footsteps above me, someone sneaking along the pitch. I sit up. Feel for the handgun I keep stashed under the mattress. I slide it out, open and close my eyes a few times, adjusting my eyes to the darkness and the subtle light coming in the windows. Then I lean out from the edge of my sleeping loft, pointing the gun at the skylight—the rectangle of gray in the middle of the roof—clicking the safety off with my thumb. I put my index finger on the trigger. I wait for whoever it is to pass by, or to become visible in the glass of the skylight, just a few feet from where I'm lying.

But whoever it is stops, stands quietly above me—exactly above me—waiting on the roof over my head. Maybe he heard me move in bed, or maybe he heard the creak of the loft as I turned over on my mattress to grab the pistol.

He's stopped for sure now, directly above me, and I imagine the bowing of the roof beneath the weight of his body, the imperceptible bending of the wood and the sheeting and the roof shingles under his feet. I wonder if the person could fall through, and what it would look like if he did, if he fell through the roof onto my mattress. I imagine shooting him from close range, the pistol flashes lighting the darkness and the pieces of roof and beams all around us as I pull the trigger.

I wait. Hold the gun. Point the barrel directly above my head.

But the man doesn't fall through. Whoever it is starts to move again, slowly and quietly at first. But I would be able to hear any noise at this point, my nerves tight as guitar strings. He takes a few steps down the roof, toward the yard, toward the gutter, hesitates, then climbs back up to the top and waits once again, shuffles his feet as he moves to the middle of the roof, moving slower now, almost to the skylight.

I think he's listening. Wondering. He's only a few feet away now, at the edge of the curved glass of the skylight, the convex window in the middle of the garage, maybe six feet from me. I point the gun and strain my eyes to see.

Then he comes into view. I take a breath and hold it, ready to shoot. I point the gun at him, at this dark shape, the edge of him. Support my wrist with my other hand. Still holding my breath.

What I see is roundish in the moonlight.

His face?

I think he's looking at me. I lean closer—toward the skylight, leading with my pistol—trying to see more clearly. Then he shifts and I do see him, the mask, the black strip across his eyes. I stop my finger from depressing the trigger when I recognize what I'm looking at.

A raccoon.

The raccoon looks all around, cranes its neck to see what's inside the skylight, pushes its face against the glass, puts its two little black hands on either side of its face and presses itself to the surface.

I click the safety back on. Exhale. Realize that I'd begun to sweat under my arms, the acrid smell of nervousness hanging in the trapped air of my loft. I put the pistol under my mattress again, and lie down. Look back at the raccoon, who's still staring down into the darkness of my garage home. I watch him still trying to look and see what's below him, probably hoping to find something to eat.

"You're lucky," I say to him. "I almost shot you."

But he doesn't hear me. He keeps craning his neck, small and humanlike, his fingers spread wide, and it wouldn't surprise me if he spit on the glass and rubbed it with his hand, tried to clear the grime and the dust from the edges so he could see even better.

Suddenly I'm so tired that I can't keep my eyes open. I shift my shoulders and readjust my head on my pillow, pull my comforter up over my chest . . .

* * *

. . . and just like that it's late morning, the bright sunlight coming through the glass of the skylight—the raccoon gone, the midday heat breathing into the garage, sweat on my skin, warm beads, salty and beginning to pool together.

It's too hot to stay in bed, and I throw my comforter off and sit up. My forehead is inches from the ceiling's sheetrock. I wipe my face with the back of my wrist. Climb down my ladder to get a bottle of water. Wonder what I should do the next few hours since I should probably stay hidden in the daylight.

21

BE HIDDEN, STAY HIDDEN

I'M UP ON the roof of my neighbor's house across the street where an eave hangs out, creating a dark space above the deck. A warped beam holds a swath of siding out, shadowing a space where I can watch the neighborhood while being invisible.

I sit and watch.

There's thirty-two percent of my phone's battery charge left, and I'm listening to "Humble," Kendrick Lamar, cranked through the noise-canceling Beats headphones I found yesterday in a desk drawer on Orchard Street. Kendrick rapping "I'm so fucking sick and tired of the Photoshop . . ." and I smile despite myself.

Looking out at this world, my neighborhood, the only world I can access, and especially now, Photoshop seems ridiculous. Even the idea of sanitizing a picture doesn't mean anything anymore—not here, not in this new reality. The idea of a glossy magazine or an internet page is so sad that I shake my head. The idea of a model. The idea of a runway. The idea of clothes too expensive and strange to wear on a daily basis.

Then I listen to Bia's "Whole Lotta Money," thinking about her first album, *Nice Girls Finish Last: Cuidado*, and how true that is.

I'm in Bia's song, in her world, with her swagger in my mind . . . when I see movement out of the corner of my eye, and I click the song off. Slide the headphones off my ears. Lean forward and look: Collection men.

They're down at the bottom of the block, and there's no way they can see me up here, but I can see them. The four of them are talking, heads leaned together, one of them scanning over their shoulders as he holds an AR-15. The four of them go up a walk, out of my view, and I want to know what they're doing. So I climb out of the roof space into the house, creep through the wreckage of the upstairs, make my way downstairs, sneak out onto the deck, then down the side into the yard.

There's a big hedge that runs from the house all the way to the sidewalk, and I crawl in there—put my face in a gap—looking down the street. Now I can see the front of that house, and every front yard down the street.

But they must've dipped in and out of that first house fast, and skipped the next three while I was coming down from my hideout because when they reappear, they're only three houses away, and I realize I might've made a mistake. They're moving in this direction, quickly, and they'll be to this hedge soon.

I reach for my gun in my waistband, and it's not there. I left my pistol under the mattress when I walked out of my garage an hour ago. I wasn't thinking. Or I was thinking of something else. And now I don't have it.

These are the same four Collection men I saw before—the ones in robes, holding guns on the flat boat—and now they're jogging in and out of houses. The two short ones are in front, the taller ones in back. They move like soldiers—rifles in four directions as the group moves. And when they go into a house, they leave a sentry on the porch. He stays low, swinging his rifle right and left, his back to the door where the other three are.

They stay in their next house for only a couple of minutes, but when they come out, one of them has a large backpack with two gun barrels sticking out from the top. Another one has a red box of something—I can't tell what. They all crowd around the box and look inside. Two of the men nod soberly, but the short man with the beard is smiling.

They're only two houses away, and I'm starting to worry. Because of their sentry, I can't sneak back to my garage. There's no time that he's not watching the street—or won't hear me if I make a sound—and I wonder how hidden I am here in the hedge, wonder if I could crawl sideways into the backyard. But I'm not sure.

After two more houses they're going to be where I am.

The three men go inside another house, then come back out onto the porch and talk to the sentry. I can hear them talking now, but can't quite make out their words.

I start to slither on my belly, army-crawling along the back of the hedge. Every few feet I stop and make sure they haven't noticed me. I'm looking sideways at the men when I get to the house and run into the corner of the porch. There isn't a wide enough space for my shoulders to fit through. I look up. Check where The Collection men are. Realize I'll have to stand and slide through the gap to get past the front corner of the house, into the side yard, then hurry through the backyard after.

If they see me. But maybe they won't?

I look at The Collection men again. They're huddled together, talking, then they turn and walk up to the closest house, only one house away from me now. I hold my breath. They're only fifteen feet from me.

I hear the tall, red-haired one say, "Still keeping an eye out, right?"

"Yep," the sentry says, "been watching the whole time." He has that AR-15 across his chest, his finger on the trigger.

The smallest man—the one with the beard—squats down and pets a cat. The cat is gray and black, rubs against his leg, walks, and turns again. He keeps petting it, murmuring and running his hand over the top of its head and back down. Then he stands up and says something too quiet for me to hear.

The other men look uncomfortable.

None of them say anything in response.

That's when I really look at the bearded man. He's so small that he reminds me more of a middle school boy or a teen girl than a grown man. He looks shorter than me—and I'm not tall—but with a brown beard on a thin, fine face. He has small hands and small fingers. He cradles that red box. It's a bright-colored, wooden, cigar box with gold cursive writing on the sides and top.

The bearded man says something again, also too quiet to hear. The men around him bow their heads and make a circle. The bearded man whispers for a moment—with all of their heads bowed, eyes closed—and I realize that they're praying. They all mumble "amen" and open their eyes again.

Then the bearded man and two others go into the house and leave the sentry on the porch. When the sentry swings his rifle away from me, down toward the water and takes two steps in that direction, I stand up quickly, slide through the gap in the bushes and duck into the space beyond the corner of the porch. The hedge runs for twenty feet with a one-foot gap between it and the house. I have to slide sideways, moving quickly, but under my feet there are dry twigs and leaves everywhere. I can't avoid stepping on them and they all make little snapping and crunching sounds. There's no way to be quiet enough.

So I just move quickly.

The sentry says, "Hey! Hello? Who's over there?"

I try to step past a small piles of dry leaves, but my feet make a loud crunch anyway. The sentry can't see me, but he can definitely hear me.

"Hey," he says again, "Stop where you are!"

The space gets so small that I have to move sideways—shuffle—and I keep snapping twigs and leaves under my feet. But I don't stop moving. I'm going as fast as I can sideways now.

"Hey!" the sentry yells to the others. "There's someone over there! At the next house!"

I hear him jump off the porch behind me.

I'm almost to the gap where the hedge ends and the backyard opens up. I keep sliding sideways. It doesn't matter what I step on now because they know I'm here.

But the gunshot surprises me. It's so close, just on the other side of the hedge, and the bullet pings off the house at the same time the sound reaches my ears. I can hear a roaring in my brain as I panic and scream, and—just then—I break through the gap into the backyard and run, run so hard for the far corner, the fence, where I hope there will be a gate, but there isn't one.

I stop and look quickly, not wanting to stop.

There's another gunshot, but I don't know where it goes. I'm not even sure that the sentry can see what he's shooting at through the hedge and the side yard. He's shooting in a general direction, but I'm sure he's coming, and he'll be able to see me soon enough.

In the other corner of the yard, there's a tree next to the fence, its branches low enough to reach, and I sprint to it, pull myself up, swing my feet over, and slide my butt up to a sitting position on the flat top of the fence, where my weight holds me suspended for a moment as I swing to get the rest of my body over and into the alley.

I'm only balanced on the fence for a second or two, but there's another gunshot as I fall forward, my weight carrying me over, into the alley, and my arm feels like it's been stung by a bee, or bitten.

I land and roll. Get to my feet and hold my arm, sprint up the alley toward Fairmount. Two houses up, there's a huge garden, no fence, and I cut left into that yard, running through the long garden beds, then past the house, into the front yard, and up that street.

I don't know if the men are behind me or not, but I keep running, sprint down the street in the direction of the floodwater, toward a house I know that doesn't have fences on the front or back. I'm breathing hard, trying not to think about my arm, telling myself to keep running, keep moving, get to safety before anything else.

I sprint through the double yard, back up that far side of the block and behind another house—open and close two gates—keep moving, gasping for breath now, past an old apartment house, over a small fence knocked halfway down.

At the third block, underneath the shadow of two downed trees leaning against a house, I stop and turn, look back. I try to calm my breathing enough so I can listen, and I hear men yelling directions to each other—maybe a block away—but I can't see them. They're calling back and forth. They're somewhere behind me. It sounds like two are out to my right and two are out to my left. They're coming toward me, sweeping in my direction.

My right arm hurts, but not as bad as I thought it would. It's shadowy where I am, and the bullet hit the back of my arm, so I can't do anything other than feel it. I move my other hand over the top—to see what it feels like, to know how bad it is—and my hand comes away with blood. I wipe it on my shorts. I can't really look at the wound here. There's no light, no mirror, and I don't have time. I jog out from underneath the trees, and keep moving.

Over the next fifteen minutes, I pick my way east toward the big hill, toward Hendrix Park and the thick woods. There are still voices behind me—every now and then—but I know there are hundreds of places to hide in the Hendrix woods if I can only make it to them without being seen by anyone from The Collection. Plus, they don't know where I've been or where I'm going. They'll have to move slower than me as they search. So I have an advantage.

I jog now. I can't sprint anymore because I'm too tired, but I keep pushing forward, keep moving until I make it to Hendrix.

I stay off the main hill road, go through front yards for a while, then cut to the back of an enormous lot, maybe four acres behind a three-story house. In the upstairs, I swear I see movement at a window—a person's face—and I duck down, run harder, hope I was imagining that face.

I scramble over a deer fence—six feet tall and metal— then I'm at the hill behind the acreage, the steep incline, and I hike hard to gain the top of a rise. When I get there, I duck under a bramble, step over a log, and slide into a space between a rock and a tree. From there, I can see everything below me: the hillside, the lot, the house, and the Hendrix road. I don't have to go any further. There's no way anyone will find me here. There are too many options in these woods, and I'm far enough up that I can't be seen.

I watch and wait. See nothing for a long, long time.

I lean forward into a shaft of sunlight and look at my right arm again, twist my hand so I can just barely see the back of my arm above my elbow. There's a fair amount of blood, but when I wipe it away, I can see that the bullet didn't go through. It only sliced the outside, left a one-inch-long cut, not too deep—maybe not even deep enough for stitches.

I wipe the cut again. Press on it to try and stop the bleeding.

I look down the hill.

Wait.

All of a sudden, I notice how tired I am. My tiredness covers me like something heavy. I want to close my eyes, but I won't let myself. And I'm thirsty too. So thirsty. My mouth feels like it's full of dryer lint. I move my tongue all around my mouth to moisten my teeth, blink a few times and yawn. Stretch my neck. I press the cut on the back of my arm and whisper, "Stay awake. Stay awake and watch."

*   *   *

It's a long wait before I see anything. Then—finally— the four Collection men come across the Hendrix road. They're moving steadily but not fast. All four have their rifles up. They're in the same formation as before, three facing forward and one facing back. They move as a team across the road into the front yard of the huge house, the three-story house that I passed earlier.

One of the men sees something and yells. Then they all run to the front of the house, and I can't see them for a minute because they're somewhere inside the structure.

I hear more yelling. The sound of wood breaking. Glass shattering.

Whoever was in the house opens the second-story sliding glass door, and she—a woman—runs out onto the back porch. It's an elevated porch and I see her stop at the rail, fifteen feet off the ground. She hesitates, and the men from The Collection come out onto the porch behind her.

They stop. Lower their rifles.

The woman looks young, maybe in her twenties, thin, with long blond hair. She puts a hand up, just one—in front of her face—as if to shield herself from whatever is coming next.

The small man with the beard hands his rifle to the Collection member next to him. Then he steps forward, slings his backpack down, unzips it, and takes out the red cigar box. He holds the box in his two hands—just like before, when I saw him on the porch a few blocks over.

The young woman tries to lean back but there's only the railing and the drop. There's nowhere for her to go.

The bearded man is directly in front of her now, the red cigar box in between them. I can tell that he's talking, even though I can't hear him. I can see his mouth moving and his head going side to side. He talks for a few minutes, one of his hands coming off the box to gesture as he explains something.

The young woman shakes her head. Then she yells, "No! Absolutely not!"

Then I hear a different sound and I don't know what it is. But I realize it's laughing. The small man with the beard is laughing, and his hands are shaking as he holds the cigar box. He's laughing and smiling at the woman.

He slides the top of the wooden box open and the woman screams. She ducks around him and runs toward the glass door, but one of the other Collection men hits her in the chest with the butt of his rifle, and she goes down immediately, slams onto the deck.

Then she curls into a ball on her side.

The man with the cigar box stands over her. He says something and she shakes her head, holds her hands in tight, her fists clenched against her chest.

The bearded man turns and walks into the house through the sliding glass door, leaving it open behind him. There's a moment when I have no idea what's going to happen. The rest of the Collection men and the young woman are still on the porch. She's lying on her side on the deck, curled up as the men stand above her. None of them say anything. But then the men reach down and grab her arms, straighten them out and drag her by her wrists. She's screaming, kicking her feet, biting at them as they drag her across the deck, through the sliding glass door, and into the house.

She goes silent, and the silence is worse than anything. I lean forward to listen. Try to hold my breath so I can hear.

Then there's screaming again—not like before—but a long, sustained screaming, the sounds of a woman coming apart, her screams vibrating out through the open sliding door, and her screams won't stop.

I want to go down and do something. I want to help her. I stand and think about it. Take a few steps down the hill, then stop, close my eyes and think.

The woman is still screaming, and I don't know what to do.

It's too much. I can't stay here, can't leave her like this. I start jogging down the hill quickly, zigzagging back and forth—taking short, quick steps on the dirt trail—and my feet slip out from under me. I fall and hit the ground, slide and stop against a downed tree branch. When I get up again, I can still hear the woman, but her tone has changed, as if something in her has been broken, as if a piece of her has already been torn away and it will never come back together again. Then I see them coming out the front door of the house, the woman in the middle of them, hunched over, them pushing her along, and their guns pointing out, covering each direction.

The woman's left arm or hand is bleeding, and the blood colors the robe of the Collection man who drags her along.

Then I know it's too late. I'm not the hero in this story, and there's nothing I can do to help her.

I take two more steps in their direction, but I look down at them hurrying along the street, almost out of sight already. I stop and turn, move back uphill, hike over the rise to where the house is no longer in view, walking along a deer path, then up the next hill in the park, into the higher forest, where the trees grow thick and close, where there are hundreds of fallen logs and ferns, spaces for me to hide all night long.

22

WAITING IN THE DARK

W HAT USED TO scare me.
What scares me now.

* * *

I don't sleep all night. Not even for a minute. And in the misty hours between night and morning—at dawn, when the sky opens gray to the east—a bear comes down the hillside. I know it's a bear right away, even though I've never seen a bear. It's funny how that works. I guess I'm starting to understand the world. For example, in the dark, at night, the noise of a small thing can sound big. A mouse could sound like a squirrel, or even a cat. A raccoon could sound like a man. But a bear sounds like a bear because there's nothing else I can imagine that sounds like one thousand pounds.

I hear the bear tearing down through the hillside like it's scraping the undergrowth raw, but it's only walking, only moving its huge bulk slowly through the blackberries and ivy, the ferns and poison oak vines.

When I finally see the bear, I know it isn't a thousand pounds even if it sounds like it, but it's at least three hundred, maybe four hundred, huge-shouldered, back bowed and wide, its weight shifting with every enormous step.

But I can't be afraid of it. Even with its dark weight coming down the hillside toward me—passing the log that I'm hiding under—there are other things in my mind, the sound of a woman's screams still ringing in my ears, the look of The Collection's four robed soldiers, hands holding guns, and the smallest member—the leader of the group—holding a red box that scares everyone.

The bear moves on. Not looking for me.

I close my eyes.

* * *

When it's late morning, I come out of my shelter and sneak down the hill, through the neighborhood, back along Fairmount Boulevard, and finally to my garage.

In the bathroom mirror, I look at the slice on the outside of my arm, where the bullet cut through. The skin has pulled away—up and down—and the line looks more like a burn than anything else. Not too bad. I pick up my tube of antibiotic ointment and smear it over the wound. Then I pull up my shorts and put ointment on the nail hole in my thigh. That puncture is looking worse lately, a big bright circle of pink surrounding the hole, and a clear, yellow liquid seeping out.

I don't know what to do about that.

I try to get the ointment inside the wound, but I can't get much inside or very far, so I find a Q-Tip, dab some Neosporin on the end, and try to mash the ointment inside

the hole that way. But the puncture has closed a little—
and swollen—and the Q-Tip won't fit. So I put an extra
glob of ointment on a Band-Aid and lay that over top, hoping the ointment will soak into the hole.

I'm not sure any of that will work, and I know it's getting infected.

23

OCEANS

THERE WERE SO many days when I didn't know how close they were, how close she was. I remember staring out at Venus in the late evening, watching it burn above the horizon, thinking of the planet setting, traveling west with the earth's rotation, thinking each day's spin might take me to where my mother was. Somehow that made sense in my mind. I was that lonely.

Or I would stare up at the night sky and wonder if she could see the same stars. I imagined some place far away, all of the possibilities of global geography. But that didn't make sense either. She had to be close. Most people don't go very far.

I have no way to describe how much I wanted her back, even though we hadn't been close for a long time. There's no logic to loneliness, just nostalgia for something that never was.

I was a girl in a garage on a mattress. Lying in a loft. By myself.

I was a girl looking out a window at a backyard she's seen a thousand times before.

* * *

I'm remembering all of that as I climb into Mr. Thomas's yard—the yard where a man first touched me. I step around the rhododendrons that have fallen across the brick path. Past the pond with the orange koi, bright against the cloudy water, the fish that drew me in, and the beautiful rose bushes. The redbud tree that I used to stand under, the trunk splintered at its base from the quake. The magnolia trellis crashed to the ground.

I've been in most of the houses and yards on my block already, but I didn't know if I would ever want to search here, didn't trust myself if I found Mr. Thomas alive. I wasn't sure of what I might do to him with all of the opportunities of chaos. So I waited, hoping he would be gone, hoping he would be injured or disfigured, then taken away, nothing I would have to see. Nothing I would feel the need to dismantle, to mangle. Nothing I might injure or kill, myself.

But I didn't have to worry about all that.

* * *

Mr. Thomas is in his backyard still.

He's been here the whole time.

I see his arm bent, his body pinned in place. His pants soiled at the crotch, which makes me smile. His face and chest under a cedar, where the tree fell on top of him. He must have run outside at the start of the shaking, trying to get to a safe place, but the rumble and cracking of the houses and structures was loud, and he probably didn't hear the first shifting of the tree's weight above him.

Some things work out. Sometimes people get what they deserve.

I step around the tree and look at his hand—that one hand sticking out from under a branch—and I think of the way Mr. Thomas first brushed his fingers over the tops of my thighs when I was twelve years old, the way the wine in my cup had turned the world soft, eased the day into something made of flannel.

Mr. Thomas was thirty years older than me. His hands on my thighs were sun spotted. I remember standing up, stepping off his porch, unsteady from my drink. I remember the wobble in my knees as he said, "Please come back and visit me again. We can have more wine together." His voice was as soft as the day around us—no worry in his throat, no hurt—just the flow of the syllables, and I stood there swaying to the music of everything, not even sure why I'd stood up in the first place.

I remember trying to blink my thoughts into focus, to close my eyes and be sure of what I'd been thinking before. Wondering which house my mother was cleaning right then, where I could even find her. I leaned against the porch rail. Stepped up and sat back down.

His hand was between my legs before I stood again— stumbling away—almost falling down the porch stairs, rolling out onto the grass this time.

I looked up at him. He put a finger to his lips as if to tell us to be quiet, as if either of us had made any sound. And he smiled. Still confident. The gold of one of his eye-teeth gleaming in the sunshine. That gold, and the grass beneath me, an unreal green.

I got to my feet again, wobbling. I had to put my hands out to balance myself on my own two feet. The wine made the yard uneven. I took a zigzag step, then another. Whispering to myself, "Just go home now. Just home."

* * *

I'm thinking of that time. And later. Other times. The bright koi in his pond as I lean and look. A tea party he set out for us. Always the best food. Cheese I had never tasted. Dark chocolate squares with sea salt. My first drink of whiskey in a teacup.

How his hands shook before he reached.

* * *

His right hand lying flat now—palm down on yellow grass—Mr. Thomas's fingers spread wide, the hand bloated and splotched with color in the heat. I see a crow waiting for me to leave, its head cocked, the black bird watching me from under the shadow of the cypress along the fence. Two other crows are above him, waiting on a branch.

I stand there. Not sure what I want.

The first crow hops forward—careful, wondering what I'll do next—so I take a step back. The crow keeps coming, hopping and hesitating, watching me, tilting his head side to side, observing me with his dark eyes, waiting for me to move farther away from the body.

So I step back all the way to the gate.

The crow stares at me for a moment longer, then drops his head and begins to peck at Mr. Thomas's forearm. Before I got there, birds or other animals had already opened Mr. Thomas's arm, the forearm split and spread, pieces pulled away.

I stand and watch. The other crows hop down from their branch and join the first crow, pecking and pulling at the meat of Mr. Thomas's forearm, then lifting their heads to swallow.

I watch as the crows hop and eat, work their way up the arm, but they don't eat Mr. Thomas's hand, or not while I'm there. I'm not sure why. His hand remains unopened, bloated and dark but the skin still intact, that palm down, his fingers against the grass, and I wonder if those fingers still hold the smell of his poison.

24

THE HORSE ON THE HILL

ASLEEP, NAPPING, HIDDEN in the ivy of Washburne Park on the hill, something wakes me. A smell. Plus a sound I haven't heard in our neighborhood ever.

I turn my head and see a big white horse on the sidewalk just above the ivy. I have no idea where the horse came from, where it could've lived before the earthquake. I shake my head. Even in the alley houses, between Moss Street and Villard—the houses with the bigger back lots—I've never seen a horse before. There are no cowboys in our neighborhood. No barns. No stalls. Zero arenas. This part of town is not rural, and that smell of a horse is nowhere.

That's what caught my attention: the smell. I didn't even know that horses had a strong smell until this horse walked past me. Woke me all the way up.

I was curled at the base of a hedge in the thick ivy—dozing—then there was a white horse above me. I sat up. The dry leaves crinkled beneath me. The horse whinnied and backed away, then turned and walked along the railing, moving uphill. I stood and climbed after him, swung my leg over the fence as he plodded up the curve of the road.

I follow, and I know which direction he's going.

I've been trying to get brave enough, to overcome my dread, my worry. I've been waiting to go up the hill to find out if my mother's there in that big Collection house, where I've read they keep people.

I've wanted to know, but not wanted to know. I've avoided the one place where I'm most likely to get answers.

But I'm following the white horse now, watching him as he takes measured steps on the blacktop, listening to the clomping of his hooves, the horse glancing over his shoulder at me every once in a while as I follow him. He's curious but doesn't seem worried.

He stops to nudge his nose at yellow grass stems in the cracks—and I stop too, giving him time to pause—then we both start walking again, and I follow along the railing at the upper portion of the park, then along the hedge as the horse turns at the Spring Boulevard cutoff. He stays on Fairmount as the road straightens. We're heading toward the wild section of Hendricks Park, the deep old-growth forest, and I stay back, giving the horse room, watching him, wondering where he'll go from here, wondering if he knows that the compound's main house is just ahead of us.

But that doesn't make sense. Why would a horse care? Why would a horse lead anyone anywhere? This is one of those moments where real life feels like a simulation, like there's a plot in this game, something I think about when I take two bars of Xanax and stare at the wall for four hours. Or stop reading a book and look at the sky, watching the clouds weave in and out of shapes.

The cars on this street look different from the ones in my neighborhood. They're all right side up—angled out, slid and bounced around, but all resting on their tires—the earthquake not jolting this hill as hard as the neighborhoods below. The houses aren't as damaged either. There are walls off-angled and carports caved, but no houses or floors are entirely collapsed. This neighborhood looks like part of a different city, like some place hit by a lesser earthquake.

There's an eeriness to the silence of this neighborhood as well, as if there should be people still living here since it's not as destroyed, as if the lack of total destruction means that more people must have stayed here afterward. It feels as though—at any moment—someone might walk out of one of the houses next to me, step into a car, start the vehicle, and drive off to work.

When we used to have work.

When we used to have school.

The horse stops in front of me. Turns and looks back. I duck behind the rear wheel of a nearby car and wait. I don't want to spook the horse or affect him in any way. I want to follow him wherever he's going. He has to be a symbol like my teacher's talk about, but he's real.

He stops, and I begin to worry. I make the sign of the cross, kiss my fingers, and whisper, "Santa María, Madre de Dios, ruega por nosotros pecadores, ahora y en la hora de nuestra muerte . . ."

I finish the prayer the way my tío taught me.

I stay down until I hear the horse's hooves clomping once again, then I stand and follow. The horse passes a big house, passes a light-yellow Mercedes Benz and a black BMW, both turned into the street from the shaking of the quake, the bumpers kissing at the corners. I'm walking past the second car, the BMW, looking left at the strip of trees and grass before the next house—an enormous white house—and the horse is right there in front of me, only forty or fifty feet up the road, when the gun goes off.

A single, loud crack.

I drop down next to the car, get low and stay low. Lie flat on the ground.

Lift my head to look.

The horse is still in the road, but its rear left leg is bent, buckles, the horse teetering. He waves his head in the air and neighs, turns and tries to bite his own back flank—the hip where the bullet entered. I see the blood run down his leg. He turns a full circle, trying to reach that wound. Then he whips his head back and forth and hobbles forward—up the road—limping forward at a bad trot, his three legs out of sync with the one.

I stay down and watch.

I'm on the ground next to the BMW, and I get up into a crouch, look through the car's side window and windshield, looking at the house up ahead of me, on the left-hand side of the street, where the shooter has to be since that was the only angle where someone could shoot the horse in that hip.

I can't see anything.

I'm waiting for a second gunshot, but no more ring out. I scan each broken window, looking for a rifle on a sill or something in the shadows. I'm scanning for the outline of a person, looking for any movement, but I see nothing.

Then I remember I have a pistol. I pull it out, click the safety off, then look back through the windshield, hoping to see something in the house. My hands are shaking, and I know I won't be able to aim well, won't be able shoot anyone with a pistol from this distance. I make myself breathe, try to calm down. Shake out one hand, then the other. Take a few more deep breaths. Hope that I can shoot straight if I need to.

I do feel like I could protect myself if someone ran out of the house and right up to the car, if they were close to me—maybe only a few feet away—I could pull the trigger and hit them. Probably?

But none of that happens. A minute passes while I stare at the house. No more shots. No more sounds. Nobody leans out a window or makes any movement that I can see. I keep staring at the house, but nothing happens.

I stay low and wait. Watch.

Up the street, the horse is almost to the top of the hill—two hundred yards away—almost to the turn in the forest. The hitch in the horse's gait looks bad. I watch him limp as he walks over the rise at the top of the hill and the turn, and then he's gone, onto the flat where the road drops down and makes a big sweeping left into Hendricks Park, back to where I was the other night.

I look back at the house, the one where I think the shooter has to be. I examine every single window one last time, trying to see a person inside, or a flash of metal. But it's as if I imagined that gunshot, as if nothing ever happened. The horse is gone. The shooter was never visible.

I stay hunched and creep back from the BMW to the side of the Mercedes, glance through the windshield, looking again for any movement in the house, then crawl past a gap until I'm behind a EuroVan at the next house down the hill. I wait behind the van, take a few breaths and watch. Then I continue to sneak back down the road—car to car—until I get to the Spring Boulevard cutoff, and once I'm there, I can finally run.

At the Washburne hedge, I slide into a gap and squat down in the ivy. Breathe and recover. Tell myself that I'll go back up the hill to find my mother soon.

STEALING

M ORNING, I ENTER the big house for the first time since the quake. I squirm through the wreckage, make my way upstairs, through the upper hallway, and into the master bedroom through a gap in the wall. I crawl past the closet doors, both of them open and splintered, jagged shards of wood. I slide past, getting to the bed, ducking under a fallen beam and rising next to the mattress.

They're both there.

John is on this side of the bed. I see the bloodstain across his pillow, the two-by-four that punctured a hole in the left side of his face. The wound and the splatter next to his ear. Julia is on the far side, but mostly hidden in the rubble. Her left arm is all I can see. At the end of that arm, her hand is outstretched, the diamond ring on her ring finger. I don't know why, but I reach over and take hold of it. Her finger has already turned dark, bloated then shrunk, her ring loose. It comes off her finger easily.

As I'm squirming back out through the wreckage, there's another aftershock—three seconds of shaking, maybe four—and the house shifts like a large animal growling. The space in front of me gets smaller and I have to kick a few boards out of the way to get through. But I hold onto that ring and don't drop it.

*   *   *

I take a walk up along the top of the block to clear my head. There are so many overwhelming things in this neighborhood—sights and smells—that sometimes I don't even know how to get away. I have Julia's ring on my left hand now, as if I'm married, a weird symbol since I never liked John. But I'm tired. My brain is fuzzy as I wander across the top of the Fairmount block.

When one of The Collection men steps out the front door of a house, right next to me, it's like I'm in a dream. I turn and face him—don't run or scream, stay right there—and a small sound comes out of my mouth, not quite a word, just a sound.

The man says, "Stay there."

He's one of the tall ones I've seen before, the red-haired man with a beard. Bad skin. He's holding a military-looking AR in one hand, the kind of rifle that looks plastic. He has jewelry in his other hand, and he looks at that handful of jewelry, gold necklaces, rings, and bracelets, a ring falling from the tangle and bouncing off the doorstep into the grass.

I look at the ring on my finger.

The man doesn't pick up what he dropped. He stuffs the rest of the jewelry into a pouch underneath his robe, pulls the strings of the pouch to close it. He gestures back at the house with his rifle, shakes his head, then lifts his rifle again and points it at me. He says, "Stop where you are."

But I'm already stopped. Standing still. I was never in motion to begin with.

This Collection man is thick armed, looks strong and a little bit fat. He takes a step toward me, keeps that rifle pointed at my chest.

I lift my hands. Wonder if I could get away now if I ran, but I don't try. I say, "What are you . . .?" and I look up and down the street, expecting to see the rest of his group coming in and out of houses in each direction, but there's no one else. I realize he's going through these houses alone, and that seems strange. I don't see The Collection out alone.

He says, "Stop," once more as he steps toward me, even though I still haven't moved.

I raise my hands a little higher.

He says, "I'm gonna have to take you with me." He has a country accent, almost southern. He makes a facial expression that I don't understand.

I say, "What?"

"Back to the compound," he says. "We're told to take everybody with us. If we find anybody."

"Who's 'we'?"

"Be quiet," he says.

I look up and down the street. There's no one else in sight. I don't know why he's telling me to be quiet since there's nobody around to hear. I say, "Are you part of the . . .?"

He shakes his head.

My hands are in the air. "Where would you take me?"

"To one of our houses." He steps even closer.

I say, "Can't you just leave me here?"

"God wouldn't want that." He shakes his head again. "Not Witness Andreas either."

"We could pretend," I say, "like maybe you didn't see me. Or maybe I didn't see you?"

The man lowers his gun. Looks at me some more. Rubs his red scalp. He's holding his rifle in one hand, and he looks tired more than anything, big and strong and tired, and also like he's not sure of what to think. He rubs his eyes.

I wonder if he's not very intelligent. Or on drugs. In the news footage from last year, most of The Collection people sounded dull or simple. Like fools that had believed an improbable story.

But I remind myself how dangerous they are. How they're all armed. How many of them went to prison for violence. How their faith makes them believe in a completely different reality.

That wakes me up, and I feel the adrenaline surge into my veins.

Then the man says one of The Collection's weird phrases, something that sounds vaguely like the Old Testament: "You could still be a vessel of help." The words don't sound natural coming from him. It's like he's trying out phrases that he's been taught out of a book.

"What?" I say.

"Something you could do to help . . ."

He sets the butt of his rifle against the step. Leans the barrel against the wall. Turns and faces me.

He's tall. Standing on the same walkway, I see just how tall, a foot taller than me. He rubs his face with his hands, huge hands, wet now with the sweat from his face. "Are you willing to . . . help one of us?"

I say, "Help you?" My heart is pounding.

"Are you given by God?" he says. "One of the . . . uh . . . one of the unfaithful?" Again, the phrases don't sound natural coming from his mouth—with his semi-southern drawl—like a farmer who's been taught Latin by a priest.

I shake my head. "No," I say, "definitely not."

He's standing so close, those huge hands between us.

"Listen," he says, "Witness Andreas has told me that the unfaithful can still aid those of the faith. So this is okay. You don't need to question this." He unzips his pants and points to the ground. Then everything is clear.

He is not subtle. He puts one huge hand on my shoulder and shoves me to my knees.

I feel the cement against my kneecaps—my mind switching to something else. I'm looking at the grass, over-grown and yellow, the dandelion tops gone to seed. There's no wind—everything still—the heat baking the world all around me.

"That's good," he says, and I blink.

He has it out now. I haven't done anything yet, but he says, "This is a good thing. I like this."

So I know what I have to do. I reach up and take it in my hand.

"Don't hurt one of us," he says. "Start slow," and now he doesn't sound religious, just like an average creep.

Us . . .

I look up at his face that doesn't matter now because he's already gone. He smiles and closes his eyes. Puts his hand in my hair.

It's out in front of me, in my hand. I'm on my knees on the concrete, and it's right there in front of me.

He says, "Witness Andreas says women can help us by taking away our desire." His eyes are still closed.

I've got one hand on it. I move that hand just a little bit and The Collection man groans, his head tilting back. I'm watching him carefully.

With my other hand, I'm reaching into my waistband—slow and smooth—pull the pistol out, hold the grip of the 9 mm. Slide the safety off as I ease the gun up between his legs. My left hand is still holding onto his thing, holding him in front of me where he can't move. My right hand is on the gun, the barrel pointing up.

"This is good," he says again. "You can take away all my desire."

I'm still watching him, his eyes closed as my left hand moves a little, but my right hand is steady, holding the pistol.

"Go on now," he says. "Take it in."

And that's when I pull the trigger.

It's such a small action, nothing really, the slight movement of my right index finger, nothing more than a quarter inch—that's all—but it's right in front of my face, the explosion of the gun, the action of the weapon, the recoil twisting my wrist, and I fall back, barely keeping hold of the pistol.

I watch The Collection man fly—as if his body is connected to an invisible wire that rips him up and away—then he falls out to my right, rolling and screaming, his voice one long sound, no real words, just that loud note, that sound, a pitch that goes up and down as he rolls and writhes in the yard.

His hands are between his legs.

I get to my feet, the gun still in my hand, my wrist hurting. I look at the pistol and don't see any smoke or evidence that it was fired. The man is now rocking on the grass, moaning. He's on his side, one hand on his stomach, the other between his legs. He makes a consistent low noise. Then he tries to push himself up to a sitting position and screams.

I'm still holding the pistol. I stand above him. The man opens his eyes, his mouth wide open, too, as he gasps big gulps of air.

I've seen the dead and the dying these past few days, but none of them caused by me, and I wonder about the path of the bullet as it traveled up between his legs. Where it went. How deep. And what it cut through as it traveled through his groin, up through his intestines and into his stomach.

The man twists his head and looks back at the house, toward his rifle. He puts his hands out on the grass and turns his body—groaning—begins to drag himself toward the step, toward his weapon.

I watch him for a few seconds. There's a red smear on the grass coming from between his legs, a dark trail following his body's path.

I stay where I am. I'm one of the solid objects of this world. I'm holding a pistol, standing above a Collection member moving along the ground. Molecules in the air expand. The house behind us is still, and I think of my garage—the days after my mom left—when I would watch the wall until a carpenter ant broke across a plane on the plaster, one object of black moving over the sheer surface of white.

The man drags himself to the little cement walkway, nearer the steps, nearer to his rifle, and I know that I can't let him get all the way there.

I walk up behind him and say, "Stop."

He doesn't listen or respond. He keeps dragging himself toward his weapon, only a few feet away now. I'm right behind him, above him, the pistol in my hand, bracing my sore wrist with my other hand. I say, "Stop," once more.

The man moans, releases a low sound from his lungs at each effort. Dragging and groaning. The bloodline flowing between his legs—out onto the grass—makes a long, red question mark.

I say, "I'm gonna kill you."

He stops and turns his head. His cheeks are red and sweaty. "No," he says, "I'm gonna kill *you*." Then he turns and continues to drag himself.

I blink and there's no longer a thought process.

I pull the trigger four times, aiming at his head,

> Pull
> Pull
> Pull
> Pull,

and the gun jerks a little with each shot. Two bullets go into him, and two bullets ding off the cement next to him.

The man's body twitches all over. Blood comes out of his neck and head, blood still flowing between his legs as well, and I stand over him with the pistol, still pointing it at him. Waiting to shoot him again if I need to.

His right hand wiggles—twitches—then drops.

His mouth makes a small sound like he's blowing out birthday candles.

Then his head turns and his whole body goes still.

I stand and wait, but there's nothing more.

This is when I finally think about the noise of the pistol, the crack of each gunshot, and the echoes afterward. I realize how loud they must've been, ripping through the neighborhood in the middle of the day—in the middle of all this silence—and I wonder if there are any other men in this area, Collection members or anyone else, anyone who might hear and come. I look up and down the street but don't see anything. No movement. Just the bright yellow daylight, the sun baking the asphalt and the cement, the grass and the trees, overturned cars.

But it doesn't matter if I can see them yet because I'm still standing out in the open. So I click the safety back on my pistol, stuff it into my waistband, then reach down, grab the top of the man's robe, where it's fastened at the shoulders, pull hard and realize how big he is, how heavy. It takes all my strength to drag his body ten feet to the bushes off the little front porch. I pull him on his back, get him to the bushes, wedge his body behind the short hedge, trying not to look at the bullet holes or his face, trying not to think about the blood on his robe or my hands.

I take the jewelry pouch and a sheath-knife from him, plus the two extra rifle clips. I wipe blood off one of the clips with a clean part of his robe. Set all those things next to the rifle, then quickly break off branches from the backside of a rhododendron—where the missing branches won't be obvious from the street—and lay them over the top of the body.

Then I snag the gear and jog to the side yard. Walk through the gate to the backyard and start sneaking house to house—over fences, through gates—until I've covered a whole block. Then I cross the street and sneak another block along Fairmount, go through backyards again, hedges, bushes, around and through fences, rose gardens, vegetable gardens with tomatoes and cucumbers rotting in the heat. I don't want anyone to see me.

When I get to Moss Street, I sneak up to the corner. Stop. Hunch behind a maple tree. Point the rifle down the block. Look at the street, expecting a group of Collection men running in and out of houses, searching for the man I just killed, searching for me, but the day is quiet, the afternoon still—even the birds resting through these baking hours when the oven is turned up and the sun sits crackling a few feet closer to the earth.

I look across the street and for the first time wonder if it's obvious that I'm still here, if somehow people can see my trail, all of my paths leading back to where I sleep, to the little garage behind the big house, to the place where I think I'm safe, where I think I'm hidden from the world.

But nobody stays hidden forever.

26

COMMUNITY

"*E*VERYTHING IS FOR *us, for the raising of the people. We are God's chosen—the elect—and there are no others. In this world, there are people of this faith, then there are those who are unfaithful. There is no middle ground.*"

Witness Andreas makes this clear. I write more of his words, exactly how he is speaking them:

"We are of God—reserved in Heaven, The Overcomers— and the rest of the depraved will be left behind for the tribulation, or burning for eternity.

"It is therefore our choice to accept what God has already chosen, the living one hundred and forty-four thousand. We are given only one opportunity to accept, and to darken another door is to give up the great offering, the purest sacrifice in all of history."

I understand what he says.

We must accept.

We must build our community.

We must be the followers.

Witness Andreas says, "We will propagate. We will multiply."

I do not understand all of his words.

But I do my part for the community, always prepare to give in my life, to allow my body as a thing for the Lord, listen to Andreas, and store up my treasures in heaven, rewards that will come to me in the next life. This life is nothing.

Witness Andreas says, "The smell of sulfur is always close at hand, the singed end of a match, the smoking stick of wood. Any turn is a trap. Never question anything because Satan is lying in wait all around us. Satan wants us to ask questions. Satan wants us to doubt. And Satan will not sleep. He will never sleep."

27

TRUE NORTH

SOMETIME BEFORE DAWN—I couldn't sleep—I'm swigging off a half-full Jack Daniels Black Label bottle that I took from 1928 Moss. Evening. Another swig. I'm an hour into drinking, the alcohol slithering through the front of my brain. If I close my eyes, I see the blood spurting from the side of The Collection man's neck. I nod and tell myself that his death was a good thing because it was.

"A good thing."

"A good thing."

I close my eyes. Pull the trigger again. Smile.

Drink.

Two rats scurry in between the jars and the bins where I've started storing my food. I raise the whiskey bottle to the rodents. "Tenemos que escabullirnos y estar escondidos," I say. I wink at them.

I'm tipsy.

The rats run out the front door that I can never quite close.

I go out for a walk, holding the pistol in my right hand, the bottle in my left. Wearing a backpack with water and snacks. I walk a block over to the park, to the wide-open space at the top of the hill.

Standing there, everything swimming below me and the Pole Star standing above me at forty-five degrees. I look straight up. Find a different star above me in a constellation I don't know—swig from the bottle. I watch that new star. Put my arms out and spin with the earth, everything curving below me, and that one star wobbling in a circle above my head.

My mother is this same sort of wobble. Even if I could see her I couldn't change anything. There's no way to fix her. Nothing in her I could trade out—because there never was—and I wonder if all children finally realize this, that the set constellations of their parents, the clear, cold stars of their reality are forever:

My mother next to a sheet-metal pile at the dump.

My mother with that red-lettered Collection Bible.

My mother staring off as the tortillas burn.

*   *   *

And now she's dead . . . or not dead. I don't know, and I wonder. Looking down at my feet, I imagine her underground, worms crawling through her loosening flesh and the chemistry of her brain leaking into one thing, the melting inside her skull.

I take a sip and allow her to be dead, but not much changes. Then I imagine her alive again, eating scavenged food after the earthquake, picking through the wreckage like me.

I know nothing. My science teacher told me that the earth is spinning at a thousand miles per hour, but I can't feel it.

I drink.

Pretend I can feel the velocity of the planet spinning through the darkness, the windshield of this vehicle driving toward the end of night and the rise of a sun that lasers through the sky without ever moving at all.

I read so many things in my stars and planets books that I can't remember them all. Tipsy now, they run together: Venus tilted and in retrograde? Two hundred and forty-three earth days for a single sunrise? Is that right? I can't remember with Mercury . . . Mercury has two or three days per year . . . or two or three years per day? Something . . .

I take a swig.

Blink.

Eyelids heavy—a little tired now—but I open my eyes again. Walk down to the bottom of the park where there's an enormous redwood tree, one I've climbed many times before. I slide my backpack off. Put the pistol and the Jack Daniels bottle inside. Take hold of a low-hanging branch— a branch drooping thirty feet out from the tree—swing my legs up, hooking my heels, and I begin to climb.

My right hand slips, but my left hand holds. I keep climbing. My foot slides off and I put it back on. Force myself to breathe and focus. I've done this so many times, but not drunk, not with Jack Daniels swimming my veins, and I'm monkeying up this long, single branch, moving toward the trunk, where I'll be able to reach the other branches.

When I get there, I have to swing my weight around to grab the next branch, pull my foot up, breathe, and make sure that I'm precise. But I get it and stand, reach the next branches, then the ones after that, and it's easy to climb from here. The branches are evenly spaced, close together. I ascend to a place I call the Crow's Nest, where I can look out on the city from an opening in the tree, an old scar on the trunk showing branches that fell off years ago.

I sit in the crow's nest and watch the light rise to the east, the morning coming, the night receding, and I whisper, "Me viene la madrugada."

*   *   *

After dawn, from the redwood tree in Washburne Park, I see motion out in front of me in the low neighborhood east of the park. It's two blocks away, but there's no mistaking the robes on the three men working house to house. Even from this distance—and up in a tree—I'm worried that I'm too visible. I make sure not to move: *don't climb up or down, just sit in the tree and look out.*

I can see The Collection men—three of them—working through the University Hill houses, searching for something, and I know what they're searching for, *who* they're searching for.

Two of them go into each house, the sentry staying at the door while the others search. I picture them searching rooms, hallways, closets. Going into the flooded basements of each house. Checking attics and crawlspaces. All the places I check for food or water, for other things. But they're checking for a body or a living person, anywhere he could be.

They keep moving house to house, and now they're only a block away from me—but down below—when they turn onto Agate Street. I watch them working parallel to the park, going south, and on their third house, they find

someone. From up in the tree, I can faintly hear the yelling, the sentry in front sprinting to a jumble of cars, three
vehicles smashed together by the quake, and he gets low
and points his rifle right, then left, scanning the neighborhood. He yells something. Waves his hands.

The other two bring a man out of the house, a middle-aged man with long, gray hair. The man isn't tough-
looking, not soldierlike. He looks exhausted, hungry, and
thin. He has his hands up—in between the two Collection
men—and he gets jostled side to side as they nudge him
forward.

There's more yelling, then the sentry stands, runs
toward them, drops his rifle and tackles the gray-haired
man who goes down hard, flat on his back, and doesn't
struggle, doesn't fight back in any way. The sentry turns
him over onto his stomach, pulling his arms behind his
back, then sitting on him while he zip-ties his wrists.
When he's got the man secured, the sentry stands him,
steps away, and picks up his rifle again. The other two Collection men lift the man to his feet, propping him back up,
and pushing him forward into the street.

The man is wobbly now. He needs help to stay
upright—he slumps a little as he shuffles along—and the
Collection men support him on both sides.

The small Collection man who seems like the leader is
leaning into the gray-haired man, looking like he's speaking to him, but I can't hear anything from so far up in the
tree. I can only see the tilting head, the nodding, and—
finally—the gray-haired man shaking his head no, then
shaking his head some more.

There is no cigar box this time, but I wonder about it.

They march the long-haired man down to the corner,
around the block to the slope of Emerald Street where the

water begins. They go out of sight and I wait. Five minutes later, there's the sound of a boat's engine starting up, the rev of an outboard motor gaining speed. They motor along, and I see that black flatboat at a streetlight before it goes out of sight again. They're boating north now—into the deeper water—and I don't see where they're headed.

After a minute, the sounds of the boat and the engine die out. I remember my Jack Daniels bottle and take it out. Sip whiskey and watch the neighborhood that's gone still again.

I wait a long time—fifteen or twenty minutes—to make sure they're not coming back, but they don't return. So I put the bottle back in my backpack, climb down out of the tree, hike up through the park, and sneak back to my garage.

I'm halfway between drunk and hungover. I climb the ladder and flop down onto my mattress, feel the start of a headache coming on. I swallow two Advil and drink a full bottle of water. Then I fall asleep.

28

NEVER SAFE

Tonight, after sleeping and eating and drinking more water—when it's dark and I'm feeling less hungover—I go out searching houses for food again. I fill a backpack with cans and boxes, food that will last, but more importantly I find a stand-up paddleboard paddle in a closet. It's not made for a canoe, but it's light and strong, and it'll work better than the broken half paddles I've been using until now.

I'm holding that paddle as I walk out the front door of a house, when the sound of a helicopter surprises me. I get low, wait and watch, and the helicopter drops out of nowhere to hover over Fairmount Boulevard in the dark—only a block away from me—its spotlight sweeping through the downed trees on the street. It's one of those military-looking helicopters that are always in action movies.

I jog to the street and slide under a car, pull the paddle in after me. I can't see the helicopter as it gets closer, but I can hear it. And when it stops midair, not too far from me, I can feel the wind off its rotors. The helicopter hovers for a few seconds, the spotlight sweeping all around, and the air blasting the dirt and grit onto my face.

Then the helicopter heads up the hill into Hendrix, the sound fading as it flies away. I'm lying in an oil spot under the car still, and I can smell the grease above me on the engine block, the rubber hoses and belts that have baked to brittle in the heat. I have dirt all over my face from where the helicopter blasted me.

I slide out from underneath the car, push the paddle and my backpack out in front of me, and I'm just clear of the car, starting to stand up, when a second helicopter drops in, only half a block away this time. The spotlight is pointing in the other direction but it begins to sweep toward me and I dive back under the car again, pulling paddle and backpack in next to me once more.

These helicopters being here is weird since there's never been another rescue effort after the first two days, no FEMA teams, no one checking the rubble, no Red Cross workers or medical teams. I don't know if there isn't enough money for all that or if there aren't enough people to help. Maybe Eugene, Oregon, isn't big enough to really matter, or maybe there were so many destroyed cities and towns that they couldn't begin to help them all. I wonder about all of this. We used to live in a world where everything felt connected to everything else, news and purchases and people and entertainment available at the tap of a finger. But now that's all gone. Each city is its own thing, each neighborhood really. How far would a person go in a day, and for what?

* * *

I hold the new paddle as I walk back to my garage, and in the first dawn hour, before it's fully light, I drag my canoe to the bottom of Moss Street, the loud rasp of metal against asphalt again, then the smooth shift to open water.

I paddle along Nineteenth Street, two deer standing in the shallows as I glide by, the outlines of them like dark etchings on the water. I think about protein, wonder if I could shoot a deer for its meat. But I know I'm not a hunter, and I wouldn't know the first thing about gutting an animal or different ways to preserve the meat. There'd be no way to keep the meat cool, no freezers or refrigerators, and no cold nights. Shooting a deer would be a complete waste. So I think about other food.

I visit two apple trees in front yards, their trunks underwater but their branches and fruit right at the level of my canoe. I pick a few dozen, the biggest ones I can find. They're not quite ripe yet, still sour but fresh, and they taste good. I've been mostly eating cheeses and bars, cans of tuna, crackers or chips, and it's nice to have something different.

I paddle all the way down to the arena, then back the way I came. It's getting light out, and I'm not comfortable staying in the open too long, even in the half-light of morning. I get to the flood line, the edge of the water, and I drag the boat up to a nearby driveway, flip it and pull the length of the hull under a carport at the bottom of the block. Slide the new paddle underneath.

Then I hear a sound behind me. It feels like this is always happening.

I duck between the canoe and the post of the carport. Look out. Don't see anything at first, but then I see movement coming right to left, something down the flooded street. I'm not sure what it is at first, not in the limited dawn light, and I stay low, stay quiet.

A raft comes into view. Standing in the middle, there's The Collection woman. She's pushing her raft along the street again, still wearing her old dirty Collection robe, still talking to herself as she slides along on her wooden raft. I see the parakeet cage and a cat, the growlers of beer and gallon jugs of water, plus a few boxes of something. All of that is piled on the left side of the raft, the side that's facing me.

Her raft is wider than the last time I saw it. She's added to it, built extensions with extra pallets of wood. It looks twice as wide as before—thicker now too, with ropes and boards connecting the whole thing, inflated inner tubes along the sides—and the woman is standing at the back corner where she can reach down into the water and push with her pole, the whole raft tilting as she leans.

She also has one of those plastic-looking ARs. It's slung over her shoulder, and I wonder how many assault rifles were in this one neighborhood before the quake. I whisper, "I guess we're all ready to go now."

The woman's raft catches on something in the water, a submerged car maybe, and the raft spins in a slow circle. Then I see the other half of the raft, the side that was hidden by the woman's boxes and jugs. On that half of the raft, there's a body just like before, another man, also naked, pale, and bearded. But this body hasn't been in the water. It hasn't been cleaned. There's blood all over the man's stomach and thighs, and a big, dark hole where his genitals used to be.

The woman says something to herself, then makes a different sound, and I realize that she's laughing. She's gliding along, pushing herself with that raft pole, talking and giggling to herself.

This time, when she passes me, I don't follow her. I don't sneak down along the block, and I don't want to know what she's going to do with the body. I can already imagine, and I don't want to watch.

29

THE RODENT LIFE

I SLEEP ALL DAY. I'm becoming nocturnal, with only short night-time naps. I wake in the late afternoon. Don't go out until evening, until the sun is down near the horizon. Every step I take makes me nervous. I don't know who I'm going to run into. I'm hoping that it's late enough that The Collection members have already been here, that they've gone back to wherever they're staying.

My leg is sore, so I put a glob of antibiotic Neosporin on the puncture hole. It's looking worse lately.

I walk over to another garden to pick tomatoes, the only produce that's still doing well in this summer heat, and I see movement along an electrical line. A squirrel jumps from the line to a branch above me, runs to the center of the tree and stops, camouflaged there. I think about how much I'm like that squirrel, foraging for small things, finding and keeping each new discovery, packing them away in my garage.

And at any noise, I run and hide.

* * *

I remember hiding from Verónica, Tío Pablo's young girl-friend, when I was little. She would call me home in the evening at dinnertime, trying to sound like a parent, yelling, *"¡Cielo! ¡Niña! ¡Estamos comiendo!"* But I never came to her. I would either duck down into a dark space and wait her out, or I'd play a trick on her, sneaking around the back of the landfill and returning to Tío Pablo's house from the other side. I'd step through a back window into the house and pretend like I'd always been there.

I liked to listen to Verónica calling me as I sat at the small table behind her back, waiting for her to turn around. Then I'd smile at her and act as if I'd never heard her call my name at all. The look on her face was perfect, exactly what I wanted.

* * *

I find a small space in the back corner of the garden that still has some green grass. There's a gravity-fed hose from a cistern, the drips of water continuing to hydrate the long strip of grass along the fence. I run my fingers over the shoots. Get down on my hands and knees and smell it. Then I lie down in the grass's lushness.

It's evening—and I've slept already today—but I still must be tired because I fall asleep immediately, sleep long and hard on that cool, green grass, sleeping most of the night.

When I wake up, it's that odd hour between night and day again, and I'm cold. I curl into myself even more. Slowly wake. Think the cool is from the grass and the nighttime, but when I open my eyes, it's more than that.

The morning is dark gray, misty, twenty degrees cooler than a usual summer morning. I stand and stretch, shivering a little as I stare at the sky, thinking how it looks like a morning in fall, how even though it's not really cold, it's so much colder than usual. This morning I can imagine this same neighborhood when it's late fall—not summer anymore—when every morning will be gray, when the mist will shift and the day will turn to rain.

I don't know what makes a day twenty degrees colder than the day before. I don't know anything about weather. But I realize—for the first time, and I don't know why I haven't thought about this before—that things will change quickly, the length of days first, then the weather, and the flooding may be still here. I realize that the city might continue to be a lake, and I might not be able to stay here in this neighborhood over the winter.

I might run out of food. Or fresh water.

As I walk back to my garage, I look up at the gray mist and the trees shivering in the wind. Think about the different possibilities, and where I could go. It's hard to imagine. Looking at other places online—the only thing I've ever done—is not the same as going to those places in real life. I don't have a good concept of the nearest cities to me. I can't imagine being in Portland right now, or on the Oregon Coast, or out east in the high desert. I've seen pictures of all those places—and my science teacher made us study the varied biozones in Oregon—but I can't put myself anywhere else. Not in my mind.

Also, how would I live and what would I do? How would I have money for anything?

Money . . .

And it hits me just like that. I need to plan for a different type of survival—the survival of afterward, of whatever comes next, of my new life and the new world to come. I need to go back through houses and search again, but not just for food, not just for water. I need to stockpile cash and valuables, get together a big pile of money, of jewelry, maybe small electronics. And . . .

. . . I'm not sure what else. Items I can sell or trade later?

I know the neighborhood well enough—I've written things down, taken notes, drawn maps. I've had a lot of time. So when I get to my garage, I look at my notes. Everything categorized:

- There are eighty-four houses between Fairmount and Nineteenth—just in those blocks—above the waterline. Plus the hill, an unknown number of additional homes.

- Thirty-seven of the eighty-four lower houses have something big and dead inside, something festering, and those houses smell so bad I can't go inside them for anything, not for food or water, not for money or gold, because it's impossible to breathe in those houses. So those houses are out.

- There are sixteen houses that don't smell at all—they're like empty boxes—unless I open a freezer or a refrigerator (which I don't anymore). Those are the houses I'll search later. I have time to go through those houses in the future.

- Then there are thirty-one houses that I wouldn't categorize as really good or really bad. They have some dead or rotting things inside, but not humans, not big bodies, and I can stomach the smaller smells. Those thirty-one houses are the ones I'll search first over the next few days.

I start, go on a planned loop, beginning on my own block with the yellow house, 1956 Moss. This is a different game, and I'm not spending all my time in kitchens and pantries. I go through side rooms, junk drawers, desks, TV rooms, bedrooms, places I haven't looked. I search night-stands and dressers, bins and bathroom cabinets. This is like when I looked for drugs and weapons, but now it's for money or anything small and valuable. I have my back-pack and I start filling it.

After a few hours I have more than $600 in cash and two or three pounds of gold and platinum jewelry. Quite a lot, actually.

The day has turned darker, and I look up at the sky. There's an enormous gray cloud coming toward me, heavy and darkening, turning to violet, a stacked storm cell, and I don't want to be caught out in the open when it hits. There might be thunder and lightning, maybe hail. The underside of the cloud is billowing, looking like a brain flipped upside down.

I find a solid, covered area behind the nearest house, a tin-roofed shed over concrete, with trees crisscrossed above. These are the structures that survived the earthquake—places like my garage—small structures that didn't have trees fall on top of them. This shed was saved by two trees falling directly next to it, nothing on top of it. I lean my rifle, my AR against the shed wall.

The wind picks up and I step out next to one of the trees and look up at the sky once again. The big, dark cloud is almost over the top of me now. I can see the fun-nels of purple spinning in the underside, ribs of deep lav-ender and gray.

There's a little flash in the southwest. Then another. And thunder claps, smacking directly afterward, no delay, and I know how close the lighting is to me. I get back under the roof.

Then the rain begins. Not light rain but big, wide drops, the weight of them banging the tin roof above me. The smell of fresh water is overwhelming, wet splatter everywhere, and a mist hitting my face. I check to see my rifle is far enough under the overhang to remain dry.

At the corner of the shed, one of the roof seams is ripped—maybe from the earthquake—and there's a run, a drizzle from that seam. I watch the water run in, pool near my feet as another lightning strike bleaches the world in front of me.

Thunder rolling. More lightning. And rain like the clouds are torn open by great claws. Swaths of water welting down on the grass next to the shed, onto the roof, slashes of rain, and it sounds like the shed will come apart all around me.

Then—just like that—the rain stops. There's another lightning strike. Then another. But they're to the northeast of me now. Thunder claps between each strike, close by, but the clouds are moving away now, going out over the water of the flooded neighborhood.

I watch the big, dark underside of the cloud cruising to the northeast as if I'm looking at the bottom of a giant ship, an improbable bright sun shining on the wet world all around me, everything turned to newly blown glass. And the smell is incredible—moist and fertile—and I lie down, roll a burlap sack from the shed as a pillow, close my eyes, and fall asleep.

When I wake, the sun has moved thirty degrees to the west, shining only on my feet, and I know a couple of hours have passed. I stand, stretch, grab my rifle. Sling my backpack, begin to walk back to my garage.

I'm thinking about all of that rain, the big storm, and the locations of each rain barrel in the neighborhood. I'll be able to wash my face and hands in fresh water today, and maybe—if I'm lucky—find a tub big enough for me to get completely inside to bathe. I've fantasized about showers and baths lately, clean water and soap, rinsing afterward, all that extra water running down the drain.

I'm imagining a good bath as I come down the sidewalk, but at the walkway to the front of my garage—the path that wraps around the side of the big house—I realize that something's different. I can't say why. It's just a feeling at first, but the feeling is strong enough that I slow down, begin to take quieter steps.

Something's not right.

I come around the bush where the path curves, and I can finally see the front of my little garage, the front door open—did I leave it that way?—and then I can hear voices inside, men's voices.

I stop.

Raise the barrel of my AR. Point it at the door in case any of them come through the opening while I'm in sight. I take a tiny step backward. Slow now. Another tiny step.

Two voices. Then a third. Quieter now. Too quiet? I wonder if they heard the sounds of my steps. I stop and hold my breath. Point the barrel at the door.

They're talking to each other in my little space, in my garage. There's a clunking sound.

I step backward again, so slowly.

Another sound inside, something being moved. My hands are shaking, and I try to take a deep, slow breath. Aim my rifle—steady now—at the open door, holding my breath for a few seconds to listen.

I hear one of the men say, "Throw that here."

Another voice says, "This?"

"Yeah, let's see what she was doing."

I keep the barrel of the rifle pointed out in front of me, backing away, around the small bush, turning at the path, and then the door is out of sight. So now they wouldn't be able to see me.

I'm still walking backward, though, still quiet, focused, placing my feet carefully, moving toward the street, until I'm out at the front of the carport and onto the sidewalk. Then I turn and run.

Run fast.

30

GREED

*O*NE OF THE *seven deadly sins. We must put this desire away like so much else. There is nothing we can take from this world into the next life, where the collected and redeemed saints will gather for eternity.*

Witness Andreas makes this clear, and I write it as he says it:

"We are not to want, or to be overcome with desire. Instead, we are to give up our desires and only ask for our daily requirements, our simple needs—nothing compared to the eternal gift, the bread of life, the cup of Christ's blood, the river of the newly risen souls. This is our vision."

He says this twice, and I write every word. Also this: "Keep your eyes peering straight ahead, even though we're in darkness."

All of this instead of greed . . .

. . . Greed would take all of this away. If we focus on our wants instead of our needs, soon we will be thinking of

nothing else. Then there will be great battles before the end—"a tribulation," Witness Andreas calls it, "even before most are raptured."

The Collection renews my mind, cleanses me to a new way of thinking. The Collection allows me to grow strong both for this world and then for the next.

"We will not be given anything here on this earth because we are enemies of this earth—inheritors of the next.

"There is a revolution coming. The just shall reap the great reward in this overturning. The fight on this earth will give us great standing in the pure world to come. But here we will see great vats of blood. Blood pouring forth."

After I hear Witness Andreas speak these words, I say a childhood prayer to myself, maybe the only prayer that is still okay to say because it is not just for a Catholic. But I tell myself to ask him if it is okay the next time we are alone together—I will make sure that I am allowed to pray these words:

Gloria al padre, al Hijo, y al Espíritu Santo. Como era en el principio, ahora y siempre, por los siglos de los siglos. Amén.

31

THE MOMENTS THAT END

I HIDE ALL NIGHT between a garden shed and a fence, a dark space, and try to sleep but can't, staying awake until dawn. In the morning, when I crawl out, the moon is a silver lozenge to the east, hanging in the late violet of the fading night, the last shades of dark, and there's a crease of expanding light coming from the direction of the Hendrix hill. It would be beautiful, but I'm so tired, so scared—daylight is something I don't want anymore.

I can't go back to my garage and hide. Or sleep.

I don't know where to go now. What to do.

I crawl back into the space between the shed and the fence, empty my pockets and my backpack to see what I have with me:

- The pistol and two clips, the one in the gun still missing four cartridges
- The assault rifle, two clips

- Two big handfuls of jewelry
- $637 in cash
- My phone, seven percent charged
- Headphones
- A mostly empty water bottle
- Half of a beef jerky packet
- Two sour apples

No extra clothes. No extra water or food.

I close my eyes and breathe, trying to stay calm. I realize that I'm crying, and I tap my fists against the fence boards. I want to punch them so hard, but I can't panic. I have to do something productive. I have to go somewhere.

I tell myself that there's food and water all over. I can find more. Plus, I can get more clothes from almost any house. I'll be okay.

I try to think through all of the houses that I've looted for food and water. The problem isn't in picking a place to stay, because I could sleep almost anywhere, in almost any house that doesn't have an overwhelming smell. But I have to know which house has already been visited by The Collection, which blocks and houses will they remember that they've gone through? Which places will they not return to? For example, if they were searching for the red-haired Collection man—the one I stuffed behind a hedge—would they come back to an already-searched house to look for him? Where would they come back again?

I replay houses and neighborhoods in my mind. Think of each location where I've seen The Collection, and what they seemed to be doing at those places. I think back, house to house.

The other problem is that I don't know what The Collection wants. I'm not sure why they're still in the neighborhood. And since I don't know what they're look-ing for, I start with that, trying to understand their motives.

In one way, they could be like me, maybe they don't trust the government or where the government would've put them if they'd gone with the rescuers that first day. But they have papers . . .

Or they might wonder if they'd run into police or National Guard if they left this area. And if they're rational—not saying that The Collection members are rational—they might wonder if the government would think they were insane or dangerous if caught. But again, I don't know if they'd think that.

So maybe The Collection stayed in the neighborhood for other reasons. The red-haired man was looting houses for jewelry. What if The Collection was looking for certain valuable items, looking in the houses for money or gold, something that they could sell or trade later when this was all over? If they stockpiled enough of those things, they could get wealthier? Or maybe if they took bank account numbers and social security cards they could commit cybercrimes later? But that's assuming that they're finan-cial criminals, or even that they want wealth. And that doesn't seem likely.

So I think about it some more. What if they stayed because they want people? What if the red-haired man was acting on his own, but the rest of them have a dif-ferent idea? I saw them take the young woman from the house at the bottom of Hendrix Park, and they also took that middle-aged man from the lower neighborhood near Agate Street. So maybe they're taking people somewhere. Maybe they need people for something. And that makes sense. That fits with what I've seen, seems more true than anything else.

So if they want people . . .

I have two houses I can choose from: The Hendrix house where they captured the young woman, or the lower neighborhood house where they captured the middle-aged, gray-haired man. I don't really want to go to either of those houses, but that's where I know they've already taken people from. So I think about my two options: The lower neighborhood house is small, which is nice, easy to defend, but also maybe too exposed, in the middle of everything. The Hendrix house is where I heard all of those screams, and I don't want to go there because of that memory, but . . .

I take a few breaths. Try to calm down and think rationally.

Which house would be better?

Even though I'm afraid of it, the Hendrix house has major advantages: It's big enough that it might hold a lot of food and supplies, and it borders the park. I'd have a quick escape path up into the woods if anyone showed up. That house also has multiple stories, and decks coming off those stories, so I'd have a high perch to see who's coming, or to shoot from with the AR.

Also, a young woman lived in that house, so I could steal her clothes. I could fill a backpack with basics like T-shirts, a sweatshirt, and maybe shorts or jeans if she's anywhere near my size. Maybe a waterproof coat for the winter.

I try to imagine myself in that house. I imagine staying there, picture myself not thinking about the young woman—not thinking about her screams—and I talk myself through it. I talk to myself out loud, saying, "You'd be okay. You're not her. And The Collection probably wouldn't come back. Plus, you didn't know the woman anyway."

I tell myself to focus on me, focus on this moment and what I need. I close my eyes and nod, say, "What do you need, Cielo? What's best for you?"

This is what I'm not good at.

My whole life I've known that survival is a frame of mind—how I think matters more than anything. Practice good thought patterns.

So I try to go further with my thoughts, create a narrative: I imagine that the young woman was a bad person, she did terrible things to people before the earthquake, so it wouldn't matter what happened to her in that house . . .

But I can't make myself believe the story. I keep hearing the sounds of her screams in my head, how terrified and powerless she sounded, and I start to cry again.

So I just sit and breathe.

Tell myself to be strong. Say aloud, "You can do this. You can do this. You can live in her house. You are strong enough, Cielo. You've always been strong enough."

That is true. I'm a survivor.

I open my eyes and pick up my phone, plug the headphones in, and slip the earbuds into my ears. Select Alessia Cara's "Here," the only lonely song I can think of right now. I say, "Fuck this world. Fuck everyone and everything they care about." Then I lean back against the fence and hit "Play." Close my eyes and let the music soak me.

*   *   *

When the song ends, I see my phone's battery is only at four percent. I turn it off. Put it away in my backpack. Stuff everything else inside my backpack as well. I don't have much with me, but it's a start. And I'll go from here, find more food, more water, make a new stockpile. Then I'll make a better plan.

As I search houses this morning, I look for three things: water, food, and weapons. And on Orchard Street, I find what I forgot I was looking for: a rain barrel half filled by the runoff from a big roof and gutter system.

I look around and don't see anyone. Go inside and find dish soap in the kitchen, then come back out. Strip quickly and using my T-shirt as a rag, I dunk the T-shirt and wash my face, then dunk it again and wipe my chest, my stomach, and the fronts of my legs. I wet the shirt again and again, and squeeze it over the back of my neck, let the water run down. Then I soap up. Lather and rinse. It feels incredible, and I scrub my body until I feel as clean as possible. My armpits are especially bad, they reek horribly, so I wash them twice, soap them up and rinse, then soap and rinse them again. Then they smell okay—not wonderful, but okay.

Finally, I pour soap directly on the puncture wound on my leg, lather and scrub it, hope the soap does something more than just help the surface be clean. The wound is pink-rimmed and raised—like a volcano with a crater in the middle, that crater getting wider—and I'm getting pretty worried about infection.

I wash the hole three times and really hope that the soap helps.

32

A NEW BEGINNING

B Y LATE MORNING, I've picked up a twenty-gauge shot-gun plus shells, and a machete, three bottles of water (I drink one), tuna cans and a can opener, a box of Cheez-Its, a loaf of stale white bread, and an unopened jar of Jif peanut butter. I eat a peppermint-chocolate-brownie Luna bar I find in a drawer.

I know this will be one of the hottest days because the early-day heat is incredible. By ten o'clock, it's at least ninety degrees. It's a swelter-blown summer day, and when I get down to the far end of Walnut Street, I can't see a wisp of cloud anywhere in the sky, just blue and wide, hard and pale above me.

I'm down by the water when the earthquake starts up again, rumbles the water as if it's made of gelatin, the sur-face alive and quivering, but then it stops—after five or six seconds—and nothing new falls down around me. This is

the biggest aftershock yet, the longest and strongest settling of the earth.

The cloudy green water is flat once again, and I look
out, see the tops of submerged cars—only the shadows
of them visible from where I am—like pods of forgotten
whales. I know I have to go up to my new house on Hendrix, have to start setting up in my new location, stockpiling, preparing to fight or run. I walk up Walnut, turn on
Fairmount, and access the park road. I don't walk on the
actual blacktop, but in the ditch to the side of the street,
past the sidewalk.

When I get to the house, I see that the front door is
open—they left it like that—but I don't feel like going
through that door. There's something creepy about it, so I
walk around back.

I pull out my pistol, flip the safety off, and start looking in windows. Most of them are broken, but a few are
intact. I keep my pistol up, point it in every direction I
look. At the broken windows, I lean over the sills, look
right and left, check to see that no one is inside, no one
hiding up against a wall, waiting for me.

The inside of the house looks like all the rest, furniture thrown in every direction: TVs, computers, books,
pictures, tables, and chairs tossed all over. Nothing's where
it's supposed to be. But I don't hear or see anything. And
when I look in the windows, I only smell a little rotten
food. Nothing else.

I go into the house through the back door. Keep my
pistol barrel in front of me. Check the first-floor rooms,
then the second floor, then the third. The stairs are tilted
but intact, and it doesn't take too long to check the entire
house. There's no one here, nobody hiding in a closet or a

bathroom, nobody out on the small roof alcoves or on the decks. When I realize that the house is completely empty, I take a deep breath and lower my pistol. Put the safety back on.

I return to the second floor—the one with the big deck out back—and I stand in the room where the young woman was screaming. I don't want to, but I know I have to. I have to face my fear right now, the very first day I'm in this house. On the floor behind the couch, there's a blood spot the size of my hand. I close my eyes and remember the woman's screams, how guilty I felt listening to them as I did nothing to help her, as I hid in the forest.

When I open my eyes again, I'm crying, but I tell myself to stop. There's nothing I can do about it now. It's over. And even then—that night—there was nothing I could've done all by myself.

I wipe my face and walk downstairs. Look around more slowly this time. The house is huge. The first floor has a bathroom, an office, an entertainment room, a dining room, a living room, and a kitchen. In the kitchen—on the cutting block—there's one large knife and a spray of blood. Droplets leading to the floor, then more droplets.

I shake my head but don't close my eyes. Don't let myself cry again.

The day is getting dark. I have to be stronger now. I take the knife and the cutting board out into the backyard and throw both of them over the fence. I don't want to have to look at them each day as I stay here.

33

MY FORTRESS

I START BY BARRICADING the front door with two couches, a table, three chairs, and a bookcase. When I'm finished, I climb over the pile of furniture and try the door, but it won't move even a quarter of an inch. I pull as hard as I can, but it doesn't budge. Then I go out the back door and around to the front of the house, try the front door again—from the street—really throw my shoulder into it, but still it won't move. I'm happy with the barricade, so I go back around through the kitchen door and start cleaning.

The refrigerator is on its side, crashed open. The smell of the spilled food and warm freezer contents is terrible, and I wonder why the young woman didn't clean this up while she was here.

I find garbage bags and gloves under the sink. Pack everything up, close the bags tight, and carry them outside into the backyard. There's a tall fence between this house's yard and the downhill neighbor's. I throw the closed garbage bags far over the fence into the next yard.

Then I go back into the kitchen to search for cleaning supplies. I find bleach, Windex, and Spray 'n Wash. I bleach the kitchen floor and counters. Spray 'n Wash over the little bit of blood that dripped off the cutting board. Then I take the Spray 'n Wash upstairs and pour most of it over the bloodspot behind the couch.

I move on to the bathrooms. Two of them have toilets broken at the bases, dirty water seeping—brown stains across the floors—so I bleach the tiles to get rid of the smells, wipe the floors with towels, then take the towels out back and throw them over the fence as well.

I scavenge the pantry for what the woman left uneaten. There's a two-liter bottle of Cherry Pepsi, half a box of Wheat Thins, five cans of black beans, half a bag of basmati rice, three empty cereal boxes, miso soup packets, hot chocolate mix, and a bag of chopped walnuts. No bottled water. No canned meat. She probably finished all that while she was here.

I put the remaining food that I'll keep on the one shelf in the pantry that's still in place. But it's not as solid as it seems, and when I turn to get the food out of my backpack, the shelf falls and lands on the two-liter bottle of Cherry Pepsi, puncturing it. Pepsi and foam spray all over me and the floor. I'm covered in stickiness.

I go outside and look for a rain barrel here, a cistern or anything that would hold water I could use. But there's nothing, and I go back inside. I can't waste bottled water on cleaning, so I sop up the Pepsi mess with a dishtowel, then spray the floor with bleach. Still, my hands, my legs, and all my food is covered in dried Pepsi, everything sticky, and I don't want to spray bleach on any of my food, or on myself. So I have to accept sticky hands for now. Sticky legs and sticky food.

I think about sneaking out to the rain barrel again, the one on Orchard Street, but I don't feel like risking it in the neighborhood twice in one day. So I set up where I'm going to sleep in the office on the first floor. I want to be somewhere with easy access to the back door in case anyone tries to come through the front. I drag a mattress down from an upstairs bedroom, plus two sheets and a light blanket. This house is not as hot as my garage was, maybe because it's bigger. The top floor—nearest the roof—is still warm, but the first floor is cool in the evening.

I set a lighter and two tea candles next to my mattress. Plus a water bottle. I lie down and try to go to sleep, but I can't. I don't feel comfortable enough in this new house to fall asleep. So I light a tea candle and get up. Look around to distract myself. Look at the spines of the books spilled onto the floor. Consider reading. But since the quake, I haven't been able to read much. I haven't been able to pay attention while worrying about other things. For the first time in ten years, I can't imagine reading a book. My mind won't focus on a page for very long.

So I do a set of sit-ups, then a set of push-ups. Lie back flat on my new bed, close my eyes . . . and suddenly it's light out. Morning. The candle burned to a small black empty tin next to me.

I look at the face of my cell phone to check the time, try to power it on. But the battery is finally dead. I imagine getting messages on Snapchat, DMs on Instagram, watching TikTok videos, how those used to matter to me.

I take a pen and a book, write inside the cover on the first page:

New Goal: Find more protein.

I can feel myself getting a little weaker lately. I can always find carbohydrates—especially bad carbohydrates—boxed or canned—but never any cheese or milk. No fresh meat. So protein is my new goal. I eat a few Cheez-Its and wash them down with a bottle of water while I write a list of proteins that might keep in this heat:

- Canned chicken
- Canned tuna
- Dry salami
- Peanuts
- Walnuts
- Cashews
- Almonds
- Beef jerky
- Sunflower seeds or other seeds?
- Hard cheeses
- Maybe look for other things that might be protein that I haven't thought of? I'm not a food expert, so . . .
- *Keep an open mind!*

I go out searching for those proteins. Sneaking through houses above Fairmount, places near this house, ones I haven't gone through yet.

There's new cottonwood haze off the river today, white fluff blowing in the air like heated snow, all of the trees releasing at once, the neighborhood drifting in its own world of improbability. It looks like snow in the rose bushes along Fairmount. Snow in the boxwoods. Snow in the cypress hedges and the borders.

I watch for The Collection men as I go. Work car to car, tree to tree, house to house. Stay against something solid before I move each time. But there seems to be nobody in the neighborhood today, none that I can see, and the air blows white.

I stay on task, fill my backpack with protein and water bottles, only those two things, and I take what I find back to my new house.

34

OTHER LOSSES

I LOVED A GIRL once, but not exactly? Well, I did love
her—I was sure about that—but I also felt confused. I
didn't know what kind of love it was because my mother
made me question how I felt. Her name was Aadita, and
she had smooth, golden skin, black hair. Her parents were
from Bengal, India.

After the day I first talked to her at lunch, I went home
from school and looked up a map of India in my ency-
clopedias, saw the provinces, found West Bengal in the
east, and no other Bengal on the map. And I thought that
must've been where she meant. She'd told me her parents
had moved to the United States right before she was born.
I'd told her about coming here when I was little—crossing
the desert.

We were in the seventh grade, and Aadita was beautiful, but she didn't know it. She wanted to be blond and
fair-skinned. She'd say, "Like the pretty girls on TV shows,

you know?" She used to talk about freckles, how her face would have freckles if she were white, if she were from Europe. She'd say, "just a few freckles across my nose, the perfect amount." She would talk about how being in the sun would make those freckles stand out a little more than they usually did. "Just enough to be sexy, you know?" She'd push her lips out, pull her hair back and tuck extra strands behind her ears.

I'd watch her and think, 'But look at you now,' even though I was never brave enough to say it.

And I wasn't blond either. We were two dark-haired girls looking in a mirror, hoping for yellow hair.

When I stayed the night at her house, we'd sleep in the same bed. We were in middle school, and a lot of girls had started to smell bad, or covered their own body odor with lots of perfume, but not Aadita. Her skin smelled like cinnamon and light sweat, plus something else too, another scent that I could never name. But she smelled incredible.

Some nights—if she'd helped her mother cook dinner—she might smell like curry or coconut milk, or chili paste, and I preferred that smell of her too, even on those nights, to any perfume a person could buy at a store.

Aadita would sleep with her back to me and if I couldn't sleep—which was most nights—I would slide in closer to her, smell her hair and skin, smell her clothes, even the washing soap they used different from the kind in my own home. Sometimes I would put my arm over the top of her hip, slide in so close that our bodies were touching the whole way, and then I might be able to sleep. Or at least I was comfortable and satisfied, as close to happy as I'd ever been.

One evening, Aadita was looking in the mirror and maybe seeing herself with blond hair—because she kept turning back and forth, smiling. "Next year," she said, "to start eighth grade, I'm gonna go by Adi, my name shortened, but with only one 'A,' not two. Don't you think Adi sounds more conventional?"

"Conventional?"

"You know, American?"

"Can I still call you Aadita?" I said. "Because I like your name."

She laughed at me. "You *would* like it. But that's because you have a weird foreign name too: Cielo." She shook her head. Stuck her chest out, turned sideways, and squinted critically at her breasts in profile. Her breasts were smaller than mine, but round. They looked perfect to me as well.

Aadita said, "You can always call me whatever you want, but at school I'm going by Adi."

But she never went by Adi at our school the next year because her family moved to Kansas. Her father was offered a job in accounting for a bank in Topeka, and he moved them there on two weeks' notice.

I didn't know anything about Kansas other than what I'd read online, that Kansas was a top producer of wheat, so I imagined her father drinking his black tea, with his legs crossed, in a cubicle that was set in the middle of a wheat field. Also, I imagined Aadita's middle school having wheat fields all around it, and the students harvesting wheat during PE classes.

We only had two weeks to say goodbye to each other after her father accepted the job, and Aadita was so busy helping her mother pack that we only had one more sleepover.

That night, when we were in her bed, I waited until she was asleep—as usual—until I put my arm over her and slid up against her. She didn't smell like curry that night because her mother couldn't dirty the kitchen by cooking in it, so her father had purchased take-out from some place downtown.

I slid up against Aadita, smelled between her shoulder blades, and tried to make myself go to sleep. But instead I kept thinking about a video we watched in geography class once where the natives on some Pacific island would chop down a tree, hack away its branches, cut it into twenty-foot lengths, then burn the middle out to make boats. I kept picturing the black center of the burning tree growing bigger and bigger, men scraping at the charcoaled mass in the middle, and my stomach felt like that, like there was charcoal burning inside of me, like I was being scraped out until I was hollow.

I thought that Aadita was asleep, but all of a sudden she took my hand, the one that was resting on her stomach, and she laced her fingers in between each one of my fingers. It wasn't a dreamy, slow, sleepy sort of action—but intentional, one by one, finger by finger—and then she squeezed my fingers between hers, and I knew she was awake for sure.

I tried to say that I was going to miss her, but it came out as a sob.

Then her whole body shook, and I knew she was crying as well.

A little later—when we were both still awake—we told stories about things we'd done together, small things like biking to all five 7-Eleven stores in town on July 11th to get a free Slurpee at each one, and how at the end of that day Aadita was sick to her stomach, leaning over her handlebars, but I finished every last drop of all my Slurpees and never felt sick at all. Or how—another time—I took her fishing at the river, but she didn't want me to kill any of the fish that we caught and she kept yelling at me as I reeled in fish. She'd say, "Oh my gosh! Look at its cute little eyes! Throw it back! Please, please, throw it back! Let it live!"

That was the Aadita who loved red lipstick and Taylor Swift, who loved to dance like a maniac in her bedroom, but never at a school dance; the Aadita who was always afraid that her father would walk in and take away her radio if we played her music too loud. For all of middle school, Aadita had carried a second outfit to school in her backpack and changed before first period: tighter shirts, shorter shorts, lower necklines.

It is Aadita I think about tonight, the second night I'm alone in this new house on Hendrix, wondering what the future will bring.

35

INFECTION

WHEN I WAKE up, my leg is sore. Really sore. I look down and see that the puncture has widened even more and is beginning to seep. The infection has turned a darker color, and there are faint pink lines going up and down my leg. I push myself to a standing position and it almost feels like I have a broken bone, the pain so sharp and specific. I don't know what I did yesterday to make it worse, but something changed.

I mash as much Neosporin into the nail hole as I can. Limp into the kitchen and find a Sharpie in a drawer to mark the edges of the infection. I saw that on a Netflix show, that you do that to check later to see if it's getting better or worse.

I sit down at the table and think. Wish I could put ice on my leg, imagine how good a cool pack of ice would feel. And this is one of those times when I think about going on Web MD or Googling what I need to know like I used to.

I'm sure I need some kind of antibiotics, pills, or a shot or something from a doctor's office, but I'm not sure exactly what that would be.

I limp into the pantry. Get a can of tuna and a few Wheat Thins. Go back to the table, open the can, drink the tuna water for additional liquid, then sit and dip the crackers into the fish.

I think about the way my leg is hurting. It's not good. I know I have to go out and find a prescription bottle of antibiotics somewhere, but I can't imagine hiking through the neighborhood with my leg feeling like this, or squatting down, sneaking, hiding quickly, and getting back up.

I take a deep breath, use the table to push up, and limp over to my backpack. I pull out the bottle of Vicodin, put a pill in my mouth, and swallow it dry. I consider taking a second one right after the first, but I put the pill bottle back in my pack instead.

I return to the table. Wait and think. Try to remember which houses had prescriptions in them. But I can't remember. I'm tired, and all of the houses and searches run together.

Then I realize that there might be an unused prescription in this house—the one I'm staying in now—and how easy that would be. I get up again and limp to the bathroom. Search there first. But all I find is bottles of Tums and Tylenol. I take two Tylenol as well.

Leaning heavily on the banister, I make my way upstairs, using only my good leg to push up each step, dragging my bad leg behind, surprised by how stiff it got in the last day. I search the two bathrooms on that floor, find a half-used prescription of Prednisone, which I don't think is an antibiotic; and an almost empty bottle of Xanax, which I know isn't an antibiotic.

I go upstairs to the third floor, and in the bathroom there I find another orange bottle, turn to the label, and see "Wellbutrin." I try to remember what that's for, ads I've seen online, ads before YouTube videos, and I can't remember. But I don't think it's an antibiotic. Drug companies make up stupid names like Wellbutrin to make people think of getting well, and not from an infection. I could be wrong, but I don't take those pills. I leave them where I've found them, then I go back downstairs—slowly—back down to the kitchen, drink a little more water as I sit at the table and wait for the painkiller to kick in.

When I start to space off, and my mind feels a little fuzzy, I know it's time. I get up from the table again and put some weight on my infected leg. It doesn't hurt as badly as before, and I'm sure the Vicodin is working. I pull my hair back into a ponytail, put my pistol in my waistband, and head out to search the next house.

There might be an antibiotic bottle in that house, but I'll never know. When I push open the front door, a rotting carcass smell hits me so hard that I retch and bend over, hands on my knees, vomiting, spilling my morning's tuna and crackers onto the doorstep.

I back away, hobble down the front walkway toward the street, and only remember to hide when I get to the rain ditch there. I duck down—trying to keep my hurt leg as straight as possible, putting it out to the side—breathing and wiping my mouth.

I move on to the next house, approach it more slowly, testing the air before I get to the front door. But it smells clean, no smells at all, and I go inside, limp through the rooms, find only two things that could be a help to me: a gallon jug of water and a bottle of Advil.

I limp through two more houses, not finding anything in those, then in the next house I do find a prescription of an antibiotic that I recognize—penicillin—but the prescription bottle is empty, every last pill gone. I throw the orange container down on the floor and it breaks, pieces of plastic scattering across the bathroom linoleum.

I rub my eyes. Take two Advil, and limp back to my new house at Hendrix. My leg hurts too much to walk around like this in the heat. The day is dry, with a hot wind licking along the street, not a drop of moisture in the air, and I drink half a gallon of water as I sit and sweat.

36

FIRE

I WAKE UP IN the middle of the night with a fever. I'm sleeping on the first floor, and I know the nights are cooler than the days, and it can't be more than seventy-five degrees in this room right now, but my covers are off and I'm sweating like it's the middle of the hottest day of summer, like it's a hundred and twenty degrees.

My leg is throbbing, and again I fantasize about putting an ice pack on my leg, feeling its cooling comfort spread over my skin and down into the wound.

I take two Advil and a Vicodin. Wait on my bed for the medicines to kick in.

It takes a long time.

My bed is wet with sweat before my head and neck finally start to go a little looser. I feel my jaw relax and my eyes get heavy. My leg still hurts, but it's separated from me a little bit, as if it's two feet farther away.

My eyes are starting to close again when I smell something in the air. I can't quite think of what it is at first, but it's a smell I recognize, and I lie there thinking, wondering, trying to figure out what it is, but then I know. It's the smell of something burning.

I sit up and look out the windows to see if it's one of the neighboring houses, but all of the windows are black. I use the back of the couch to stand, hop on my good leg up the first flight of stairs, then the second flight, to the third floor, to the northernmost bedroom. There's a small deck off that room that goes out toward the street, and I can see the city from this elevated perch.

The fire is way out to my left, to the northwest on University Hill, at least a half mile away. Two big buildings are burning, and it takes me a minute to realize that they're two of the historical sites on campus. I don't know the names of any of those places, but I've seen them before many times—the ones that are burning—some of the oldest wooden university buildings, built more than a hundred years ago, a few stories tall and right in the middle of campus.

Next to them are three brick buildings, a little bit newer but still old. There's an intermittent wind coming in my direction, and I can smell the fire in the small gusts, smell it as it grows in the structures, the third and fourth floors catching, then filling, with flames. The fires burn bright orange, exploding all the windows, and a roof on one of the building goes, the fire pushing through and taking the top. Then, soon enough, the other building's roof goes as well.

The fires are burning vertically, and it doesn't look like they'll spread to the next buildings over. I'm mesmerized by the sight of the fire, the flames pulsing into the dark sky from the rectangular frameworks. I've just decided that the brick buildings next to them won't catch on fire when the wind changes—a steady wind suddenly in my face—and I see all of the fire arcing out to the right. Pieces of orange float over the tops of the next two buildings, and some low sparks drop to the ground. Grass or bushes catch fire, low down, then trees along the building's walls. Something on the front ignites as well.

I'm standing on my little porch—staring in a Vicodin haze—as the next three buildings burn. That they're brick buildings doesn't seem to matter. Everything on their insides burns, and their roofs as well, and—after a while—only the walls remain, standing hollow and dark against the bright flames behind.

On campus, there's a big gap across a street before the next buildings, and that room seems to be enough to keep the other buildings safe. The wind dies down, and now there's just the smell of smoke in the air, nothing more sinister than that. But I wonder what would happen to this neighborhood, my own—with its tightly spaced houses, almost all of them wood—what would happen if something were to catch on fire here. I don't know why I haven't thought about that possibility until now. But as I stand here, leaning on the porch rail, I'm worried.

37

NEEDING

WHEN I WAKE up, my leg is throbbing. I'm sweating again, and I feel disoriented, like maybe it's not me lying here in this room, staring at the ceiling. I look down at the puncture wound on my leg and see the infection has spread an inch past my Sharpie circle in every direction. Dark pink lines are running up and down my leg. I have to get antibiotics this morning. I have to find them or this might get really bad.

I take another Vicodin and three Advil. Drink the pills down with water. Reach over for a few Wheat Thins and find the cracker box covered in ants. The ants start to crawl up my hands and I brush them off, hope they're just interested in the Pepsi spilled on the outside of the box. But when I reach inside, they're on the crackers as well. I say, "Fuck," and throw the box of crackers against the wall, crackers spilling out onto the carpet.

I reach inside my backpack for a granola bar that I think I still have in there, but then I remember that I ate it already. The days are really starting to run together, and I can't remember which day of the week it is or how long it's been since the earthquake. I lost track somewhere, and I wonder if it's because of the infection or my weird sleeping habits, or everything. I lie there and think about it as the pain pills start to kick in, but my stomach cramps from taking pills without any food, and I roll into a fetal position and wait for the Vicodin to fully kick in.

I think about getting up and eating some food in the pantry, but the pantry seems far away, and my leg is hurting too much to get up right now. It feels like a coal is burning deep inside, next to the bone, a coal that alternates between red and black, pumping with heat, then dropping off before pumping again.

I check my phone to see what time it is, but the battery's dead. I think of other ways to check the time, but I can't think of any as I lie here. Everything in this room is digital, or was digital—electrically run—and I'm not one of those people who can tell time by looking at the sun.

I close my eyes and wonder if I can sleep until the Vicodin takes away the pain, but the Advil is tearing apart my stomach, and that feeling—along with my leg pain— makes it impossible to go back to sleep. So I count for a while, count up to a hundred and back down to zero a few times. Then I lie back and listen for sounds: I hear birds outside and my own breathing in this room. Nothing else. I listen hard, but that's it.

I continue to lie there—sweating—until the Vicodin makes my head swim, and I finally have enough relief to move around.

Then I get up and walk out into the kitchen, drink some more water, and eat some food—crackers and another can of tuna—then sit there as the burning in my stomach lessens. I take the Sharpie from the counter and circle my new infection line, a circle outside of my old circle like rings on the water. At the puncture site, the hole is raised now, looking more and more like a mountain. I'm going to search until I find an antibiotic today because I can't let this get any worse.

I start out in the opposite direction from yesterday. I've searched the houses on the wrap-around road, but only for food and water, nothing else. I limp and hop, take another Vicodin after an hour to keep the painkillers overlapping since I don't have a choice about walking on my leg today. No matter what, I have to keep pushing through the pain until I get what I need.

In the sixth house, I finally find a prescription—for Amoxicillin—and I swallow two immediately, wash them down with a Mountain Dew and a dozen saltine crackers from that house's kitchen. There are only twelve antibiotic pills remaining in the bottle, not a full prescription, but the instructions read, "Take one pill three times per day with or without food," so I know I have four days' worth.

I limp back to my house slowly. My leg hurts more than ever, and I wonder if it's too late, if I'm beyond what a prescription can do to help me. I don't know much about infections—or pharmaceutical drugs—but I remember a history teacher last year telling our class that more soldiers in the Civil War died of infection than on the battlefield. I think about that as I drag my injured leg along the road, consider swallowing the whole bottle of pills to try to get a big enough dose to really knock out the infection. But I also wonder if that would make me sick, and vomiting up the only antibiotics I have would be the worst thing yet. So I keep limping and hope the drugs work.

Back in the house, in the kitchen, I tell myself that everything will be okay, but I know that I'm lying to myself. Everything isn't close to okay now—everything hasn't been close to okay for a long, long time—and nothing will ever be the same after all of this is over.

38

FATE

I'M SWEATING ALL night. Powerful fever. My hands feel hot, my face and feet too. At one point in the night, I touch my leg and it feels like a piece of meat that's been roasting on an outdoor grill. I lie in the dark and cry, letting my tears stream off the side of my face.

My English teacher at school last year had us read a Haruki Murakami novel where fate was a sandstorm. We learned that the sandstorm followed the main character because the storm is inside all of us, not outside. Our teacher looked at us and she said, "That's the problem with people: They think they can avoid their own sandstorms." Then she had us read *Oedipus Rex*. We read the play aloud in class—comparing the two stories, each with their fated endings, then writing about them after. I argued that fate could be determined by the individual because otherwise I would still be living in Mexico, and my teacher liked my argument. Sometimes, after that, I would go get the free lunch food in the cafeteria, then take it to that English teacher's classroom. She was young—or youngish—and I liked how her bottom teeth overlapped. I thought her smile was pretty too, and I tried not to get caught looking at her too often. I also thought about fate and wondered if she was fated to be an English teacher or if we were both fated to sit in her room during lunch.

How can a person ever know if she's making her own choices or if her choices were already predetermined? What if she thinks she's making a "different" choice, but that her "different" option was actually the choice she was going to make all along?

I think about that now, the sandstorm inside of me or the prophecy I can't avoid. I wonder about fate and destiny—or the God my mother believes in—wonder if there's a path marked out for me, and I imagine what that path might look like. And could I leave that path, or would any branch or turn I choose to take only be the direction that I was destined to go all along?

I fall asleep thinking about these things, and in my dream The Collection man with the cigar box comes and places birds inside my ears. The birds are small and white, and they peck at the tissue of my brain, and the tissue spills out when I sit up, and it drips onto my infected leg, which has gotten so hot that it's beginning to smolder, then catches fire and burns completely.

* * *

When I wake, the sun is out.

I've slept a long time and it's somewhere near midday, maybe early afternoon. I start to stand, but my injured leg is so stiff that I can't bend it very well. I look at the infection lines I've drawn with the Sharpie. The infection hasn't gotten worse, but it hasn't gotten better. I swallow two more antibiotic pills and drink some water. I know I have to wait it out now, wait for these pills to start working—for the infection to recede—but it's hard to do nothing all day. I need more food and water. I also need to figure out what I'm going to do long term. Eventually, summer's going to end. Fall will come, with its heavy wet rains; then winter, long and cold and dark.

I swallow a Vicodin and lie on my mattress, planning for the next few months. I wonder how long the neighborhood will stay this way, wonder if there's a plan already being made to rebuild the city. But who would make that plan? And how many cities and towns look like this on the West Coast?

The earthquake's shaking felt like it went on for a full five minutes. I saw houses buckle, trees fall down, telephone poles topple, cars bounce out into the street and flip upside down. And anything that powerful must've extended for hundreds of miles in every direction.

In school we had earthquake drills, and one teacher even told us that nothing we were practicing was sufficient. He said, "It won't matter. Everything here will be destroyed anyway." Then he made a few of the students cry as he told how the earthquake would stretch from Canada to California and a hundred thousand people would die. He described tsunamis ripping through coastal towns, drowning and crushing everyone. He said, "Most of the coastal towns you know will be gone after that event. They'll have just vanished along with their people." He snapped his fingers. He was smiling, but his smile didn't look happy.

But being here in this neighborhood, in one small place, it's hard to tell how much of what he said was true.

Was the destruction as widespread as he'd predicted? What if it wasn't that bad? Or what if it was worse? There's no way to know.

I get a piece of paper and write ideas. Wonder if I can scavenge enough water to stay here long term, wonder if I'll be able to go back to my garage and collect all of the food and water I stored there or if The Collection took all of it when they found my hiding spot.

I write down different places I could go: across the mountains to Central Oregon, or into the Coastal Range or the Cascades. The mountains would be fine except in winter. Maybe stay here until the winter is over, then move? Could I survive a winter here? Or should I go up to Portland? Or just up the river valley far enough to be above the flood line? I write a pros and cons list for each idea as I lie on the floor and wait for the antibiotics to help my leg. But after a while I get tired and overwhelmed, and I go back to sleep.

When I wake up, I take another Vicodin and write lists while the pill kicks in. After a while, I feel fuzzy, warm, and floating, and my leg separates again from my body, so when I get to my feet, it doesn't hurt too much to put weight on it. I hope that the antibiotics are starting to work, not just the Vicodin, but I'm not sure.

I'm hungry. I walk into the kitchen . . .

. . . and stop. There's a dead rat there, big and brown, with a long, scaled tail. It's lying in the middle of the floor—on the tiles—next to my box of Cheez-Its, as if they were laced with poison. The rat has its front feet on the cracker box. It doesn't move.

I don't know what killed it. But I know it can't have been here long since I've been to this kitchen recently, and I can't leave it to start rotting. I already have ants and rats in everything. A dead rat might bring in something even worse. What bigger animal eats dead rats?

I can't wait around and see.

The rat's head is tilted back and its mouth is open. It doesn't move. I go get a plastic bag and pick up the rat with the bag inside-out. Set it off to the side. Then I use an old T-shirt as a rag and spray bleach where the rat had been lying on the floor. I bleach over everything, hoping I've gotten all of the dead animal scent off the floor.

When I'm finished cleaning, I throw the bleached T-shirt into the plastic bag with the rat's body and step out the back door, limping slowly around to the front of the house, looking for an outdoor garbage can.

Most of the garbage cans were knocked over and spilled with the quake, emptied out onto the street or at the sides of houses where they were sitting before the shaking started, but I find one garbage can that was pinched between two cars and is still upright with the lid on. I scooch sideways between the cars, get to the garbage can and hold my breath, creak the plastic lid open. I'm about to toss my bag on top when I see movement inside. I lean in to look, forgetting that there were fourth of July parties right before the earthquake, garbage cans full of picnic and barbecue leftovers, and this garbage can is filled like most were: beer and soda cups, food plates, grease-stained napkins, plastic wine glasses, old food, salads, meats, and side dishes. The food that used to be on the disposable plastic plates has morphed into piles of yellow maggots, and I stare at the writhing, globular masses for a moment, the movements of them mesmerizing, how the larvae swim over each other, traveling continually without going anywhere, but then the smell of the rotting in the can fully hits me, and I gag.

I lower the lid, bend over and take a big breath. I'm so high on Vicodin that I think of lying down right where I am then, just going to sleep on the bright white concrete of this neighbor's driveway, in between these cars, next to this full trash can, holding a rat in a plastic bag.

But I stand upright again, lift the lid, and toss the bag on top, unsettling the pile of garbage in the can, and something explodes out from underneath the stack of old food plates. I see black in the air, small flashes of a brighter color too but I don't recognize the cloud in front of me until it's too late.

There's a whoosh, something spinning, an expansion around me, and the sound that a cup of lighter fluid makes when it's touched by a match. And before I even know what they are, the yellow jackets are on me, their little bodies upside down, V-shaped, biting and stinging my skin at the same time, and I swat at them, crush some, crush as many as I can, but each one is replaced by two more, and I realize I have to run—not fight—if I want to get rid of them. But I can't run. Even on the Vicodin, my leg is too tight and painful.

So I fast-limp down the driveway, swatting and crushing yellow jackets on my arms and face, prying the wasps off as others sting my fingers and hands, and there's a smell in the air now, the smell of their smashed bodies, new yellow jackets replacing the old ones as I limp up the road. I'm screaming as I peel more off my neck, raking them out of my hair, quite a few still following me up the street.

I'm still being stung as I go through the back door of my house, close the sliding glass door, and stand there in the protection of the house, killing the last few yellow jackets on my body.

Then I lean against the counter, gasping for air, my skin hurting, big red welts all over my arms. I can feel more welts rising on my scalp, on my neck and upper chest. I peel off my T-shirt and find one final yellow jacket near my armpit. It bites and stings me on the soft skin where my chest meets my shoulder, and I scream as I crush it, then pick it off.

I open a bottle of water on the counter, drink some, then splash the rest on my skin. I clean the pieces of wasp bodies off my arms and chest, splash a little water on my scalp where my hair is parted.

I find Benadryl in the bathroom, pink tablets, and I swallow two, knowing that they'll add to the Vicodin and make me so tired. I look at myself in the mirror and say—aloud—"Overdose, anyone?" and swallow another antibiotic pill as well.

Anything to feel better.

39

MORE

FOR THREE DAYS, I pop pills and try to sleep as much as possible. Benadryl and Vicodin. Antibiotics three times a day. On the fourth day, the swelling in my leg diminishes around the puncture, and my whole leg doesn't hurt nearly as much. I draw a new circle inside the original circle, and I'm able to walk to the back corner of the yard—where I've dug a latrine—without limping as much as before. I still squat only halfway as I pee, but I'm definitely feeling a little better.

I need more antibiotics, so I head out into the neighborhood to search again. Walk up Hamble Drive, a tiny dirt road on the hill into the park that I haven't searched yet because the two houses at the bottom of that road were so completely destroyed that I never thought about going inside them. I imagined the rest of the houses on this road looked the same.

The houses are set close together, and the first two are completely torn from their foundations, sliding downhill, looking more like tornado wreckage than anything else. The third house isn't much better. I'm able to get in the living room through a shattered side door, but I can't get to any other part of the house, and the only thing I find in the living room is a headlamp.

But the fourth house is mostly upright. It's sitting at weird angles, still standing, and I find two gallons of water, more Benadryl, Band-Aids, and a box of Nature Valley granola bars.

At the sixth house, I find the antibiotics I need—half a prescription of penicillin—plus ten Valiums. I take those back to my house on Hendrix, pop a Valium and a new antibiotic pill. Then I look at the pile of books on the floor to the left of my mattress, paperbacks, twenty-five or thirty, all of them by Danielle Steel: *A Good Woman*, *Big Girl*, *Precious Gifts*, *One Day at a Time*. More of the same. I open *Precious Gifts* and read two chapters before I fall asleep.

* * *

I wake to the smell.

Sit up. It's the middle of the night, and so dark that I can't see my hand in front of my face. The moon must be completely clouded over.

Some things—like this night's darkness—are hard to get used to. My whole life, the halogen lamps above Fairmount Boulevard and Hendrix have burned all night long, the yellow light glinting off parked cars, even making the blacktop shimmer. But now those light posts are just dark sticks hanging in the air, the curved heads of the lamps hanging thirty feet up in the black.

It takes me a minute to remember that I have a new headlamp. But then I reach for it, click it on, and it shines a steady beam. I stand and make my way to the stairs, tripping a couple of times on things just outside the flashlight's beam. I climb up to the second floor, then the third. I step over a shattered TV and get to the door that leads to the balcony.

Outside, it's a little lighter—orange reflected off the bottom of the clouds—and I click off my headlamp to save its batteries. Out in front of me, the drowned city is on fire, burning left to right, all of the houses and buildings and apartment complexes that are sticking out of the water. It's hard to tell exactly where the fire started since so many buildings and houses are up in flames, but I can feel a steady wind from west to east, see the arcs of fire coming off each structure, flames making turns at their tops like waves of orange, cresting swells.

So the fire must've started somewhere over by University Hill, moving east toward The Glenwood. I watch the fire working left to right across the city's black water, the transitions of the blaze like a living thing: birds of sparks flying to a new roof, then small flames, then bigger, as the upper stories begin to burn big and bright, then fire catching on another house. And another.

And another.

The entire drowned section of the city is raging, just a few blocks from me, west to east. I watch five news houses burn in a matter of a few minutes—I'm entranced by the burning—feel the wind against the left side of my face, and know that the fire will move out to my right. In that direction there are the drowned trailer parks, the I-5 overpass, the Sanipac Waste Management complex, Papé Machinery, and Springfield. I wonder how far the fire will travel before it burns out.

The water is still and dark, an ocean of ink surrounding each burning building, the structures like Vaseline-dipped cotton-balls, waiting for a spark, waiting for an ignition, a quick rush of flame and the burning of everything down to the waterline where the fire goes out again.

I look at my hands, illuminated orange from the fires out in front of me. I think of the July-heated grass up on this hillside, everything dry and yellow, even the underbrush looking dead throughout the park. This is the blind heat of late summer—August—and I shake my head. Think about my world waiting for a spark. And then what would I do?

I watch a roof lift on a house down at the bottom of Walnut Street—red-orange and glowing—the roof lifting into the air and seeming to float, the entire roof disconnected from the house below. The peak of the roof holds in the air for a moment, then implodes, drops, and shards of color spray in every direction, cinders arcing out into the water and over the adjacent house that has already begun to burn next to it.

If this were another life, I would call this beautiful. Watching from here—on my elevated porch on this hill, the fire both gorgeous and terrible, vibrant oranges gashing the black of the water, slices of light lifting into darkness. But there's smoke in the air—even here, out of the wind—the creeping smell of burning wood and metal, and I know my neighborhood is next. The fires are starting, and it only makes sense that this neighborhood will eventually burn too.

40

CLOSING THE DOOR

THE DAY IS bright already. Noon-bright I think. I get up to stretch, the air in the room feeling hot. A little bit of sweat on my face. I think, "What time is it?" Glance at the blank face of my dead phone for the hundredth time.

I think about what I heard from my history teacher last year about time—the concept of time—how a researcher somewhere decided that Hopi verb tenses proved that the Hopi people didn't understand time. The researcher made a big deal about it, then white people ran with the idea and believed that Hopi people were "beyond time." It became a new-age idea spread on the internet. There was a belief that the Hopi people didn't speak of time because they were enlightened somehow regarding time. It was all because of verb tenses, but it wasn't even true. The researcher wasn't correct about their Hopi language. My history teacher said, "But politically correct white people are pretty stupid for something that they think might be 'amazing' . . . or 'different.'" He made air quotes. "People will believe whatever reinforces their world view."

I think about that now.

What reinforces my world view?

How would I know? How could I tell whether I was being biased from the start? How could I tell if I was only finding something that I already agreed with?

And everything around me now makes my old life seem stupid. Why did I care about my Instagram account? Snapchat and TikTok? Why did it matter if somebody Snapped me back within thirty seconds or liked my story or kept me on read? Why did I care about my clothes or the brands of my shoes? Why did I care what other people thought of my music or my playlists?

I fold my sleeping blanket and set it on the coffee table. Try to imagine where everyone else is right now, people my age—who is dead and who is still alive. Then I imagine the world where electricity is still running, where plumbing still works in other parts of the country and other parts of the world. Are they hearing about us? Did they hear about the earthquake, and do they know what's happening afterward?

I try to picture my high school with the hallways full of people. But I know that's not possible. So I picture other high schools in other places. I picture popular girls, always girls with money, how mean they are, how hard I tried to go unnoticed by them.

I shake my head. Think, *But what matters now?*

What matters here? In this moment?

My leg feels better this morning, improving every day. That matters. And I have enough food. I'm still not starving. I have water as well. I haven't seen The Collection in days. Every day here is like a hundred days, and The Collection feels like a bad memory.

I check my leg, draw a new circle inside the older circle, the infection going down even more. But it still hurts, so I pop a Vicodin, just in case, swallow that pain pill with a big swig of Mountain Dew. Then I swallow a penicillin afterward.

I stay in the house all day. Since I don't have to go out to find anything, I don't leave. I'm too worried about being seen in the neighborhood. So I lie on my mattress and read the Danielle Steel novel. Eat food. Go outside only to use the latrine.

In the afternoon, I fall asleep.

*   *   *

Midnight.

Above me the sky is salted with stars around a full moon, and I glance up at the brightest constellations—the only ones still visible with the enormous moon—as I make my way slowly along the sidewalk, stepping around the brambles of downed treetops, trying to go easy on my leg, even though it's been better the last two days.

I move out into the street. The bright moonlight and no clouds make me feel exposed in the middle of Fairmount Boulevard as I walk along the crest of the road, the rain arc just noticeable under my feet. But even traveling in the street, there are downed trees to navigate, one huge maple hiding the crushed hulls of two cars underneath its trunk, and the wide perimeter of its downed branches extending twenty feet in each direction.

This is the last time I'm going up the hill. Once more to visit the compound and find out, then never again.

There's not much left for me to find or do here in this neighborhood—except for this—and I need to plan my exit, my leaving.

But I need to do this one last thing before I leave.

I have a bandana tied around my neck—to pull up and disguise my face, as if that will work. The full moon is my only light right now, but I have a headlamp in one pocket as a backup. Two pistol clips in the other pocket. I hold my pistol in my hand. Ready.

I walk up Fairmont Boulevard. Walk past cars, see no one inside and no one outside. Just silent houses. No wind in the trees either. Even walking quietly, my footfalls are louder than I'd like them to be. Everything is too bright, too loud. I try to calm my breathing.

As I merge onto Spring Boulevard, something is behind the wheel of a car, and I lift my gun, pull out my headlamp, stop, and wait. Something crawls out into the street, and I shine my headlamp. It's an opossum, and it stops when my light beam hits it. The animal stays still, its mouth open in the light; short, sharp teeth glinting; and its breathing sounding like a wheeze.

But it's no danger to me and I walk past it. Keep moving. A hundred yards later, there's the first Collection house on the left, the three-story white one, then the compound up on the right, an even bigger house set back behind the fence and its enormous, sprawling lawn.

I keep my gun up and watch the house on the left until I'm past it, until I'm to the big fence and the gate up right, the bigger house way up on the hill.

The fence is wrought iron with spikes on top. I'm not sure if I want to go through the gate or climb over the fence. The gate is open a foot, but I don't know if someone is watching that entrance. So I wait and watch. Stand back and look at both options. I doubt I can climb the fence without getting hung up on the spikes—and my leg still isn't one hundred percent—so I decide to go through the gate. It's one or two o'clock in the morning, and I'm hoping that no one is watching the front of the property. But—just in case—I slide the pistol's safety off and point the gun in front of me as I step through the gate. The hinges squeak, a sound that seems incredibly loud in the silence.

I step through and point my gun all around. But I don't see anyone, just the shadows of the trees out in front of me. There are the long spaces of lawn on both sides of the path, and then oak trees. I wait and hold my breath but don't hear any sounds other than crickets, don't see any movement. I slide the safety back on, lower my pistol, and move quickly to the trunk of the nearest oak tree.

I wait there. Look around some more. There are no dogs barking, no sounds of people. The white house is big and still in front of me, waiting silently up on the hill.

I move tree to tree until I'm close enough to the big house to get a better look. But even with a lot of moonlight, I can't see clearly enough. I can't see into any of the dark windows, can't tell if they're broken or if the glass is still intact in the frames.

I can see the clean, bright white of the paint on the house, and the dark rectangles at each window space, and an even darker rectangle where the front door of the house looks like it's open. I stare at that door for a long time. Wait for someone to come out. Close my eyes and listen, then open my eyes and stare some more.

But the only sound I hear is the crickets in the grass.

I don't know what to do. I have to go inside the house, but I also don't want to. The house is forty or fifty feet away from me now. That's the distance from the trunk of this last oak tree, and I'm stuck here, looking at the big structure, so scared that I'm shaking.

I close my eyes, breathe, then open my eyes again. I slide the pistol's safety off—ready to fire—and move forward with the gun up in front of me. I'm breathing hard, and I try to calm myself down, try to breathe slower, try to be as quiet as possible. But it's difficult. The gun is trembling in my hands. I bring my elbows in, try to calm the shaking in my limbs. There's a strange taste in my mouth, something I can't name. It feels like there's metal in my lungs.

I'm creeping forward, moving through the open space in front of the house—visible in the moonlight if anyone is awake, if anyone is looking out any of the front windows. But I still don't hear anything, and I get to the steps, then the front door, the door not just open, but wide open, peeled all the way back and stuck in that position. I point my gun into the darkness of the house. Step inside and put my back against the wall next to the door. Then I blink and try to adjust my eyes to the lack of light inside. I keep my pistol out in front of me.

Something moves near my feet and I point my gun at it. Follow it out the door and into the moonlight. It's a cat walking smooth and slow, exiting the house and walking off, down the front steps. It walks out onto the grass where I just came from, then past an oak tree where I can't see it anymore in the shadows.

Then there's quiet and no movement all around me. I'm inside the house. Pointing my pistol out into the dark.

I've smelled so many things this last month, but the smell in this house is stronger than anything I've ever encountered—completely overwhelming—and I put my bandana to my nose, clamp my nostrils shut with one hand, hold my gun with the other as I walk into the front room. I look around. See furniture at odd angles, indistinguishable things lying on the floor. Even with four windows on the front side of this room, I can't see well enough to make anything out clearly. I think about the headlamp in my pocket, but I'm too scared to turn it on.

I go to the next room, a huge dining room with a table at least thirty feet long, fifty or sixty chairs tipped backward or forward all around it. A chest of something along the wall—near a window, under moonlight. I start to walk up to it, but my shoes crunch on glass, the sound too loud, so I stop. Listen. Close my eyes to hear if the crunching of the glass woke anyone up. I listen for people moving upstairs, but I don't hear anything. If there's someone else in the house with me, they're completely quiet.

Sleeping or waiting.

I leave the dining room. Go down some kind of short hallway. The smell is stronger in this space. Even with my nose plugged and the bandana over my face, it seems like the smell is forcing its way into my mouth. I try to take smaller breaths, try not to think about it.

I turn into the kitchen. There's a big pile of something in there, and movement, things moving on the floor, scurrying, rats or mice.

The reek in the room is penetrating, coming in waves—even with my nostrils pinched shut and my mouth clamped on the bandana—the profound stench getting through. I hold my breath, let go of my nostrils, and reach into my pocket to pull the headlamp out. I keep holding my breath, point the pistol out in front of me and hope no one sees my light when it flashes on. But I have to see what the pile is in front of me. I have to know if my mother is here.

I turn the light on and there they are. Bodies. Nine or ten of them, rats working over the pile, disappearing into tangles of arms and legs, blood and flesh and hair, hard to distinguish as individual people.

My vision gets splotchy, and I have to blink away the blackness at the edges of my eyesight. I feel almost too light-headed to stand. My head swings. I stagger and my stomach clinches. I bend over, take a quick breath, and hold it again, crushing the bandana back into my mouth. I bite down and fight the urge to vomit. Close my eyes and stay like that for a moment. Then I push myself back to standing upright. Blink and wipe my eyes with the back of my hand. Shine the headlamp directly on the pile of bodies once more, see that all of the people were shot—in the head or in the face, who knows why—bullet and exit wounds on every single one. They're also all missing a finger on their left hands, pinky fingers gone on the arms that are outstretched.

I take a step forward to look more closely. They're all men, each one wearing a Collection robe, the nearest robe covering a man with a long brown beard, a gunshot hole in his cheek—under his eye—his mouth open, and a rat dipping its head inside his mouth.

The rat makes a sound as it chews, and I feel like I'm floating, drawing up into the air, swinging down. Then there's weight in my legs again, the force of gravity doubled, and I retch and bend over, pull the bandana from my mouth and splat vomit onto the floor. My stomach tightens and I vomit again. I watch a string of dark bile come out, something connected to the bottom of my stomach. I bite the string off and spit. Stumble back into the hall. Turn my light off.

And now I can't see anything, just the black space of the hallway, the former light of my headlamp blinding me, and the dark dining room somewhere out in front of me. I close my eyes, then open them. Do that twice more. And after, I can see a little bit, so I walk forward. Turn left at the dining room—toward the front of the house, the bank of windows and the door not too far away.

My right hand is shaking so hard—still holding the pistol—but my finger isn't on the trigger. The gun is loose in my hand, and if someone came at me right now, I don't know if I could raise the gun up steady enough to shoot.

I lean against the dining room wall. Wait to pass the stairs. Take a deep breath and try to calm down. Peek around the corner, pointing my gun up toward the second floor, but I don't see anyone or anything—not even the outlines of anyone—just a big, blank space where the stairs rise to the upper landing.

I wait for a person to appear—someone who heard me vomit in the kitchen, or saw the light from my headlamp—but no one does. And I finally realize that there probably isn't anyone here, not anymore, not with the smell of those bodies like that. It would be too overwhelming. The house is ruined, and nobody could live here anymore.

So I step out the front door, move through it again, and hurry back to the nearest oak tree. I walk fast down the hill, tree to tree, then out across the open space to the gate, onto Spring Boulevard. I keep walking fast until I'm all the way down to the park, to the turn at Fairmount, to the hedge where I can duck into a small space and catch my breath.

I crouch down and let myself cry finally. Rock lightly with my arms wrapped over my knees, my pistol still in my hand. My stomach doesn't feel right, but I don't think I'll throw up again.

When my crying winds down, I straighten out my injured leg. Rub my thigh and try to loosen the muscle around the puncture hole. Then I get to my feet, look in both directions, and hurry back to my house on Hendrix.

Lying on my mattress in the house, I wonder about my mother. She wasn't in that pile of bodies—I looked to make sure—so she has to be somewhere else. She could be living or dead nearby, or she could have left the neighborhood completely.

41

SEPARATION

*I*CANNOT BE OF *this world. I must choose to be set apart.*

Witness Andreas has touched each of our ears, and now he stands up front and says, "We must step away from our worldly existence and cloak ourselves in a new righteousness. This action—this choice—determines eternity." He says, "The coming of a new heaven and a new earth, these earthly shambles gone away. We will be raptured before the Tribulation."

I write these words down in my spirit journal—even what I don't understand—and I plan to ask him myself, to go to him for his teaching, for him to explain.

This is what I do know: I am a soldier for the next life— as he demands of us—as many have become soldiers before me. We do not fight in flesh and blood, but against darkness, with angels and demons. Even the flesh we tear is not real.

Following evil is not hard to see. I think of the people who follow Nuestra Señora de la Santa Muerte, but not only them because there are also evil forces that can work inside of any person.

If you let the demons inside of you.

If you are not careful in every moment not to let the darkness settle.

¡Cuidado! ¡El Diablo acecha!

The existence of evil means I must be a watching person. At any moment, I can lose the good favor that I have with God. At any moment, I can be possessed by something from the world around me, or the world beneath me, the burning world where the brothers and sisters of The Collection cannot go to help me anymore.

Witness Andreas says, "Stand vigilant! Keep your eyes open."

He also says, "We must always be afraid. We must be afraid every second that we're alive, so we're not overcome by the darkness."

42

IN REAL LIFE

WE AREN'T WHO we say we are—not to the government. We don't exist. There are no papers to prove anything. We don't have Social Security cards, passports, tax IDs, tax returns, state IDs, or birth certificates. We can't afford to be pulled over when we drive. We can't show a license or registration. We can't step to the side and identify ourselves. We can't produce proof. Or—in my case, here in this neighborhood—we can't go with the rescue workers right after the earthquake.

Last spring, I learned that my condition was permanent. I was hoping to change things.

I'd read my learner's permit manual. Studied it while lying on the floor of my garage. Quizzed myself. Put the strange rules up on the ceiling above my bed, rules about roundabouts and yielding to pedestrians who are still standing on the sidewalk, or how to pass a horse and buggy on a two-lane highway.

My dream of driving was the booklet in my hands and the car I'd eventually own someday, a red 1964 Mustang convertible, the silver trim along the windshield buffed to shine, the black cloth top oiled. I looked at '64 Mustangs on Google images and pictured myself driving the coastal highway as my hair blew around in the wind. I found an app where you could photoshop yourself into a classic car, and I did.

I skipped my afternoon classes and took the bus out to West Eleventh. Got off two blocks from the DMV and walked the rest of the way. It was a gray, rainy day, but I didn't care. I was so happy to almost be a driver.

When I put my two pieces of mail, my school transcript, and my birth certificate on the counter at the DMV, the man looked down at the paperwork, then back at me. He said, "What is this?"

"Those are my forms."

"No," he said, "what is *this*?" He held up one of my papers.

I said, "That's my birth certificate."

"See, the thing is . . ." he said, "I don't know how to tell you this, but this isn't a birth certificate. This isn't how a birth certificate looks in Oregon." He shook his head. Then he set the paper down on the countertop and tapped it with two fingers.

I said, "What do you mean?"

"I mean, this isn't how they're set up, this isn't how they look, and this doesn't have a state seal either. None of this is correct."

I took the birth certificate. Looked at it. There wasn't any kind of seal, but it was a form. It had my information. It was typed, and it said "Birth Certificate, State of Oregon" at the top. I thought my mother had ordered it.

I said, "Are you sure? Maybe there are different kinds?"

"Look," the man said, "is there any chance that your dad or mom just sort of, ya know . . . made this thing on a typewriter? Cause that's what this looks like to me."

I shook my head. "I don't think so."

"Well," he said, "is there any chance they just decided to do their own 'birth certificate' thing?" He made air quotes as he said 'birth certificate.' He said, "Maybe they put a real nice piece of paper in a typewriter and spaced things out. This does look pretty good for a fake. It has a lot of info."

I was sure my mother ordered it. I remembered her talking about how you can order them online. How real they look.

"Here's the thing," the man said, "there's no way for you to get a learner's permit today without this. But your parents can write a letter to the state and order an official document. Or maybe they have another copy of your birth certificate somewhere, or something from the hospital where you were born?"

"But what if they don't?"

"You could bring your passport then. Any of those would work."

"My passport?"

"For travel, for anywhere you've been overseas or anything like that." He pushed the rest of my documents back to me. Said, "I'm sorry about this. I really am. But the good news is that you don't have to pay me any money today." He smiled.

I took all of my paperwork and turned, walked through the crowded lobby, pushed out the front doors past an old lady and another teenager, and stepped outside into the gray day already turning to a heavy rain.

43

NO PLAN

AFTERNOON, I'M DAY-DRUNK on a bottle of Captain Morgan's Rum that I found in a nearby house, and now I'm stumbling around the living room of the Hendrix place. Earlier, I'd been crying and couldn't stop myself. So I started to drink.

Even drunk, my throat feels thick, like I'm getting a cold. My shoulders are so tight they feel bound by wire, fastened together, bolts on my shoulder blades and a wrench turning everything tighter.

I take a swig from the bottle.

That same wire comes around the front of me and tightens across my chest. My ribs feel pressed together.

I take another drink.

Only two inches left in the bottom of the bottle, and it was half full before I started. I'm eight or ten drinks in. I sip again, the liquor tasteless now, not warm or sweet like it was at first, but now a nothing taste because I'm this far along. I trip over something on the floor and fall down, the bottle hitting the rug but not breaking. A small slosh of rum spills out of the neck.

I pick up the bottle. Sit on my mattress and sip. Then I stand back up. But the angles of the room are all wrong, and I have to lean against the couch, blink, clear my vision so I can lean solidly.

I take one final swig. Set the bottle on a chair. Go outside into the backyard to my latrine in the corner, pull down my pants, and pee.

* * *

Later, in the dark, I have night sweats, not sleeping but fighting, my mouth full of old sugar. Don't remember lying down. Or standing up again. Hazy and wobbling on my feet, I get a large metal pot from the kitchen and put it next to my bed. Feel the hot flashes in my body, the poison running through my liver.

Head on my pillow again. Regular images: I think of people scrolling their phones after work. Cars driving down the street. The sounds of sprinklers greening lawns. The sound of a lawnmower somewhere in the neighborhood.

I think of other normal things, one by one:

The sounds UPS trucks used to make coming down the street. Their hydraulic brakes.

An air conditioner humming next to a house.

A garage door opening.

A car's double beep as it's locked.

* * *

When I look at the window, there's a face. Eyes above a beard.

I reach underneath my pillow, pull my pistol, stand up and wobble, take an unsteady step.

Breathe deep. Cock the pistol.

At the window, I hold the pistol against the glass. This window not broken. No light behind me and no light outside. I don't see the face anymore.

I blink and look. There's the outlines of the rhododendron leaves, withered flowers, the heat-limp branches, and nothing else.

I slide the window open and the smell of the yard rushes me, summer-bent and dry. I stick the barrel of the gun through the opening, point up and down, left and right. But I don't see anything. Don't see anyone.

I'm still so drunk I have to lean on the sill, lean heavy, and my eyes blurry. I shake my head. Don't hear anything, and I realize I might have made up the face. But I keep the pistol in my hand, stumbling back to my bed and lying down again.

*   *   *

Sometime in the early morning, I throw up in the kitchen pot—violently, but just once—and then I'm through. Over and over my mouth fills with saliva, and I can smell the bile in my nostrils, but I don't vomit anymore, nothing else to get rid of, and then it's light out, my head feeling like long nails have been pounded deep into my skull above my eyebrows.

The morning lengthens and warms, and there's a steep angle to my headache.

I drift and wake again, drift and wake two or three more times, so thirsty that I turn and drink a whole bottle of water, only to throw it up again a few minutes later. The metal pot is half full of vomit now, sloshing, a yellow color, the new water mixing with last night's vomit, and I think how nice a shower would feel—warm, not hot—and a wet washcloth over my eyes. Then lying down again, a washcloth full of ice cubes.

I close my eyes again.

Images float through my mind, but not the good neighborhood images of before. I see distended bodies, limbs turned black, a face in the window, dried blood, a crack in the skin releasing trapped gases. I gag. Breathe through my open mouth. Close my eyes and fall back asleep, but only for a little while.

*   *   *

Awake again, I turn slowly and sip water. Wait. Sip some more. Swallow a Vicodin. Wait and drift.

This is what I never thought of when I thought of survival or the apocalypse. Those types of movies are all action and motion. But in the real world, if you survive, most of everything is waiting. Lots of sitting and thinking, lots of sleeping. Maybe one of the tougher things about survival: too much time.

The Vicodin kicks in, and I drink the rest of my water bottle. I wait a few more minutes, then roll to my knees, put my hands on the back of the couch, get myself slowly to my feet, walking into the kitchen to get saltine crackers and a bottle of Tums antacids that I left on the counter. Plus another small bottle of water.

I suck on the Tums while I pack two backpacks. Eat one saltine cracker in between each tablet of Tums, chewing slowly, swallowing, taking a sip of water with every cracker, just enough to keep my mouth moist, but nothing more. I try to rebuild my stomach from scratch.

*   *   *

We took backpacks when we came across the border ten years ago—those days and nights in the desert something I will never forget—my backpack holding a water bottle, two of the dehydration packets, plus a small paper bag of tortillas from Tía Verónica, and my pink Minnie Mouse sweatshirt that I loved. My mother's backpack held more items, meat and beans and rice wrapped in tinfoil and plastic bags. Extra water. Extra dehydration packets. Two blankets for sleeping. One extra set of clothing for each of us.

At the last stop in Mexico, my mother refused what the medical woman was offering her. My mother said, "Estará en las manos de Dios."

The medical woman looked at her and shook her head.

My mother pressed her lips together and held her chin high.

But she was not so confident when the coyote left us in the desert, shrugging his shoulders, saying only, "¿Desde aquí?" and pointing. Then he walked back in the direction where we'd come.

I remember the next day too, with the desert seeming to go on forever, my mother pointing at the mountains way out in front of us. She was trying out English, going back and forth between the two languages, speaking in Spanglish when she could think of the English words. She said, "Es América . . . just there."

I pointed at the peaks. "¿Están en los Estados Unidos?"

"But before," she said, "antes de las montañas." She paused. "The desert aquí, m'hija." She knelt down and drew a line in the dirt, her finger going back and forth. Just a line, nothing else.

I looked at her line, then up at the desert. There wasn't a line or a fence or a wall. No buildings. It was nothing like I'd imagined. "¿Dónde está la línea?" I said, "¿Cómo conocen?"

"They only know, claro que sí," she said. "Es muy importante for they to know."

I remember that moment well, but I'm not sure if I asked anything after that. I can't remember. I only remember the feeling that nothing made sense. How could two countries look the exact same? Where were the things that told someone they were in a new country? It seemed impossible. There was just desert and then more desert. But two countries?

We hiked and hiked, all day, my legs heavy and stiff long before we stopped. I wanted to whine and complain to my mother, but I'd never seen the look she had on her face, and it scared me. So I kept quiet, kept lifting my feet and moving forward.

Then there were the nights: the sounds of owls and coyote packs, stars multiplying in the black above us, and a curve of moon. I lay flat on a blanket on the ground, with another blanket spread over me. My mother poured our dehydration packs into our water bottles.

Even though the days were hot, the nights were cold in the desert, cool winds gusting as we drank our salty-sweet dehydration mixes, ate tortillas with beans, lay back down, and pulled in the corners of our blankets.

I watched for shooting stars and made wishes, imagined a new life so different from the old one. I imagined something better, but I wondered.

The first place we stayed after my mother told me we had crossed into the United States was a metal shed in the middle of nowhere, near nothing, with a tarantula that crawled out of the corner in the afternoon. We stayed two days, drinking a full gallon of water left by border angels under a tree. When we found the water, my mother made us get down on our knees. She whispered, "Dios, gracias por mantenernos a salvo, y . . ."

I remember that I made the sign of the cross and kissed my fingers, but my mother slapped my hand. She hissed, "*¡Somos evangélicos! ¡No católicos!*"

I looked at the set of her teeth, her upper lip curled. I started to cry, but I didn't want her to see. So I looked away. Stayed silent.

* * *

I think about that desert crossing as I load my two backpacks now. I make a small pile of water, food, medicine, money, jewelry, my pistol, and all my rounds. Put my AR and two clips next to that backpack, plus a few items of clothing. This is what I'll take with me if I have to leave quickly.

I pack a second bag full of extras, extra food, extra clothing—warm clothing for the winter—and a few books. If I'm able to, whenever I leave, I'll take this second bag as well. One bag if I have to run. Two if I can carry.

I realized that eventually there will only be one place to go: out across the water. On the water I could decide which direction to paddle, north or south, east or west, but I won't have a choice between water and land. This hill is an island, and eventually there will be nothing for me up on this hill. The floodwater seems like it will be here to stay, and when it begins to rain in a month or two, the water will only rise, the flood will only get deeper.

INFIDEL

I CARRY TWO PACKS with me for a week, then one, then sometimes neither. I don't see The Collection, and it begins to feel like they were never here, like I've always been alone in this neighborhood. I've found more antibiotics and taken them. There's no pink around the scab on my thigh and my leg feels all the way better.

I don't decide on a day when I'll leave. I never make that decision, and I'm stepping over a month-old bag of garbage on a kitchen floor when I hear the click of a gun behind me. I wasn't even being careful anymore.

I turn around and it's the woman from the raft, her head full of dreadlocks, her old robe so dirty that a person couldn't tell now if it was ever white in the first place.

She says, "No one believed me, but I'd been prophesying for months." She's sitting in a chair, her feet spread over the curdled chunk of an old gallon of spilled milk. A blue-oiled pistol is in her hand. The pistol is pointed at me.

It looks like one of those Old West guns from a movie, the ones where you can spin the cylinder.

She says, "God had revealed the truth to me."

"What?" I say. I'm sweating, feeling ghostlike, heavy and light at the same time. My heartbeat is in the front of my forehead.

"I knew the truth," she says. "I knew it all, and I told them. God whispered in my ear, in a dream, that this was coming." She motions with the end of her pistol. "But they wouldn't listen. No, they never did."

I don't have my hands up, but I'm standing still. Waiting for her to tell me what to do.

But instead, she says, "People don't like to hear bad news. They don't want to hear about the world falling apart. That's all we got for news the last two years. Social discord. Viruses. Maybe a coming civil war."

I nod. "I remember."

"But things kept clicking. Society adjusted to new realities. So the vast destruction I was talking about?" She laughs. Then she squints her eyes and shakes her head like she's trying to get rid of some bad image she's seeing.

She moves her pistol in a small circle, outlining my face.

I say, "Are you living in this house?"

"No, no," she says. "I live nowhere. I only sleep where God tells me to. When he says to lay my head down, I do. And in this way, I'm like you, Narco."

"Narco?"

"Narcoleptic. Insomniac given to sleeping spells . . ." She doesn't blink. "That's you."

So I know she's been following and watching me. I have this feeling like all the blood in my body has turned the color gray.

She says, "Do you believe in God?"

This question makes me feel tired. I've been asked that too many times. I hesitate.

But the woman doesn't seem to notice that I don't answer her question. She says, "The earthquake was inevitable. That was fine. But they didn't want to hear the *real* truth."

I look at her face, her eyes a little out of focus.

"About the wrath of God." She squints again and her head tilts to the side.

I say, "Is that what you think this is?"

"Wrong," she says, as if she's talking to someone else, not to me. "No one wants to know. Even the earth's crust and mantle, all of it. Of course it all belongs to God. And he's sick of us, of our choices here. 'And the Lord said, I will destroy man, whom I have created from the face of the earth; both man, and beast, and the creeping thing, and the fowls of the air; for it repenteth me that I have made them.' And 'behold, I will destroy them with the earth,' and 'I will strike down upon thee with great vengeance and furious anger.' And that's the truth. That is a promise he's made, this catastrophic act of God. That's what we're seeing here, a purging. We are—collectively—evil people in an evil time."

She stands up and I take a step back. But she turns away from me and spreads her arms, her pistol in her right hand, now pointing at the wall. I look at the back of her head and see fat, white lice crawling from her scalp. I realize she's facing a window as she says, "Behold, the Lord lays the earth to waste, devastates it, distorts its surface, and scatters its inhabitants."

I think about shooting her in the back. Slowly, I slip my right hand into my waistband, feel my pistol's grip, the gun there.

The woman turns around quickly and shakes her head. Looks directly at me, but doesn't point her pistol. Instead, she holds it at her side. Stares at me without blinking. She says, "Only a fool would think this is anything else. So— let me ask you a simple question—are you a fool?"

"About what?" I say.

She smiles. "Don't you listen? This is the scariest thing of all. He leans down. He leans in. He says, 'Those who have ears . . . let them hear.'"

I want to turn and leave, but I'm not sure if this woman will let me go. I look down at her pistol. My right hand is still on the grip of my own pistol, under my T-shirt.

Neither of us move, and I wonder if her last statement was a question.

She says, "It's okay to be a fool if you admit that it's true, that you *are* a fool . . . and then you make a decision to change." She puts her index finger up in the air. Holds it there. Then points at me.

I take a step sideways. Hold both of my hands up. Say, "I have to go now."

"Leaving is a bad decision. Running away." She holds her one finger in the air, very still. She says, "When you begin to talk about what's important, you have to be willing to stay forever, to hear the eternal truth. You are a field ripe for the harvest."

I say, "But maybe I'm all wrong?" Somehow this seems like something she'll understand.

"See that?" she says. "That right there is honesty. That shows me something. And now I see that you're not with them."

I say, "With who?" But I know she's talking about The Collection.

"You know who." She nods her head. "You've been watching them, and I've been watching you, and—again—this is about eternity, about God's wrath, about your soul. So let's not pretend."

"Okay," I say, but I take another step sideways. Say again, "I have to go." I'm at the start of the hallway.

The woman puts a long, yellow thumbnail to her nostril and scrapes the inside. Her nose is red-rimmed and crusty. She says, "In the dark, we remain unrepentant."

I nod and walk backward, ease my way down the hallway, my hands still up.

At the door, I step outside. I still have my hands up. I wait for her to shoot me, but then I step off the front stoop, and I'm out of her sight. Then I run.

45

RUNNING

I DON'T SLEEP WELL that night. I'm not sure if the woman knows where I sleep, and I don't know if she'll come for me. I wake up multiple times to sounds, but then I listen and hear nothing else. I try to go back to sleep but don't for a long, long time.

Sometime just before dawn, I wake to something more solid—a definite sound, a clunk—and I sit up, pull my pistol from under my pillow. Stand and look around in the dark. Wonder what made the sound and where it came from.

I check the lock on the back door and my barricade of the front door. But neither is out of place. So I check each window. Put my head and gun out past the shattered glass, over the empty sills, looking in every direction. The windows are big, though, and any animal could crawl in through any of them.

Then I lift the only two windows that didn't shatter. But I see nothing through those either.

I walk into the kitchen and check that my two back-packs are ready to go. I add a bottle of water to each of them. Feel how heavy they are. Remember which one I'll wear and which one I'll carry as a secondary pack.

And that's when I hear an explosion—something like a small bomb.

I run up the stairs to the third floor; go out on the balcony. I scan the neighborhood, looking north, down to the water, then west. And I see it there, toward College Hill, a house far off to my left is burning. Heat explodes the upper windows and the roof comes apart in less than a minute. I count blocks and figure out that it's on Columbia Street, a block over from where I used to live.

The next house goes up quickly, then the fire spreads three houses wide, multiplying, creating an expanding triangle of burning homes, the fire moving east, coming in my direction and widening.

So this is it. I'm out of time. I hurry back down the stairs. Go into the kitchen to see if there's any food I might want to take with me.

There's my headlamp, in the kitchen, where I set it on the counter before I fell asleep. I pick it up and turn it on, everything in front of the beam too bright and everything outside of my light becoming completely invisible.

I shine my light into the pantry. Go shelf to shelf and see if I missed anything that I'll regret leaving here later. I shake a half-empty box of Rice Krispies. Set the box back down. Open a bag of white bread, cram a slice into my mouth, chew as I look at Oreos, a quarter jar of Skippy peanut butter, miso soup packets. Leave those. I think I have what I need in my packs.

I turn to exit the pantry, holding the flashlight up in front of me, and as I step out into the kitchen—out of the pantry door—there's an arm swinging, a gun and a handle of that gun, and I start to scream as it hits my head.

*   *   *

We do not run because we are afraid of bears.
    We are afraid of bears because we run.

*   *   *

The flashlight. Light and dark. Then just dark.

46

INNER DARK

I'VE NEVER FELT my eyes so heavy. Like a hand over my face, holding my eyelids shut. I try to open them, but they only go to slits, and I see gray white. I can tell it's daylight, but I'm too drowsy. I try to talk—one sentence to ask where I am—but my mouth is full of something.

My head tips forward.

Back to the shadows.

And black.

47

OUTER DARK

I STRUGGLE TO WAKE again, like waves are holding me down in the dark water, and I come up three times before I break through the surface. I open my eyes, close them again. Open them a second time, this time wider. I fight to keep them open.

It's nighttime now—no daylight coming through the window to my right. This isn't my room. Not where I've been staying on Hendrix. This isn't that house. I'm somewhere new, somewhere else, not anywhere I've been before. There are candles lit around the room. All the candles flicker and separate. Come back together again. The room is painted red—the walls dark in the candlelight—only one window, and it's all black. I lift my head, try to open my eyes fully, but my left eye is swollen partway shut where the pistol hit me. As I try to open it, it catches and stings. My other eye isn't injured, but I'm tired.

So tired.

I think I must be drugged.

*　*　*

A while later—it's impossible to know how long—I open my eyes again and see that I'm in a wooden chair that has arms. My wrists are tied to the arms of the chair with rope. Duct tape running a loop next to the rope—reinforcing the bindings—everything so tight that I can't wiggle my elbows. I try and fail. Try again. But it's useless. My arms won't budge.

My ankles are tied to the chair as well. I can move my knees just a little, but not my lower legs, and I imagine there's rope and duct tape down there as well.

Across from me—facing me—is another chair, an empty chair. I stare at the chair a long time, trying to understand why it's here. I wonder if there was someone else bound in that chair, someone who's no longer in this room. And where did they go?

I close my eyes and open them again.

It could've been five minutes. Or an hour.

That chair across from me is still empty. But something to my right catches my eye. A white cat hops onto a long side table set against the wall. The cat weaves in between the candles, its tail trailing near the flames, and it looks like it'll light on fire, but it doesn't. The cat makes its way to the end of the table and hops down, walks over to the empty chair across from me, starts scratching at the wood, rasping its claws on one of the chairs legs. There are old cat scratches from before, from another time.

My whole body feels heavy.

I close my eyes and open them again, and now the cat is gone. It must be a while later again. I squeeze my eyes together and try to wake up completely, but that feels difficult. Something's stuffed in my mouth so I take a deep breath through my nostrils. Exhale and take another deep breath.

I seem to be alone. I don't hear any other sounds in the room. I try to say, "Hello?" but it comes out garbled. I try to scream, but whatever's stuck in my mouth doesn't come out, and my scream sounds like someone moaning under a blanket. My mouth is cottony, full of something that feels wet. Claustrophobia is not a strong enough word to describe that thing being in my mouth. I start to panic.

I hyperventilate through my nose. The corner of my vision turns black, and I drop my head. Exhausted.

It feels like there's sand in my blood, the grains catching, thick and heavy. My heart can't pump quickly enough for me to think at any normal speed, and I wonder about the thickener they must have put inside of me. I try to shake my head to clear the haze. Pull breaths through my nose again, but I realize that one of my nostrils is partly clotted with blood . . . or snot? It feels like I can't get enough oxygen to my brain from my single nostril.

I try screaming again. But my mouth is so full.

Someone comes into the room.

They walk behind me. Fumble with something. I try to turn my head to see them. Say, "Who's there?" but my question is muffled.

The person sounds like they're directly behind me. They're doing something, maybe setting objects on a table? I can hear what sounds like metal clunking against wood. I can also hear feet on the floor, then a door creaking and some other sound I can't identify.

There are no sounds for a little while, and I wait— with my eyes open—listening.

Finally, someone is in the room again, and a person walks past me. He's tall and big and has a beard, and he's carrying something in his hands. He steps to the empty chair and sets the object down. Doesn't say anything. Steps back behind me and is gone. The door closes and clicks.

Then there are no more sounds in the room.

On the chair, across from me, is the red cigar box. It looks like it's made of wood, painted with gold lettering. The writing says:

Maduro
Gran Habano
Imperiales 6 x 60
No. 5

I realize that there are new smells in the room that I can't quite place, but I've smelled them before. Some kind of cleaner, plus something else. Some kind of rot.

48

AND THEN SHE WAS GONE

I NEVER THOUGHT SHE'D leave, even though I knew how much she was caught up, how much she was obsessed. Right away, it was like her clothes were on fire, as if she were alight, burning, raging. Something had changed in her face after the first meeting, then the second, then the third. I was always worried by her choices of churches, but this time it was like she was speaking a different language. Even how she chewed her food had changed, like the muscles in her face had been altered by the new things she was learning.

She told me about the meetings—not everything, but enough. She told me about the video releases, how on the first day of each month they would all go early to the meeting, how the deacons would lock the congregation inside the church, how no one was allowed to come into the building or go out during the entirety of the video's running time. No one was allowed in late either. They had to be on time and all in.

She also told me about the first time she was blessed by Witness Andreas, how he smiled at her, how he closed his eyes to say the blessing, and how the warmth of his small hand spread throughout her entire body.

This was last year. There had been so many strange churches during my lifetime, but this one sounded like the weirdest of them all. She told me I was required to go on the next Saturday night, that everyone would bring their family members, but I refused to go. I was beyond all that with her. She couldn't make me anymore, and if she tried—if I actually went—she knew I wouldn't stay silent. She knew I would embarrass her.

Before this, I had endured a different church that was similar: Women were not allowed to show their ankles or bare their wrists, a church where they called me "Sister Wagner" as if I were a nun, but when I made a joke about being a nun, everyone frowned at me, and an old woman narrowed her eyes and took a step forward. She said, "Satan is in the Roman Catholic church. Satan has led that congregation for a thousand years."

So now there was The Collection and its weekly video releases that I knew to avoid. I was hoping that something made my mother move churches again, something that wouldn't seem right to her. But nothing changed. She kept going.

We grew further apart. The garage space was so small with both of us in it, me doing my homework as my mother sat on the floor and memorized verses from The Collection's new translation of the Bible. If I caught her eye, she would stare at me and shake her head.

Then—so many evenings—she was gone. The services lasted for hours, so I had our small garage space to myself. It was like I was living alone even before I was actually living alone.

49

CHOSEN

SOMEONE ELSE COMES into the room, not the big man who set the cigar box down, but someone shorter, and I recognize him. He's the leader person I saw in the neighborhood many times.

He holds his hand to his chest. Says, "Let me introduce myself. I am Witness Andreas. I am The Witness to The Collection of Redeemed Souls. And as its witness from God, its guide, I lead my brothers and sisters in the circumspect reverence of the Lord Almighty, the God of all eternity."

The white cat is in the room still. I see it rub against the man's leg, wend a figure eight around his ankles. Witness Andreas bends down and runs his small hand over the cat's body. The cat's mid-back bows, and it purrs loudly.

Witness Andreas stands back up and takes a deep breath. Reaches toward my face, but I flinch, pull my head back as far as it can go, turn away from him.

"Shh," he says, and takes ahold of my head with his two hands. "I'm only removing this." He holds the back of my neck firmly with one hand as his other hand pulls a big wad of wet cotton out of my mouth, sets it on the empty chair next to the cigar box.

"I've seen you," I say. "I know about you. You're the creepy leader person."

Witness Andreas smiles at me. His smile is the smile a person might make when talking to a very small child. He says, "You will learn to understand things—maybe—but not all at once. I won't give you a long speech. But there are those who choose, and then there are those who are chosen. But in reality, both are one and the same. Who can tell which one is first? And even a choice . . ." He makes a motion with his hand, a circle in the air. "Well," he says, "even that is of God. He chooses whom he will redeem, and I am happy to bring you the good news that you have been chosen."

"No," I say, "I haven't."

"Hmm," he says, and his index finger makes another circle in the air. "It has been revealed to me that you have indeed been chosen, whether you know it or not. To be clear, anything revealed to me is of absolute truth. The Lord reveals. But this is also true: the chosen must make a first act—a sacrifice, something visible, something tangible—even if they don't understand what they're doing or why. Maybe your ears aren't open yet, but we could pray for that together?"

I struggle against my bindings, try to wiggle my arms to see if there's any chance of getting free, but there's no point. I'm bound too tightly. My chair doesn't even move. I say, "I don't want to pray for anything with you. I'm not doing any sacrifices either."

Witness Andreas bends down and pets the white cat at his feet once again. He runs his hand over its sleek head, and its purring is loud.

"Because you are young," he says, "you think that what you say is true. And I was foolish when I was young as well. I believed in my own understanding, in what I said, in what I thought I saw. But I didn't know that God had chosen me."

"I don't care about all that," I say. "I don't care about this or about your religion. It doesn't mean anything to me."

"Religion?" he laughs. "Religion is for the small-minded. Religion isn't of God. Religion is of man. It's a warped thing. There's nothing in religion, but we all do—however—need to know the Lord, and there is a God-sized hole in all of us that the Lord can fill."

I shake my head. I wish my thoughts were clearer. I say, "Did you drug me?"

Witness Andreas smiles again. "You do seem"—he makes a circle motion in front of my face—"unclear."

"Listen," I say, "I don't believe in your religion. You can't make a person believe."

"No, no, of course not. People who call themselves religious do not understand anything. Even people who call themselves Christians are not true believers. They are not the chosen people of the Lord." He shakes his head. "People who go to their little churches on Sundays, people who read other people's translations of the Bible."

"So do you read your own?"

He taps his fingers against his chest. "No," he says, "I don't trust other men. I've translated the entire Bible myself, Old and New Testament. I am called to be The Witness to the Lord God of all eternity."

He takes a breath. Says, "But that's enough for now."

He smiles again, tilts his head and looks at me. Then he walks past my chair, and I hear him close the door behind me. The latch clicks. Then I'm alone with the cat again. It hops up on the chair opposite me. The cat smells the saliva-soaked cotton ball, then the box.

50

THE COLLECTION

I'M SO UNCOMFORTABLE—MY whole body cramping—but whatever drug they gave me was strong. I fall asleep again.

When I wake up, it's dark, none of the candles lit. I wonder if someone came in the room and blew the candles out or if they burned out on their own. I wonder how long I've been in this chair. My lower back is aching. I try to arch and shift, but nothing feels good.

I stay awake for a long time. My back throbs. I try to imagine my escape, try to picture some way that I'll leave this place, get out of my chair, and I remember the girl I saw at the Hendrix house the night when they caught her on the porch, how I listened to her screams, how I didn't help her, how I couldn't help her or how I chose not to.

I'm thinking about her when I fall asleep again.

I dream about the bear.

*   *   *

Something slides underneath my left hand and I jolt awake.

It's not Witness Andreas in front of me, but a much taller person, a spiderlike man with long, thin arms. He's younger than Witness Andreas but with the same type of beard. He's sliding a wooden cutting board underneath my left hand.

I say, "Wait . . . no! Hey, stop!"

The man doesn't say anything. He doesn't look me in the eye.

He picks up the wad of cotton from the other chair and grabs my face. He tries to stuff the cotton in my mouth, but I keep my jaws clenched, my lips sealed. I shake my head, and he waits for me to stop. Then he grabs my face harder, stabs into the side of my cheek with one of his thumbs, gouges hard into the muscle on the side of my face, and my mouth pops open. Then he stuffs the cotton into my mouth, and I gag on it. I try to bite his fingers, but he pulls them back.

He stands again, walks past me out of the room, but doesn't close the door behind him. I don't hear the door creak, and there's no click of the latch. So I know the door is open behind me.

I try not to cry, but tears spill down my cheeks as I hear footsteps behind me once again. I turn my head, but I still can't see.

Then Witness Andreas is in front of me again, and he taps the cutting board with the tips of his fingers. I try to scream but it's muffled.

"This is a good choice," he says. "It will hurt of course, but then you will be redeemed. You will be collected by the Lord, and we will welcome you among us."

That's when I see the wide-bladed kitchen knife in his other hand.

He adjusts the cutting board once more, slides and angles it so it's centered underneath my smallest finger, the pinky of my left hand. The bindings are too tight for me to pull away.

I shake my head and cry even harder. My vision goes blurry.

But I feel the blade of the knife against my skin—at the joint where my pinky connects to my hand—and I open my eyes wide, shake my head to stop crying. Feel how sharp the knife is. Witness Andreas puts his other hand on the back of the blade for leverage.

I wiggle my finger just a little bit, and feel the sharp edge of the knife.

Witness Andreas says, "We are allowing for the eternal."

Then he pushes down on the back of the blade.

HOW IT WAS EVERY DAY

WHEN YOU HAVE nothing. When you don't fit into any culture. Middle school and you can't tell people that you live in a one-room converted garage. That your mom doesn't own a car. That you sell Marinol and Xanax, Valium and Ritalin to anyone who will buy them. Percocet when you can get it. That every stray purse in every restaurant or coffee shop has pills like these. That a quick dip of your hand is all it takes.

This is how you bought your first iPod and—later—your first phone.

You can't afford popular clothes, so you steal those as well. You've been practicing invisibility your entire life, so this is not as difficult as it sounds. You are a ghost on a foggy day. You are the background extra in a movie scene. You are a droplet in a glass of water.

You walk into the Valley River Center mall with a messenger bag slung on your hip. The bag looks like a purse but will hold more stolen items than anyone could ever imagine. You buy one T-shirt as cover, and walk out with a full wardrobe. You do this three more times at three other stores to begin ninth grade.

You study hard in school and your A and B grades keep you out of trouble with your teachers and the school counselors. Staying out of trouble is your cloak. The principal walks by you in the hallway and doesn't know your name. That is important. The assistant principal points at you one time and says, "Um . . .," then snaps his fingers and smiles. "You go here, right?"

You nod and smile back. Say, "Of course!" But you don't offer your name. You turn and keep walking.

Even if you want to, you can't afford to join the soccer team. You can't afford to join the chess club. But you have a library card, and you take the maximum number of books each month—ten—and those books are your world. You lie on the roof of your garage and read novels as the daylight fades into evening. And on weekends, you sit up on the roof and read in the sunlight.

You see your mother come back from a full day of cleaning houses. The big house on Monday. Other houses in a rotation—one each day—Tuesday through Friday. Your mother's ankles look swollen, and she sits on the floor, leaning back against the wall, eating a 7-Eleven hot dog. She hands you the other hot dog (mustard, no ketchup). She rolled your dinner in a double napkin and stuffed it into her purse for the bus ride home. She says, "I don't like you to stare at me after work. *Déjame sólo.*"

So you don't look at her as you eat your hot dog. You give her space.

A moment to relax.

She takes a shower in the zinc stall in the back of the garage, the showerhead a cut length of garden hose. She puts on a long-sleeved dress, long socks, no makeup. Covers her head. Walks around without talking to you because you have told her—finally—that you will never go to another church with her ever again. You told her that all of her churches are nothing like your Tío Pablo's church in Mexico where you went when you were little, where the family was all together, and they smiled at the priest, who also smiled back at the family, and everyone made the sign of the cross, and everyone ate food together when mass was finished. But she was never with you.

52

METAPHYSICS

Witness Andreas says, "This will be an addition to The Collection," as he drops the lid on the red cigar box.

I glance down and see the blood run off the edge of the cutting board. I feel light-headed. Black coming in from the sides of my vision. Dreams of beauty, the past, kaleidoscope twists, one and then the next:

> Catching a gopher snake in a company field near K-59, the quick flick of its black tongue against my palm as I sit among the bright green heads of lettuce.

> Holding a bottle of Coke on a summer day next to the sheet metal of the tienda, Tío Pablo smiling at me, the smell of cane sugar as he tilts his Coke bottle and the glass clinks against his silver front tooth. He says, "Cuando el sol brilla, siempre es un buen día."

I felt bad for thinking, "Pero el sol brilla la mayoría de los días, y la mayoría son . . ." I mean, how could all sunny days be good days?

But he was still smiling, and his smile was always good.

Sitting on the roof of the garage as the constellation Orion rises in the east, the Pleiades above it, putting on my black hoodie after I shiver for the first time.

The night Aadita and I skinny-dipped in the eddy pool below the Wave Train on the Willamette River, the way water beaded on the curve of her naked back, both of us laughing as we pulled our T-shirts back on.

I take a sudden breath and open my eyes.

The weight is heaviest where the pinky used to connect. I hear a click. Look down. Witness Andreas has a Butane lighter, the blue flame steady and straight next to my left hand.

IN THIS CHAIR

I WAKE IN THE daylight, my left hand throbbing. There's a white bandage over the hand, one spot of blood on the gauze. I'm so thirsty. My throat feels like it's lined with steel wool. My pants are wet and my legs itch where I peed myself.

The candles are out, but light is coming into the room. I see where someone has peeled back the foil that was covering the window. I'm still tied to the chair. The empty chair is still facing me, but the red cigar box is gone.

The white cat leaps from the side table, walks up to me, and rubs against my leg, purring.

I realize that I'm not gagged anymore, wonder if I have a chance of someone hearing me if I scream. Somebody not with them. So I yell, "Help me! Is anyone there?! *Help me!!!*"

No one answers.

I scream again. "Hello?! Anyone?! If you can hear me, *help me!*"

I hear something move in the house above. The sound of a chair scraping across a floor. Footsteps. The door opens behind me. Then closes.

Witness Andreas sits down across from me. He says, "I'm glad you're awake. I was waiting for that. We need to talk through our possibilities." He leans forward. His robe is newly cleaned, incredibly white.

I yell again. *"Help me! Someone please help me!"*

Witness Andreas sits and looks at me. Doesn't speak.

I stop yelling. Wait and listen for anyone else, anyone who might help.

Witness Andreas blinks and shakes his head. "There's no one who could hear you. And—anyway—we need to talk more productively. We need to discuss a plan."

"What are you talking about?"

"About what you are going to decide." He presses his palms together. Puts his lips to his fingertips. "Your future," he says, then he stretches his arms wide. "And about God."

I say, "About God?"

"The only thing that matters . . . the one, true thing in this universe. God is waiting for you, either in this life or the next, but you have to call out to him. You have to choose wisely."

I say, "That's where people like you are so stupid. Before, you told me that I was chosen. Now you're saying I need to choose."

"Well, of course," he says, "it's really simple." He smiles again, like he's a grade school teacher and I'm a child who doesn't understand a math problem. He tilts his head. "But now you have to respond. With God, it is always about the call and the response."

I look at the bandage on my left hand, the blood spot on the gauze, and I think about my missing pinky. I start to cry. I don't want to cry—I don't want to give him that—but I can't stop myself. I look away and close my eyes.

Witness Andreas waits. He doesn't say anything.

I keep my eyes closed and think. Force myself to stop crying. Then I clear my throat, gather phlegm in my mouth and open my eyes. I lift my head and look at Witness Andreas. Then I spit, and the wad of phlegm hits him on his robe, high on the right side of his chest. He looks down at it—the spit yellow with a line of red in it—a chunk dripping from one fold of his robe to the next.

He shakes his head and looks at me.

I say, "You don't know anything about God."

"I am afraid," he says, "that the truth is the other way around. You are the one who does not know anything about God." He looks up at the ceiling. Tilts his face and breathes through his nose like he's sniffing the air. "I am the called witness to the Lord God of the universe, the guiding light of The Collection."

"You might think that," I say.

Witness Andreas closes his eyes and exhales. "If you were humble, you could learn from me. And you may still."

"But what if *you* were humble?" I say. "Do you even realize how ridiculous it is that you wrote your own version of the Bible?"

Witness Andreas shakes his head. Takes a big breath and exhales.

"You and your stupid red-letter version of the Bible," I say. "You don't have anything that I want to learn. Not a single thing."

He looks at me again. "That is one option that you might decide upon. I cannot force you to change your mind, and you will have to make your own eternal decisions, or . . ." and he trails off. Looks out the window now, where the foil has been peeled back.

"Or what? Are you gonna hurt me again? Are you gonna fuckin' . . ." I shake my head. I'm angry and I start to cry again, which makes me even more mad that I can't control myself, that I can't stay calm in situations like this, even if I want to so badly.

Witness Andreas is still staring at the window. He doesn't look at me. He says, "Or this is not going to work out."

"Right," I say, "this isn't gonna work out. So you can just let me go."

Witness Andreas makes a clicking noise with his mouth as he turns back from the window and looks at me. "Unfortunately," he says, "I cannot let that happen."

"But say I don't change, and you don't change either. Say neither of us agree on anything. What then? What would your brilliant plan be? I know how smart you must feel."

He closes his eyes and presses his hands together. Rubs them back and forth. Then he gets up and walks to the door. I hear it open, the hinge creaking, then the click of the latch as it's pulled shut behind him.

*   *   *

I sit for another hour or two. My back seizes, and my neck is so stiff that I can't roll it in either direction without it making a popping sound. My hand is throbbing and I fantasize about an ice pack again, or a field of snow, to lie down and feel cool and painless all over.

I'm thirsty too. I think of filling a pitcher of water and drinking glass after glass. Then I think of Gatorade. A full bottle of yellow Gatorade. Or a cold soft-drink, a Dr. Pepper with ice cubes floating on top. Crushed ice. I think of swallowing a mouthful of liquid and pain pills, drifting away from this chair, from the pain in my lower back—all the cramping—and the burning sensation in my left hand. I imagine not being in this small, hot room—not being in this house, breathing fresh air, not having these stupid little discussions with Witness Andreas.

After a while, I fall asleep again. It's not good sleep, but it's sleep. I dream about high school, what seems like a normal day of walking through the halls, trying to speak to teachers without my accent giving me away, staying silent when I'm not called on in class, watching the loud boys joke back and forth across the room—how much those boys want everyone's attention. Witness Andreas probably didn't get much attention when he was younger. Or maybe he did, but he's a man who feels he should've gotten just a little bit more.

I dream of my past, a real moment: doing all of my homework in the library after school. pulling on a sweatshirt when I feel the cool air blow down from a ceiling vent, the librarian walking up to me and saying, "Cielo, it's time to go home now."

CHAPTER

54

ASSASSIN

I WAKE UP TO a thump. Shouting. Then gunfire.

I look side to side. My neck pops and seizes. I cramp, cry out, and try to lift my hands, but I'm still tied to this fucking chair. My neck releases its cramping, and I gasp, trying to roll it out, trying to see anything, trying not to think of how my low back feels.

I think it's the middle of the night, dark windows just a little less dark than the rest of the room. Maybe moonlight? Or starlight?

There are gunshots back and forth outside. I see the flashes. Then they sound closer. Gunshots inside the house. Big sounds in the room above me. Then behind me, scraping and a thump.

Silence for ten or fifteen seconds.

Then three more gunshots—pop, pop, pop—and the sound of glass breaking, something hitting the wall or the floor inside the house, I can't tell where. Then a man screaming. Another thump, and a scraping noise again. Two or three different kinds of guns going off back and forth. Yelling, then a really loud gunshot.

I try for the hundredth time to move, to turn and look behind me, but it's useless. The ropes and the duct tape are so tight. My injured hand feels as if it's been dipped in fire. I try to breathe deeply, take big breaths and blow them out. Try not to panic.

But my low back hurts so much. And my hand. And I wonder if I'll ever get out of this fucking chair.

More glass breaking. More yelling. Furniture turned over in the next room, then three more gunshots followed by silence.

Total silence.

Then a man begins to groan. It starts so low that I don't even know what the sound is, for a minute. But it gets louder and I realize that it's a man making an animal noise—a low, injured moaning—and it goes on and on. Then a door creaks. The sound of something scrabbling.

Another gunshot.

I wait and hear nothing. Realize I should maybe start yelling again.

I say, "I'm in here! Please help me! Please!!!"

The door opens behind me, and a flashlight beam swings around the room, trains on me, then swings around the room again.

Someone steps toward me. I can smell the person in the dark—standing behind me—someone filthy, with overwhelming body odor, smelling like old food and rank sweat, oil and animal.

The person is breathing audibly, panting just behind me.

I say, "Help?" But I'm not sure who this is or if they will.

The person stands behind me for a long, long time, and I don't say anything else. I wait.

The flashlight beam goes around the room one last time. Then it shines on my chair again, the back of my head, then each of my arms, the right one, then the left. It stops on my injured hand, hovers there for so long that I wonder what the person is thinking.

I don't speak though. I don't know what else to say. I've yelled and cried so much already, and I'm in incredible pain. I guess I'm in shock as well. I'm breathing through my mouth, and my head feels heavy. I try to hold it up, but I'm just too tired. I drop my head.

The person steps forward, right next to me now, and I see the blade of a knife in the flashlight's beam.

"Don't hurt me anymore. Please, God," I whisper.

"I won't." It's a woman's voice.

I look up but I can't see her face.

The knife cuts the bindings on my right hand, then moves over to my left hand. Even the wiggling of the ropes and the duct tape as they're cut hurts so much. I cry out.

"It's okay," the woman says.

She finishes cutting the bindings on my arms, and I bend over with nausea, gasp with my head between my knees.

She says, "Give me a little room to cut your legs out too."

I move my head, and she crouches down in front of me, cuts the bindings on my legs and ankles. She's so close to me and she smells horrible, a human-animal reek that I've never smelled on a person before. I can see her thick, dark hair, matted chunks in the shaky light, but I can't see her face. She stands back up.

"Get up slowly," she says.

It's the woman from the raft. I see the outline of her robe, her wild hair, the knife in one hand and the flashlight in the other. She sets the knife down on the chair behind her, extends her hand to me. Says, "Can you stand up?"

"I don't know. Maybe?" But when I try, I stumble and fall to the floor. She lets me.

"Maybe stay there a minute. Let your body relax."

When I try to use my left hand, a white-hot light of pain streaks up my arm. I yell.

"Shh!" she says, and nudges me with the toe of her boot.

I roll over on my back, groan with pain.

"You're gonna be okay," she says.

I nod but I can't talk yet. Tears come out the corners of my eyes.

"Try to move the rest of your body a little bit," she says, "You were in that chair too long. Stretch and move, let the circulation do its work."

My back is so cramped that I'm on my side on the floor. I try to straighten out, but even that hurts.

"Move more," the woman says, "Get your blood going. I'll give you a minute." She unloads her rifle, checks the breach, and loads it again. Then she does something with her pistol as I move my arms and legs around.

I say, "Thank you for rescuing me." I get to my hands and knees, careful with my left hand.

"Okay," she says, "we need to start moving pretty soon. We don't want to stay here too long."

"Are there more of them?"

"In this house?"

I nod.

"No," she says, "I took care of the people in this house. But they have a lot of houses."

I stretch a little more, and my back starts to loosen.

The woman goes over by the door of the room and looks out. Shines her flashlight through of the doorway.

"Are we okay for a few minutes?"

"Maybe," she says, and walks back over to me, "I don't know." She holds out her hand to help me up. I take it with my good arm and slowly get to my feet. My back feels terrible, like it's been bent wrong. I try to twist side to side slowly. That helps.

The woman has her pistol in her hand. She cocks it. Says, "I'm gonna go and look for something. Be right back."

"I'll go with you."

"No," she says, "keep loosening up." She disappears through the door, pointing her pistol and flashlight out in front of her.

I'm alone in the room again. Scared. I want to follow her—even though she doesn't want me to—but I'm worried she might shoot me, might think I'm one of them if I come up from behind her. So I wait.

I hear the woman doing something out in the kitchen, rifling through drawers, opening and shutting cupboards or something. Then there's the light of her flashlight returning, in the hall first, then the doorway, and then she steps back into this room.

She hands me something. "Here," she says, "drink that. It'll give you blood sugar." She's taken the cap off already, and some of it spills on my hand. It's apple juice— a sixty-four-ounce jug—and it smells amazing.

I take a long drink. After being stuck in that chair, it's the best thing I've ever had in my entire life.

"Drink it slower," she says. "You don't want to throw up."

So I force myself to sip, but it's difficult.

"And move," the woman says. "Keep in motion. We need you loosened up."

So I move my legs as I drink, stretch different parts of my body.

The woman's looking me over, and it's like she knows what I'm thinking. "Stop doubting," she says. "You'll feel a lot better soon. You're young and fit."

I nod. Keep drinking the apple juice.

The woman shines her flashlight around the room. Finds the butane lighter and lights two candles. She sets her rifle on the side table. The rifle looks like something soldiers have in movies, black, with a wire stock.

I think I've had my limit of apple juice. It feels like I might puke. I burp and breathe. Roll my neck side to side. "I'm feeling a little better." I burp again.

"Okay," she says. She lifts the rifle to her shoulder again, sights down the barrel, pointing at something imaginary, then relaxes and lowers the gun. She says, "There's one other Collection house that has most of them. Most of the important ones that are left. And I'm God's wrath, the extension of his hand."

"So we're going there?"

"Soon." She nods. "Once you're feeling a little better."

My body's starting to feel a little better, but my stomach is too full. "I think I'm gonna throw up."

"No you're not," she says. "Keep it down."

I offer her the apple juice. "Do you wanna drink the rest?"

She takes it and drinks it down. Sets the empty on the side table. Says, "Stretch some more. You need to be loose enough to move well on your own. I can't take care of you out there."

So I bend and stretch. Straighten back up and reach to the ceiling, tilting one way, then the other. My back pops a few times. I say, "Thank you again for getting me out of that chair."

"Well," she says, "I knew you weren't one of them, so God wouldn't allow me to kill you." She makes a circling motion with her finger. "Walk it off. Move some more."

I guess I'm still in shock. I just do whatever she says, walk to the wall and back. Then walk in a circle around the chairs.

"When that apple juice gets in your system," she says, "you'll actually be doing better. There's a lot of sugar in that."

"All right," I say. "I can already feel it starting to work. I can already move better."

She watches me like she's trying to figure out what I'm worth. I walk around the room a few more times.

She stops me with her hand. "Ready now," she says. "We have to get you guns." She walks to the door. Turns and looks at me. "But I'll warn you: there's a lot of blood out here."

I realize that even though the apple juice helped, it's like I'm not quite in my own mind. It's like I'm detached still, watching a movie of myself looking around. I glance down at my own gauze-wrapped left hand, then look away again. That can't be my hand. That can't have been my finger.

55

GEARING UP

B UT THE KITCHEN is a different movie scene: broken furniture, shattered glass, pools of blood, everything illuminated by candles that are burning on the countertops. There are three men on the floor, none of them moving. I walk over to the smallest one and turn him over with my foot. But he's not Witness Andreas. He has a different beard, different face.

The woman says, "Did you think that was Andreas?"

I nod.

"He's not here," she says. "I haven't killed him yet."

The woman's looking around, trying to find something.

I say, "He was here before."

She points at my hand. "I know."

There's another Collection man by the refrigerator, but he looks strange, almost unhuman. His head is too small or weirdly shaped or something. It's half in shadow, and I can't quite see it in the candlelight.

The woman shines her flashlight that way. Says, "He was still breathing when I got to him, so I stomped on his face."

That's what it was. His head was too flat.

I look away. "How are you such a . . ."

She nudges the crushed head with her boot. Says, "How am I such a skilled soldier?"

I nod.

"God prepares us, even though we don't know that he is." She turns and opens a kitchen drawer, rifling through it. "My father was in the special forces," she says. "He didn't have a son, so I was the son he never had."

"And he taught you?"

"Everything," she says. "All the time. He'd say, 'This is how you take apart an AR-15. This is how you build a bamboo trap with feces on the stakes. This is how you purify water. This is how you kill someone silently with a piano wire."

She closes the drawer and opens the next. Finds a Gerber pocket knife and hands it to me.

I take it and put it in my pocket. "But then you were part of The Collection?"

"At first," she says, "because I thought they were following the will of God. But then God began to speak to me, and I began to understand them for who they were."

"So you left?"

"Yes."

"But you stayed nearby?"

"I did His will." She closes the drawer. Points to the ceiling. "God whispered a new message in my ear, and I followed His orders."

"Did God really whisper in your ear?"

She stops pawing through the drawer and looks at me. She's doesn't smile now. "What are you asking?"

"I'm asking if God really whispered in your ear."

She shuts the kitchen drawer. "Of course," she says. "Are you doubting?" She steps across to the third body on the floor, a skinny man. She reaches down and goes through his robe, then turns him halfway over. "Right here," she says, and picks up a pistol. She uses his robe to wipe the blood from the gun, then holds it out to me. "Have you ever shot one of these?"

"Yeah, but it looked different."

"Well," she says, "this is a single-action, semiautomatic revolver, so you cock the hammer like this." She demonstrates. "Then you pull the trigger, and the hammer cocks itself from the recoil. Ready to shoot again." She lowers the hammer. Hands the revolver to me.

"Okay," I say, "so I just cock it once."

"Yes, and maybe we find you a shotgun as well. Those are the easiest to use." She shines the flashlight around—in the corners and the pantry, and a closet as well—but doesn't find what she's looking for. She turns and her face is close to mine. She holds me firmly by the elbow, and I hold my breath. She closes her eyes. "Lord, we need a weapon for vengeance. Grant us this gift. In Your name, amen." Then she opens her eyes again.

She walks into the living room and I follow her.

Everything still feels real and unreal at the same time. I watch as the woman shines her flashlight all around. There's another dead Collection man in this room, his body twisted and blood sprayed out to his right. I look at the spatter and think of rain on a windshield, wonder what would happen if windshield wipers were turned on in this room.

My head feels like it's filled with gas, too light, everything I'm seeing strange and untrue, like I'm reading a book that I don't quite believe. I wonder if I'm high on pills right now and don't know it, if they gave me something. There's a thin layer of cellophane between me and reality.

I say, "Am I on drugs? Did they give me something?"

The woman doesn't answer me. She kicks the dead man's arms out of the way, one at a time, searches under the folds of his robe. But there's nothing there, or nothing she wants.

I watch her search the rest of the room, see her look in a box, under a chair, beneath a blanket covering a pile of canned food. She says, "I'm going to look upstairs. They have so many weapons in each of their houses that I can probably find you a shotgun. I'll be right back." She turns, then stops, slides off her backpack, and unzips it. She reaches inside and pulls something out. "Take this," she says. "Eat it while you wait." She hands me a Snickers bar.

That's not what I expected her to hand to me. "Okay," I say. I realize that I don't feel sick anymore.

"You have to eat it," she says.

"Okay."

She takes it back, unwraps it, and hands it to me. "You're in shock," she says. She snaps her fingers twice. "We have to get you out of shock." She pushes the candy bar toward my mouth, and I take a bite.

I eat as the woman jogs up the stairs.

I'm chewing on a bite of candy bar in a house full of dead men. I haven't had a Snickers in a long time, and it tastes delicious, chocolate and sweet, peanuts and caramel. It's like there's no blood at my feet, like I haven't been tied to a chair for a couple days.

I take another bite. Think, *Something's definitely wrong with me.*

The woman thumps around in a room above me, sounding like she's throwing things, like she's sliding furniture across the room. Then it gets quiet before I hear her coming back down the stairs. She says, "The Lord provides," as she holds a shotgun in one hand, six red shells in the other.

I drop the candy bar wrapper. "How do you work it?"

"Pump the action like this." She shows me. Then she raises it to her shoulder, clicks the safety off, puts her finger on the trigger, and pretends to shoot.

I nod.

She unloads the gun and dry-fires it. Then loads it again and hands me the extra shells.

I put them in my pocket. Then she hands me the gun. "It's already loaded," she says. "Those other shells are extra."

"Okay," I say again.

"Not gonna lie to you. It's gonna jolt your injured hand—holding the grip—but it'll be worth it. A shotgun sprays wide, so you'll get whatever you're aiming at." She walks toward the door. "Are you ready?"

I nod.

We walk out of the house, and I follow the woman.

The moon is out. There's a warm wind, and the green leaves of an oak tree shiver a little above me. I look around and realize that I forgot about the earthquake, forgot how everything was destroyed, the toppled trees and tilted houses, cars crushed together, a motorcycle on its side, an empty helmet like the rider fell off into the road, then his body disappeared.

I have a funny thought that everything is made of plastic and miniature. Maybe I've been shrunk down. Maybe I'm inside a smaller world.

The woman shakes me. "Are you okay?"

"What?"

"I just had to walk back to grab you."

"Oh," I say. "Sorry." I close my eyes and open them again, try to clear my head.

The woman pulls me down next to a car. She says, "Do you want your backpacks?"

"You have my backpacks?"

She pulls them out from underneath the car.

I set down the shotgun and the revolver. Look at the backpacks and try to remember what I put in each one. Then I remember, and I choose my emergency pack. Leave my second backpack next to the wheel well of the car to return for it later.

I say, "How did you get these?"

"For a long time," she says, "they were following you, and I was following them. It was a game, a hunt, a sort of dance."

"So you saw them take me?"

"Basically. I saw them go into your house, and I waited. I needed to know where the last two houses were."

"So I was bait?"

"Not exactly. They were going to take you anyway, no matter what. And I knew they'd take you somewhere important, somewhere I could watch and learn, figure out how and when to attack."

"But you left me in there that whole time?"

"I'm sorry," she says, "but the only way to end this is to know their last two locations. So I had to wait until he went back and forth."

"Who? Witness Andreas?"

"Yes," she says.

I look at my left hand, the gauze and the blood stain.

She says, "That will heal. Then she holds up her left hand, also missing its pinky.

I shake my head, look at the plastic world all around us. None of this is real.

"Wiggle it," she says.

"What?"

"It'll hurt, but you'll be okay."

I wiggle where the finger used to be, and the pain is incredible. I bite my lip and groan. But the pain makes everything more real. I can't separate myself from that pain.

"You're going to be okay," the woman says. "We're tougher than people think."

"Who's tougher?"

She cracks her neck one way, then the other. "Women," she says, "but also all of us. We're all tougher than we think—humans in general—God made us capable of suffering more than we think is possible."

I take a deep breath. Put my pack on. Ask, "When did you grab my backpacks?"

"Right after they took you. I thought you might need them later. And I've been staking out this house for two days, waiting for them to make a mistake so I could come in and get you."

"And what was the mistake?"

"They don't pray, and cast lots. So they rotate their watch, even if someone is incapable. When it was that man's turn, I knew I had them, knew the rest of them wouldn't be ready for me inside."

I nod, and my nod means "thank you."

"Of course," she says. "And it was good too. God blesses us in moments. It gave me a chance to kill five more of them."

"Five?"

"Four inside and one out. The sentry. Now, if we can get Andreas at the next house . . ."

I try to picture killing him myself, but I can't imagine that.

I root around in my backpack with my good hand, find my Vicodin and take two, swallow them dry. I say, "I hope these will kick in by the time I have to use the shotgun."

The woman says, "We could wait for that. This next part is all about stealth anyway. We need to set up slowly and be quiet. I'll tell you what to do, where to position, and how long to wait. Then you will be the other angle."

"The other angle?"

"I'll explain everything, but it doesn't matter what I say. God is guarding me, and he's everywhere at once, omnipotent, omniscient, and omnipresent," she says, and makes a circle motion with her finger. "I will only die when he wants me to die, and I am living blessed."

I put my backpack on carefully, wincing with the pain in my hand. But there's no avoiding it. I pick up the shotgun in my good hand and cradle it in the crook of my left elbow. "Okay," I say. "We can start walking."

56

THE FINAL HOUSE

I SOMETIMES DIDN'T KNOW what the point was. Middle school, there were girls starving and cutting themselves. Then there was a girl who said she was "clinically depressed" because she got a B in social studies. It was hard to feel sorry for her. I watched girls eat edibles in the bathroom, giggling and talking about the party they were throwing that weekend.

It was hard to listen to those types of girls talk in the lunchroom too, to hear them criticize the brands of jeans other girls wore, to hear them make fun of people's outdated phones, to complain about a scratched screen on their new phones.

I drank my free-and-reduced-price chocolate milk. Ate my plate of Tater Tots. Dipped my tots in ketchup even though I didn't like the taste of ketchup. I didn't want to be mocked for liking the flavor of mustard.

I ate quickly, kept my outdated phone hidden in my pocket.

* * *

I follow the woman along the block. She has her rifle in her hands. I have my shotgun. Each of us has a pistol tucked into her pants as well.

I whisper, "How many of them are at this next house?"

She holds up three fingers.

"That includes Witness Andreas?"

She looks back at me and nods. "You want to kill him, don't you?"

"Yeah, I think I do."

She stops suddenly, and I run into her back. She says, "You need to be serious about this. God is watching." She's so much taller than me. She tilts her head back and looks at the sky. Points at a cluster of stars. Says, "Do you know how to read the constellations?"

"I don't know."

"Are you ready to do what God tells us?"

"Well . . . I . . ." I wonder if she is as crazy as Witness Andreas, if I've just traded one for the other.

The woman points at two different places in the sky. "See those stars?" she says.

"Yes?" I say, but I have no idea what she's talking about. I still don't feel in my right mind. The Vicodin hasn't kicked in yet, so it's not the pills. I feel like I'm swimming through cotton, parting the fibers with my hands, moving so slowly, unable to see out in front of me.

The woman stares at the sky for a long, long time.

I watch her face.

She doesn't say anything. She stands there with her head tilted, staring at the stars.

I finally say, "Should we keep going?"

"Okay." The woman nods, and doesn't explain anything else about the stars. She starts walking again. "It's not far."

We walk another block. Stop next to a dark-colored pickup in a driveway. We duck down. The woman points at a house two houses away. She says, "That's the house."

In the moonlight, I can't tell what color it is, but it's a pale, single-story home, wide, with at least four bedrooms. I can see low windows along the ground, meaning the house has a basement as well. I've been in a lot of houses like this one. I'm so used to searching houses that I know what they'll look like inside even before I enter.

We crouch behind the pickup, and both stare at the house for a while.

I point to the low windows. "We better be careful. They might have someone watching from those basement windows."

The woman shakes her head. "They've blacked them out."

"How do you know?" I say.

She looks at me. Wipes her face on her shoulder and shakes her head again.

"What?" I say.

"That's where they keep a nest."

"A nest?"

"For the woman who is populating The Collection."

"One woman?"

"One woman in each nest house."

"So did the other house have a nest."

"Yes."

"Then why didn't we save the woman?"

She looks at me. "I did."

"What?" I say.

"You," she says. "You were going to be that woman."

"Oh shit," I say.

She flinches when I cuss. She takes hold of my good hand and prays quickly. She whispers through a series of words spoken so fast I can't understand them.

I say, "Sorry for cussing."

The woman looks at me, then spits over her shoulder.

"Wait," I say, "were you one of the women too? I mean, before you left The Collection?"

She doesn't answer me. She unslings her rifle from her back. Looks through the sights at the house.

I say. "I'm sorry you had to be a part of that."

"Sometimes," she says, "God, in His infinite wisdom and ordainment, doesn't make a womb fruitful, and therefore saves a person."

"A womb?"

"And to Him be the glory, in times of full and in times of empty," she says, "and I know now that He had no desire to gift them from my body."

I close my eyes. Shake my head.

I hear the action of her rifle. "To Him be the glory, forever and ever, amen," she says. "Are you close to ready?"

The Vicodin must be kicking in because the world is starting to feel a little different, and my hand on the shotgun doesn't hurt quite as much as it did before. "Yes," I say, "I think I am."

"All right then."

The moonlight comes over my shoulder, like a gray flame. I say, "What do we do now? What's the plan?"

"It's going to be like this," the woman says, and she points. "You'll go to the front door. You'll knock, be straightforward. They'll open it, or you'll open it, and you'll say 'Hello?' They won't think that you're harmless. They won't believe that, but it doesn't matter. You'll be at that front angle. You'll draw someone forward. Make sure your gun's up when he opens the door. He's gonna be moving slowly. He's gonna be facing you." She makes a "T" with her hands. "Then I'll have the side angle through the window. He won't have a chance because he won't ever know I'm there, or ever see me. Even if he's ready to shoot, he'll be facing the wrong direction."

"So you'll shoot him from the side?"

"Yes. Through the window."

"So I don't shoot him?"

"Not unless something goes wrong. But if it does, fire that shotgun and things will be all right again."

"And what if there's more than one of them?"

"There will be." The woman shakes her head. "But not at first. They'll only send one to the door. There are three men inside, and they wouldn't send two to the door. There's going to be one in the kitchen and one down in the nest."

"Okay," I say. "You know them well."

"I've been watching." The woman taps the shotgun in my hands. "Pump that now," she says. "But not too loud—not too quickly—just slide the action until it clicks both ways. We don't want them to hear anything until you knock on the door. Then I'll be ready."

She screws something onto the end of her rifle.

"What is that?"

"It's a type of suppressor," she says. "Sometimes you leave it loud, to draw them out. But sometimes you make it quiet, to take them out. Don't worry about all that. You just get ready to go up to the door."

I nod and slide my shotgun's pump action. It makes more noise than I'd like to. I look at the woman's face to see if we're okay.

"We're fine," she says. "That wasn't too loud."

I stand there as she stares at the house for a moment more. Then she says, "Ready?"

"Yes," I say.

"Okay. Walk right up and open. But if the door's locked, knock away," she says. "And don't look at me. Don't look right or left. Pretend you're all alone in case someone looks out the front window before he opens it."

I take a deep breath. "All right," I say, "but if he's gonna shoot me before he opens the door, make sure you get him. And don't miss."

"I won't miss," she says.

"And wait, what about when I'm inside?"

"It'll already be over. Don't worry about that." She looks at me and nods, then creeps quickly forward and to the left, into the side yard.

I wait and take a deep breath. I don't feel ready for this moment. My hands are shaking as I hold the shotgun. The pills are surging and the world feels fuzzy. I walk forward onto the sidewalk until I get to the house, then go up the walk, holding my gun in front of me, forcing myself to go forward and to only look forward, not to the right or to the left.

When I get to the door, it's not closed. It's a few inches open, jammed like almost every other door in this neighborhood. But it looks like it could be pushed open. And I don't want to knock. I'm not sure if anyone's there behind the door, waiting. I push lightly, but the door doesn't move. I think about pushing harder—the noise it will make— and my blood pumps in my ears.

I don't know about the woman's plan. It seems crazy. It seems like I'll get shot on the doorstep before she can shoot them. I sort of trust her, but I have to protect myself most of all. If I've learned anything, it's that no one will ever take care of me in this world if I don't take care of myself. So I don't knock.

I go in. I shove hard and the door creaks, pops, hits something behind it, but I keep pushing until there's enough space for me to step through. It's so loud that there's no way someone didn't hear all that noise, so I yell, "Hello?" to tip off the woman. Then I lead with my gun, creeping into the front room.

Nothing.

So I crouch down, the shotgun ready.

Listening.

But I don't see anyone. Or hear anyone.

My heart is beating fast. I blink a few times, try to adjust my eyes to the mostly dark house. I open my mouth to get more oxygen to my brain. Yell into the rest of the house, "I'm here! I'm at the front door!"

There are movements in the hallway, the sounds of feet, but I still don't see anyone.

I whisper, "Fuck." This isn't going how the woman said it would. I slide behind a couch. Crawl to the other end of it, propping the shotgun's barrel up over the armrest.

Nothing. I'm pointing into the dark.

There's moonlight shining in the window, but it's only enough light to illuminate the left side of the room. The rest of the house is too shadowed. I'm in a good location—down low, in the dark, where I don't think anyone can see me—so I wait for someone to enter this room from the hallway, or for the woman to come from behind me into the house, or to shoot her way in from one of the side windows. But she doesn't do any of those things, and nobody comes at me from the hallway. So maybe by not knocking, I changed the whole plan?

There's silence.

I don't hear any loud noises inside or out. There's just a big, long wait as I crouch there in the dark. And somewhere near me there's the sound of a clock ticking, a big, old clock.

I don't yell anything else. The Collection men know I'm here, but they're not coming into this room. I look around and see a desk near the hallway. It's tipped on its side, and I think that if I can get to that desk, it'll be good enough cover, and I'll be close enough to the hallway, where I can maybe see down the corridor. But I'll have to crawl across a gap, and I can't see down the shadowed hall. Someone could be right there, waiting for me to make a mistake.

I hear a quick movement at the far end of the house—in the kitchen or in a back bedroom; I'm not sure which—then quiet again, just the sound of the clock, the seconds ticking away.

I crawl across the gap, anticipating gunshots, flinching and keeping my head down. Halfway across, I don't chance it. I aim down the hallway with the shotgun and pull the trigger. The recoil wrenches my wrist and the explosion deafens me. The hall is lit up for a second and I see two people's heads—both men—one head sticking out of each doorway down the hall. But my shot is low, knee-level at best, and I don't think I hit either one.

I dive behind the cover of the desk. Pump the shotgun to put another shell in the chamber. Place my finger on the trigger and wait for the creeping noises of the two men coming toward me. But then there's nothing again. Relative silence after the blast of my shotgun.

Just the ticking of the clock.

I wait and blink, try to adjust my eyes to the dark. Imagine the faces of those two men in the hallway. I keep the stock of the shotgun against my shoulder.

A minute passes.

Two minutes?

I wonder if my sense of time is off, maybe because of the pills, or if being tied to that chair and the loss of my finger have warped everything in my brain, and now I'm operating on a different plane, a different schedule, the world altered permanently.

I'm sitting. Waiting.

Then the sound of breaking glass. The quiet *tsh, tsh, tsh* of a suppressed rifle and the boom of a bigger gun going off somewhere in the house. I think the woman's still outside, to my left. It sounds like she's outside? Maybe she's shooting through the windows, but I'm not sure anymore. I can't see the flashes of her shots out there.

Someone shoots again.

Then screaming in the hallway.

Tsh, tsh, and a big bang, and the sounds of bullets ripping through walls. Bright flashes, then the thwack of a bullet hitting something solid in the room right behind me.

I stay low. Keep hold of my shotgun, ready to shoot either of those two men if they try to escape in my direction. I look for the big outline of a Collection robe, plan to aim middle, cut a target in half. That's what I whisper to myself: "They're targets. They're not people."

Then one of them does run down the hall, at the far end, and I bring my barrel up quick and pull the trigger.

But the blast illuminates the robe and hair of the woman, no beard on her face, and her dreadlocks flying back as she's hit with my shot. She screams as her body spins, her rifle flinging out to the right, bouncing off the wall.

After I shoot, I stay where I am, unable to move, shaking my head, gripping the shotgun. I'm crouching and listening. Starting to cry.

There are no more gunshots. I hear a man moaning from somewhere in one of the rooms. He makes a long, low sound, then coughs. Then gets quiet again.

I whisper, "Fuck." Set my shotgun down. Stay crouched behind the desk. I rub away my tears with the heels of my hands. I have to be ready for whatever's coming next, so I pick the shotgun back up again, slide the action. Blink a few times.

I whisper to myself, "Do whatever you have to, Cielo. Kill them all."

I point my gun down the hallway and wait. But nothing happens. No one's moving around inside the house. No one's coming toward me. I don't know who's left. What if there were more Collection men than the woman thought? What if they have another house nearby, and at that house they heard all of these gunshots. What if those other men come here too?

How could I know until it was too late?

"Be brave," I whisper to myself. "Finish this."

I look behind me, over my shoulder at the front door, then back down the hallway where my gun is pointing. I can't see the floor of the hall—not with the furniture in front of me—but I don't hear any movements there either, and I don't think the woman is still alive. And in the side room, the man has stopped moaning.

It's so quiet that I can hear the clock again, the second hand ticking away, time moving on.

I think of the woman coming toward me. And before that, how she saved me from that chair, from Witness Andreas. "I'm sorry," I whisper. "I didn't mean to. I just . . ." I start to cry again. I shake my head and close my eyes. Take a deep breath. ". . . but I'm still alive."

I say it again. "I'm still alive."

The house creaks, settles in around the new bullet holes and shattered glass, the ripped plaster, plus anything else changed by the bullets and the bodies.

Suddenly the man starts moaning again—up the hall—quieter now, but he's still alive.

I don't want to wait here forever—not with the open door behind me, not with the sounds of the shots ringing out into the neighborhood—so I step over the furniture in front of me, drop down low again, crawl into the hallway and up to the woman.

It's too dark to see, but I feel around until I find her headlamp, slide it off her forehead and pull it free of her tangled hair. Holding it in my hand, I click the light on to see if she's still alive. But the headlamp is so bright that I turn it off immediately.

I saw enough, blood covering the front of her robe, blood spilled out of her mouth. Nothing about her looking alive at all. Nothing to save.

I whisper, "Thanks for helping me. Thank you for saving me."

I touch her shoulder and wish there was something else I could've done. I wish I'd known that she would run down the hallway like that.

I whisper to myself, "You're still alive, Cielo."

I rub my face, wiping away my tears. Take another big breath, exhale, and breathe in again.

The man is moaning in the room up the hall, and I have to go finish him.

I put the headlamp on my head. Get to my feet. "This is it," I say. I pull out my pistol. I don't know how many shells are left inside the shotgun, but I know the pistol has six shots.

I point my pistol down the hallway and click the headlamp on. There are two feet sticking out of one of the doorways—the one on the left—feet with leather sandals. The feet aren't moving, not even twitching, so I glance in—just to be sure—then keep going up the hall. It wasn't Witness Andreas anyway.

In the next doorway, the man's robe is ripped to the side—a bullet hole in his stomach and another going through his neck. There's a pool of blood behind his head, his beard soaked in it. I nudge his face with my foot and see another bullet hole next to his ear.

He's not Witness Andreas either.

I shine my flashlight back down the hallway, see the feet of the man, and the body of the woman back next to the living room. I turn and keep going, toward the kitchen, toward the back of the house. I hold my pistol ready, and point the barrel out in front of me.

There another room, some kind of office or study—full of books all over the floor—and this is where the moaning man is. So there were more of them than the woman thought. Maybe that's why she ran down the hall like that?

There's a big blood trail where this man dragged himself over behind the desk, trying to get to something or to hide. He's staring at the ceiling, making a tiny sound with his mouth but not turning toward me, even when I shine the flashlight on his face, so I know that the wires connecting his eyes and brain aren't working anymore.

I point at the middle of his chest and pull the trigger. The bullet jolts his body, and then his head turns to the side. He doesn't make any more noise.

I lean down to make sure he's dead, see the blood he spit up on his chin. He's not breathing, not moving at all. I watch and wait, but nothing changes.

So I move on.

The kitchen is neat and tidy, the cleanest kitchen I've seen since the earthquake, so I know people have been living here for a while, organizing and stockpiling. Cereal boxes are lined up on the top shelf. Jars of mixed nuts and tuna cans are on the next shelf, clean bowls and plates stacked below those. Silverware is divided into three ceramic mugs, one for spoons, one for forks, and one for knives.

On the other side of the sink are thirty or forty types of water bottles—of various sizes—all full. A water-filter pump is next to the bottles. I slide off my backpack, put the water-filter inside, take three thirty-two-ounce water bottles as well, then put my backpack back on.

In the bathroom off the kitchen, there's a stash of medicines. I open my backpack again, and scrape everything into it—all the pill bottles, all the ointments, all the Band-Aids and medical tape. My pack is nearly full and I stuff everything down, click the buckles that secure the top. Then I put the pack back on, shift and center its weight. I refasten the waist belt and tighten the straps.

I walk over to the kitchen door and look out into the yard. The doorway is open wide, the door jammed in the open position, and I wonder if the woman came through this entrance, if that's how she surprised The Collection men from behind.

Thinking about the woman makes me upset again, so I stop myself before I really get started. I shut my eyes, tilt my head back, and take deep breaths until the feeling passes. I tell myself, "She helped you, but she was crazy." I nod and whisper, "And you survived. You're still here."

I open my eyes again. Standing in the doorway, I can see the whole backyard, objects illuminated by my headlamp as I look at them, and everything else lit fainter by the moon. There's a toppled apple tree covered in apples, a metal shed off to the left, a table with tools, and some garden beds along the fence.

I can't hear anything. There's no wind out there. The night is quiet.

I turn back to the kitchen and shine my light around. See the pantry. And next to the pantry, I see—finally— a closed door. It could lead to anything—or only be a closet—but I know as soon as I see it. I know what it leads to. It's the only door that isn't open. It's the only door that I haven't been through.

57

HOW THEY GROW

WHERE DO WE go when a catastrophe happens? What should I have done? Maybe I should've left the neighborhood when all the other survivors went with FEMA. Or later with the Red Cross. Maybe I should've trusted that I would've been safe, that I would've been taken care of, that I didn't need paperwork or citizenship to get food or shelter. Maybe no one would've required anything of me. Maybe I didn't need ID or proof of who I was—such an odd idea since I obviously existed, and shouldn't that have been enough?

Maybe the time period right after the earthquake was the perfect time to leave, to become legitimate, to integrate.

I told myself that it was about lack of paperwork—that it was about my fear of being discovered—but I knew it wasn't. I knew my mother was somewhere nearby, and I needed to find her. I knew she was still in the neighborhood, and that if she'd lived through the quake—*if*—then she would've stayed right here. So I couldn't leave.

Or even if she was dead, by staying I could find her body. That was important to me as well. I needed to know.

So I asked, *Where* would she be?

I didn't know which houses they owned. After she got obsessed with The Collection, I'd read every article about them in the paper and online, about their formation, about their growing numbers in the state. I learned how they sprang from the paranoid, religious right wing in Roseburg, Oregon.

But it wasn't just reading on my own. My history teacher made the class study examples, showing that this is how people radicalize anywhere in the world: Islamic suicide bombers, Central American government sympathizers, splinter cells of rogue Russian agents. My teacher said that the great irony is that the far right-wing movement in the United States thinks it's different from far right-wing movements in the rest of the world. In an essay we had to read and discuss in class, I remember reading the line: "They chant freedom slogans as they support fascism with no understanding of that paradox."

I'd looked up The Collection's social media accounts before they went offline as well, before their leader banned social media completely. That was what he was known as, last year, by the media: "Their leader." None of them ever wrote his name in online posts. Back then, everything in the articles said "their leader" or "the head person" or "the man they call The Witness." Nobody knew his real name. None of the articles said anything about a "Witness Andreas." I didn't know that name until I read my mother's journals, and I wondered about how much trouble she'd have been in if anyone found one of her journals.

I knew about The Witness locking the doors of his church to teach his congregation in isolation and purity, how his videos spread his revelations, how people were unable to leave the room during the entirety of his testimonies.

So I had known about The Collection's growing numbers, about their obsession with guns, pictures of guns, pictures of themselves with guns, pictures of guns and Bibles, memes of patriotism, patriotism and Bible verses, posts about hating liberals, posts about hating the mainstream media, posts about hating the radical left and people of color. Once I learned about The Collection, I couldn't stop myself. I read about them obsessively because I knew that they hated me, and they didn't want anyone like me, even as they preached about God giving us freedom.

They had meetings. Online chat boards. They bragged that their enemies were unarmed, that the revolution would be too easy. Then they disappeared from the internet, went underground, and not long after that, my mother disappeared as well.

I kept thinking about something I'd read in an online weekly newspaper, something a reporter got from an informant: "The Collection is infiltrating. They are dressing as normal people, saying they are tricking the unbelieving, that they will go back to the symbolism of their white robes when the appointed time comes to claim the middle earth, when that has been revealed to them. So no one knows how many of them are out there in this city. They say they are waiting for that preamble to the Kingdom of Heaven. The moment of pre-tribulation."

I read everything, and I knew my mother was still with them because she wrote "in death or in life."

58

THE FINISHING

I SET DOWN MY backpack and click off my headlamp. Take a breath, turn the handle, and open the basement door, the hinges squeaking slightly. I cringe. Take a step. Every stair creaks, so there's nothing to be done. I descend with the gun in front of me.

At the bottom of the stairs, there's a faint light off to my right, a flickering, and I know that there are more candles lit somewhere. I turn and walk in that direction.

The basement is big and old—cement and stone— with rooms partitioned by plywood. One of them glows, the plywood painted red, the flickering of the candle flames like the pulsing of an enormous heart.

The makeshift door is at the back left, covered by a red sheet, and I hesitate before I push it aside. A spider crawls across the top of the door and disappears in the seam between the sheet and the plywood. I wait for it to reemerge but it stays in that space, in the shadow between the cotton and the wood.

I move aside the sheet-door with the barrel of my pistol, step into the small room, and there they are—Witness Andreas and my mother—both of them sitting on beanbag chairs on top of a king-size mattress. To the right and left of the mattress are side tables covered with lit candles, six or seven on each table, so the space is brightly illuminated.

Witness Andreas says, "Come in. Come here." He beckons with his hand like he wants me to join them, to sit between them on the mattress. There's an empty beanbag there.

My mother doesn't say anything to me. She looks at me like we are strangers.

I point my pistol at each of them, back and forth, but neither of them holds a gun. I thought they'd be armed. I thought this would be different.

Witness Andreas waves his hand. "No need for your pistol. Put it down."

I take a step toward him. Stand at the end of the mattress. Point my revolver at his chest.

He puts his arms out wide. Turns his palms up. "See?" he says. "I am completely unarmed. You can search my robe if you like."

"I'm not touching your robe," I say. Then I look at my mother. "Vamos."

She shakes her head.

I gesture with the gun barrel.

"You do not understand," she says. "I want to stay . . . of course."

I'm still pointing the pistol at Witness Andreas.

"Here," she says. "I will stay here."

"Pero vine a llevarte conmigo." I'm staring at my mother. She shakes her head again. Takes a breath and closes her eyes.

"It's not a question," I say. "You're not staying here."

She holds up her left hand, which is missing a pinkie. Like mine. The way she holds it so steady overwhelms me, and I feel like crying again. But I refuse to. I bite my lip on the inside, bite down until I taste blood. Hold back tears.

My mother says, "I'm part of The Collection now. I have chosen this for eternity. On this earth, and in the heaven above that will come after." She puts her left hand across her stomach. Pats it.

And at that moment, I know what she means. "No," I say. "The Collection is finished. There are only the two of you now."

"Is that what you think?" Witness Andreas says. "That we are few? That there are no more of us, no more witnesses to the eternal?"

The way he looks at me, I know how wrong I am. I know the difference between what I hope to be true and what is real.

Witness Andreas sees me understand, and smiles. "There are so many of us. Maybe not in this room, but in this city, yes, and in this state, even more, all waiting just to the south of us, an enormous Collection of Redeemed Souls."

"You're lying," I say, but I know he isn't.

He smiles again. "That is the great failing of people like you, of the misguided, college professors, high school teachers, foolish reporters. You think there are few, you who call us 'a fringe movement.' But God is never on the fringe. He is always in the center. And the center is always growing."

"You're not with God. God wouldn't like any of . . . this." I make a sweeping motion with my hand.

Witness Andreas rubs his beard. Looks at the wall, then back at me. "The other thing you said was wrong as

well. You said two. But there are three of us in this room,"
he says. "You are with us as well."

"Me?"

"Yes, of course."

"No," I say, "you're wrong about that. I'm definitely
not with you."

"Aren't you, though?" he says. "Please show me your
left hand." He tilts his head and smiles.

"Fuck you." I cock the pistol, aim right at the middle
of his face.

He blinks slowly. Keeps smiling. "What people believe
is that we *feel* and we *choose* in this world. But as your
mother said, we are chosen. So it is"—he points at me—
"in your case. You have been chosen—in heaven and on
earth—regardless of your current . . . feelings."

I shake my head. "I didn't choose anything, and you
know that. I also wasn't chosen by anything other than
you, just a short, weird, delusional, angry man."

"I am short," he says, "but since God has chosen me, I
am clearly enough."

"No," I say, "since nothing has chosen you, but you're
obsessed with that nothing, you are clearly nothing. You're
just a worthless little piece of shit."

"¡Cállate!" My mother points at me. "You stop your
filthy mouth in his presence!"

"Really? Then fuck you too!" I say. "You're nothing as
well. Just a crazy person who abandoned her own daughter."

Witness Andreas is still smiling. "What is and is not
true is not for you to determine," he says. "It is not for any
of us. Just because you *believe* something to be true doesn't
make it so. But let me assuage your fears: it was never up to
you."

"Oh, you know what I fear now?"

"Yes," he says. "I do. Because I am the bridegroom—the church—I know a great many things that other people do not know. And as the bridegroom, I helped you choose what was already chosen for you. Therefore, you should be filled with gratitude."

When he says that, my hands start to shake. I say, "This is the real truth: you kidnapped me and cut off my finger. There's no other way to look at it."

"Someday," he says, "I will uncover your eyes and help you to see that there is another perspective. I will help you to see the true perspective, the angle from God's perspective: the truth."

"No, you won't," I say. It feels like there's a faint aftershock underneath me, like the world is shifting under my feet once again. I'm shaking and I'm crying a little bit. Trying not to cry, but I can't stop myself.

Witness Andreas says, "And even if I am gone, even if I leave this physical earth, there will be another witness. I have prophesied as much already, and he is rising in the fields of harvest even as we speak."

My vision is blurred by my tears. I wipe at them with my injured hand. Try to clear my head. The gun is shaking out in front of me, so I step forward and put the barrel of the pistol against Witness Andreas's forehead.

He smiles because he thinks I won't pull the trigger.

My mother knows me better. She says, "You do *not* do this. She clasps her hands to pray. "Dios todopoderoso, por favor . . ."

But I don't wait for her to finish the prayer. I hold the gun as steady as I can, hold it steady against his forehead as I pull the trigger.

The back of Witness Andreas's head spatters across the wall behind him.

THE RIGHT CHOICE

THE SOUND OF the shot dissipates, and I can hear screaming now, my mother's screaming as she lays herself across the body of The Witness, covering his body with her own. She turns and yells at me, "¿Por qué harías? . . . You killed The Witness, the prophet of God!"

"No," I say, "he was never any of that."

I feel so tired now. I want to sleep—not sleep here, but somewhere. I'm exhausted. I want to close my eyes and sleep for a long time.

My mother pulls him close. His blood is dripping onto her shoulder.

"Let go of him," I say. "He was just a crazy person, a loser." I want to break the spell.

But she's cradling his face, the hole in his forehead circled by a burn mark. The back of his head is drizzling onto her, but she doesn't seem to notice.

"It's time." I try to take her hand. "Let's go."

But she brushes me off. "How could you?"

"Mamá, get up. We're going now."

"No," she says, "I will stay here."

"In this house? There's nothing to stay for, not anymore. That was it. Look at him now." I point at Witness Andreas. "It's finished. He's dead."

"No, you are wrong." She rubs her stomach. "I have the future of The Collection right here."

I squeeze my eyes shut. Try to breathe in enough air to deal with this. I feel so tired that I could almost lie down on this bed, right here, right now. But I force myself to open my eyes wide. Shake my head.

My mother says, "You cannot stop The Collection because The Collection is the people of God. And if God is inside of us, then we *are* God."

"Oh no." I look down at the revolver in my hand. It's as if the gun is in someone else's hand. I lift it like a stranger lifts a gun. The world is so hazy right now.

"What can you do?" my mother says. "What can *you* do?"

I lift the pistol. Point it at her.

She says, "Are you willing to shoot your own mother as well?"

"I need to," I say. I keep the pistol pointed at her. "I should."

"But you will not"—she shakes her head—"because of what I have inside of me. You will not kill a child."

"No, you have it backward. The child is why I *should* kill you," I say, "but that's not . . ." My hand starts to shake again, and this time I can't keep it steady.

"Will you put the gun to my head as well?" she says. "¿Me matarás?"

My hand is shaking so wildly. I try to cock the revolver, but my thumb slips off the hammer, and it's already cocked anyway.

My mother touches her stomach once more. "Con el niño, continuaremos, m'hija. Seguiremos. Nosotros. Porque te conozco." Her eyes are blazing.

It's true. She does know me.

I'm crying and my vision is watery. I point the gun at her. I know I have to pull the trigger. I want to end this.

I need to.

"Like this," my mother says. "It will be like this?"

I want to shoot, but I can't. I lower the gun.

"You will do what is right for the future," my mother says. "You will allow for this. You will step aside in your own life because you are not a wise girl."

"I'm wiser than you think." I'm holding the pistol, but it's pointed at the floor. I can't make myself raise it again. I can't point it at my mother again.

She says, "Sólo Dios da sabiduría."

I say, "What's right and what I can do are two different things."

My mother glares at me.

I can't do anything else here, so I turn to leave the little makeshift room. Move the red sheet to the side, ducking through, walking to the stairs, and heading back up into the main part of the house.

CLEANLINESS

I WRITE THIS JUST *as I learn it—word for word from his mouth—as I hear him speak the truth:*

> "We become washed for God. Pure white. None of the filth of this world can cling to us. As with baptism, we lower in sin and rise in perfection. I keep us in this perfection—this state of holiness—as the fourth part of God:
>
> - *God the Father*
> - *God the Son*
> - *God the Holy Spirit*
> - *Plus The Witness to the eternal. And me with him.*
>
> "It is God's revelation to me that keeps you clean from the world. It is my anointment that cleanses you. It is my consecration that saves this church, the

one and only true church of the living God of the universe. Stay with me and remain clean. Stay with me and remain in the pure, white goodness of The Almighty."

CHAPTER

61

AWAY

I FILL A CANVAS duffel bag with food from the kitchen, grab another gun and two clips from bodies in the hall, don't look at any of their faces. I walk out of the house into the early morning, through the neighborhood to where I left my second backpack by the wheel well of the car. I pick up that second pack and hike over to Moss Street, where I stashed my canoe.

When I get to the boat, I slide it out from behind the hedge, and drag it down to the water. The morning light hits the foam sticking to the divots in the curb. The cement is zigzagged above a drain that doesn't drain anymore.

I'm about to push off into the deep water when I think of everything I have stored in my garage, how stupid it would be to leave everything I stashed there. So I walk up the street, turn at the big house, and go back along the little path to my old apartment.

The Collection men threw everything around when they discovered this place, but they didn't take much. There's still a pile of food and water. Other things too.

I pack everything I want to keep in plastic bins: chlorine tablets, a Coleman stove, fifteen green propane bottles, Quick Ties, cooking pots, raft straps, and kitchen utensils. Then I fill a bin with mixed nuts, a case of Powerade, thirty cans of tuna, a box of Luna bars, and a few sixteen-ounce bags of beef jerky. I put two tents in another bin in case one of the tents gets torn in a future storm, then a sleeping bag and a pillow. Three different kinds of shoes and a pair of Chaco sandals only one size too big. Finally, I pack a bin full of warm clothes, two warm hats, and a raincoat for the winter that will arrive in a few months.

I have to carry each load down the block to the canoe, and I'm sweating hard, resting between trips, rehydrating on each return trip to my garage. Packing and carrying loads takes a couple of hours, and it's hot by the time I finish, the sun roasting the asphalt and the yellow grass. I still haven't slept, and I'm so tired after I carry the last load down to the canoe that I consider lying down in the grass and taking a nap right there. But I want to leave the neighborhood today, get out of here before I let myself relax.

I try to push my canoe into the water, but it's too heavy. I heave and pull, but it won't move anywhere. I try sliding the nose sideways, moving half of the canoe at a time—to walk it back and forth to the water—but it's stuck, and I have to unload it again.

Once the canoe is half empty, I can just barely push it, move its weight, and I slide it halfway into the water to take the weight off, leaving only the stern to rest on the grass and the lip of the curb. Then I start to load the boat again, carrying the plastic tubs into the water and heaving them into the canoe, centering them carefully, balancing each one's weight, then going back for more. I'm so tired now— beyond exhaustion—wading in and out of the water with my heavy bins, and I don't hear her walk up behind me.

She says, "Listen to me," and I spin around. See her standing there with a gun in her hand, a black pistol.

I feel for the gun in my waistband, but it's not there. My revolver and Taurus pistol are both sitting on a bin in the bow of the canoe, less than ten feet away but too far to reach.

My mother says, "You have to choose to stay with me. I gave you too much free will for a long time, but I will not make that mistake any longer."

I say, "I'm not staying here."

"You do not understand me." She shakes her head, keeps the pistol pointed at me. "It is a choice, but it also is not a choice."

"You sound like him," I say. "Like that creep."

"If you mean I sound like Witness Andreas—The Witness to the God Almighty of the universe—then thank you. That is a compliment."

I'm standing next to the water. I look out over the flood. Say, "He was crazy."

"¿Quién dice?" She tilts her head. "¿Tú?"

"Yes." I look her in the eye now. "Me. And anyone logical would agree with me."

She is not the mother of my childhood. Or maybe she is. Maybe she was always this way, some other kind of thing, some animal with eyes that see different shapes in the dark. I don't know why I didn't see that when I was younger. Or maybe I did. I never felt safe.

She says, "¿Qué te da a ti la autoridad para juzgar? ¿Y qué es la lógica comparada con la fe?"

"Faith?" I say, "You think you believe in something real?" I take a step toward her.

She raises the gun.

I say, "And now, are you gonna shoot me?"

"If I must."

"No," I say, "you won't. We were just in this same position a little while ago. One of us had a gun, and the other did not. And no one got shot."

I take another step toward her.

"But there is a difference," she says. "I have the gun now."

"It doesn't matter. I couldn't shoot a family member, and neither can you."

"So are you choosing to be my family?" she says.

"What?"

"So," she says, "you're choosing to be a part of The Collection?"

"No." I shake my head. "That's not family. But you and I, we're blood. We're real. We're something that does not require faith."

"Earthly blood is nothing. Witness Andreas taught us that earthly treasures cannot compare to the treasures laid up in heaven."

"Stop," I say. "All of what he said was manipulation. Now that you're—"

"There will be another man," she says. "They're coming here, and we could . . . repopulate. Maybe God will speak to me as a new minister. Or maybe I will be a future prophet."

"You think they'd let a woman be in power? You really believe that?"

"God has always been with me," she says. "I have always heard his revelations. From before you were born."

"This is crazy," I say. "All of this."

She raises the pistol, points it at my head. "I do not need anyone to doubt me. Doubting me or doubting God is the same thing." Now it is her hand that's shaking. Her face is flushed and tears are leaking down her cheeks. Her eyes look like an electrical fire.

I hold my hands above my head. I say, "Look at me. I don't have a gun. I don't have anything. My hands are empty." I take another step toward her. Her pistol is only two feet from my face now. I say, "Don't pull the trigger. I'm your daughter. I'm your family."

"No quiero matarte." She takes a deep breath. A tear drips off the end of her chin. "And we need you because you are . . . fertile, because you could be . . ." She closes her eyes. Shakes her head.

The gun is raised but she lowers her head.

And that's when I jump forward, knocking the gun to the side. She pulls the trigger, but the bullet travels up through the trees.

My mother tries to punch me, and I grab her as we slip. Then we're wrestling on the ground, rolling in the grass, across the sidewalk, into the bark mulch of the next yard. I try to hit her, but her face is too close and we're still moving, rolling. I don't get a good swing at her, and my fist goes through her hair. Then her fingernails are gouging my cheek under my eye, and I scream as I squint my eye closed. The gun is between us—somehow still in her right hand—and I push it, push the barrel away from us, angle the pistol up and to the side. It goes off again but neither of us is shot.

We roll over—I'm underneath her now—then we roll over again. I'm above her once more, in the bushes, and there are rocks next to us. I'm holding the wrist of her right hand, her gun hand, and I beat that hand against a rock. The gun comes loose, flips and slides down a small gulley in the side yard.

I watch the gun settle in the rocks, stare at it for a second, and that's when my mother punches me, when she really connects, her fist hitting me directly in the eye. My head snaps back and I lose my balance, tilt, and gravity takes me over the embankment. But I have ahold of my mother still, one of my hands caught in her hair, and I rip her down with me. We roll twice, and there's a crack sound as we land in the bottom of a dry pond.

Then everything stops.

She's not fighting anymore.

She's not moving.

I untangle my hand from her hair, push up to a sitting position. Look at her.

The back of her head hit a rock, and she's unconscious. But she's still breathing. She's taking loud, short little breaths, whimpering a little bit, whispering something in Spanish with her eyes closed.

I see the pistol next to her in the rocks and I grab it, toss it over by the canoe. Then I feel my eye where my mother punched me, feel the swelling, the bruise rising. I can feel a small cut at the corner of my eye as well.

I lean down and roll my mother over, see a large egg-sized lump growing on the back of her head, a spot of blood on the rock that she hit. I let go of her and stand up. She opens her eyes and says something I don't understand, then closes her eyes again.

I look up at the sky, cloudless and pale blue, realize how hot it is and how much I'm sweating in this heat. Everything is too bright—the sun rotating on a burning spike in the middle of the sky—no shadows anywhere. I feel dizzy and I stumble. Go down on one knee and catch my breath. I realize I need water. Sleep. Food.

I walk over to my canoe at the waterline, toss the gun in. Retrieve a bottle of water. I drink the entire thing. Then I reach in and get another. I start to drink that one too, but then I stop, put the cap back on. I walk back over to the yard, to the embankment and the gulley.

My mother is lying down in the bottom still, but her eyes are open. She looks at me and doesn't say anything. There are bark chips in her hair, bark chips all over her clothes. I look down at myself and see that I've got bark mulch all over me as well. I brush some of it off the front of my pants. Shake out my T-shirt. Then I step over next to my mother, lean down, and set the water bottle next to her head. "Drink this when you feel a little better. But take it slow. Stay down until you're feeling okay."

She doesn't respond. She doesn't say anything.

"This is it," I say. "I'm going now."

There's nothing else to do. If I stayed, I wouldn't change her mind. I'm already gone, and she'll never be the same. She'll never be who she was ten years ago, when I was a little girl. And I'm not little anymore either.

My mother licks her lips. There's a cut on her tongue, and the blood paints her lips red. "You are without God," she says. "Estás sin Dios, m'hija. Perdida."

"I've been stuck here," I say. "I've been stuck for a long time, but I've never been lost."

She stares at me, and her eyes look hateful. She doesn't say anything else.

I turn and walk to my canoe. Push the stern and step into the boat as it glides out into the floodwater.

EPILOGUE

PORTLAND IS A hundred miles north, a large city, much larger than Eugene, but I know it could be more destroyed than here since it's closer to the coast and between two rivers. Plus, any survivors in a big city might be scarier than what I've already encountered. So I cross Portland off my list of possibilities.

In that same direction, downriver—north on the Willamette—there are two medium-sized towns, but I know both could be full of Collection members. There were so many articles about The Collection "owning" those towns the last two years. Maybe many of The Collection members didn't survive the earthquake, but still I don't want to chance it.

So where do I go?

I drift and think about the options. Above me, the cottonwoods shiver in the afternoon breeze. Their leaves make a sound like rain, and I paddle through their weave, hear an osprey calling its hunt, and something turning over in the water a few feet behind my canoe, a carp or a nutria.

My hand throbs, and I daub triple-antibiotic medicine on the thick burn scab at the stub of my pinky. Swallow a Vicodin. Feel the current of my pumping blood soften in my brain.

I paddle northwest, across the widest part of the river, turn up-flood—east—at the high plain of the old city landfill, the former county dumpsite now covered, long grass waving a yellow color in the water beneath my canoe.

I paddle all afternoon, through the slack floodwater between the two rivers, making my way north toward the waterway of the McKenzie River. But before I get there, I turn east, toward the mountains, in the direction of the old dams that crumbled in the earthquake. I choose the east fork and begin paddling to the foothills and the rising ground.

When it's late, almost dark, I tie off to backwater branches, eat a dry dinner and drink a Powerade, then squat on an island hummock to pee, my feet and ankles submerged in the river water. Then I lay my sleeping bag across the tops of the gear bins in the canoe. The lids of the bins make ridges in my sleeping pad, but I fall asleep immediately, regardless of the ridge that digs into my hip.

I'm so tired from the last few days that I don't wake up a single time all night long.

In the morning, my injured hand has stiffened to a claw, and I have to work the tendons to get them to relax. I kneed my palm with my opposite thumb, open and close my remaining fingers. I swallow more Vicodin and wait to paddle, eating a breakfast of granola bars and drinking some water.

I paddle on, continuing all day east. In the afternoon, two peaks of the Cascades rise up through a gap in the foothills, the snowy summits of Middle and North Sister making white triangles in the glare of the late orange sun.

I continue to paddle and struggle to stay awake, telling myself stories, repeating lines from books, and rap lyrics; humming melodies from pop songs and quoting movies and jokes I can't quite remember correctly—anything to keep my eyes open as I paddle.

But I get more and more tired as I go.

Exhausted now. It feels like a plaster cast is settling on my shoulders, hardening and growing heavier with each passing hour. It's not that my arms are tired from paddling, even though that's also true. I feel emptied out from the last few weeks, like something has reached inside of me and scooped everything out—and now I'm this hollow shell that can barely support the weight on my shoulders.

I fall asleep sitting up in the canoe, wake later to a spinning boat, in a space between three huge trees on the side of what might be a branch of the river? I don't know. I'm not sure if I've floated down or been pushed to the side. I can't tell how long I've been asleep. Nothing around me looks familiar.

I drink a bottle of water. Eat a few crackers. Look around.

Then I paddle out to where I can get a better view, gaze at the hillside beyond the water, the fir trees on the ridge to the north, a red tail turning a wheeling arc, and—late evening—bats coming down to hunt bugs on top of the slack water, fluttering and weaving like wax paper lifting from fire.

Every day the same: dry food and water. Paddling and resting. Paddling some more. And nowhere that appears safe to stop, where I might feel comfortable sleeping out alone. I wonder about the millions of insects that die on earth each day, scrabbling and flying and dying in the fields and woods and water, against doors and windows, enclosures and open spaces—so many ways and places to die—and I know that I'm nothing more than one small life as I scrabble and paddle in my loaded canoe each day.

Close my eyes and open them again. Eat and drink. Cling to the possibility of something. The verb *esperar* en ingles means "to wait," but also "to hope," continuing this paddle each day as a small prayer for some unknown future.

I move east.

I tie off each night to tree branches or trunks of submerged trees, sleeping on top of my gear bins, far enough from any shoreline that people would never be able to see me in the dark.

I soak my finger stub in gluts of triple antibiotic.

Sometimes I pass houses like islands in the floodwater, more and more of them above the waterline as I move further east and rise slightly in elevation. All of the houses are abandoned until the first one that isn't empty has an old man on the porch. He stands up out of the shadows, with a deer rifle that he raises to his shoulder. I'm way too close, only a hundred feet out, and he's pointing the rifle at me.

He doesn't say anything. Levers the action.

"Please don't shoot!" I call out to him. "I'm not stopping! I won't bother you!" I hold up my hands for a moment, then continue paddling—away—turning even farther from his house. I call over my shoulder. "I don't have a gun! I don't have any weapons!" That's not true but seems like the wisest thing to say.

I keep paddling, look over my shoulder, and see that the old man is still following my motions with his rifle, the barrel still pointing at me as I continue east. Just before I get to a copse of fir trees, I look back one final time and see that he never lowered his gun, never sat back down. I slide into the dark grove, snake my canoe between flooded trunks until I'm deep in the shade—out of the old man's sight, finally—and then I can breathe again.

I hold a low branch. Take a moment.

My finger stub is bleeding. I rebandage the wound, then drink some water.

* * *

I try not to sleep during the afternoons on open water, try not to fall asleep while holding my paddle, even when I'm thick with the midday heat and drowsiness. I don't want to drop my paddle and lose it, or drift and stop my progress. I want to keep moving forward each day, keep moving in the direction of something, of another place, somewhere I might be able to stay during the winter.

On the fourth day, I notice that the water is getting significantly shallower. Four feet deep, then three. Far off to my right, the cars abandoned on Highway 126 are visible now, the water only to the middle of their wheels. I paddle past a farm that looks inhabited. I hesitate for a few minutes, consider stopping and talking to whoever might be there, but something about the house doesn't feel right, and I trust my instincts. Move on again. I won't stop unless I feel safe, unless something about the situation makes me feel at least mostly certain.

* * *

Finally—on the fifth day—I step out of my canoe onto a piece of property with an old farmhouse exposed, clear of the waterline, a two-story home on a small rise that looks like it was built in the last century along the McKenzie River. The house has clapboard siding and a tin roof gone to rust. I stop because this is the first place that seems okay. It looks like there might be only one or two people living here. Something about it feels right to me.

The raised garden beds next to the house are well tended. I see potato plants, bright green leaves, carrots and cucumbers, zucchinis and tomatoes. A few beans and peas still drying on the vines. Cornstalks taller than me along the southern side of the house.

I reach back into my canoe, retrieve my rifle. I lever a cartridge into the chamber and look around.

Behind the house, there's a clothesline: a women's underwear, skirts and T-shirts, and a brown dress, wet and clean, hanging on the line strung between the house and an outbuilding. I don't see any men's clothing. I walk up and touch a dress to see if it's still damp, and it is.

I look at the house and hesitate.

The low ground between the buildings is newly freed from floodwater, and there are footprints, but it's hard to tell if they're man-sized or a woman's. Only one set. Only one foot size.

I stand and think. Take a few breaths. Shake my head. Then I walk back to my canoe, hold the bow, the front of the boat resting on the angled bank.

I try to decide what to do.

I'm looking at the only house in this section of the valley, the submerged fields all around me part of what must have been a huge farm. I examine the open space, not sure what was growing on the acres near the house, but I see hazelnuts in a big section off to my right, old trees with moss-covered branches and new saplings with their green leaves just poking above the water.

I decide to walk back up to the house.

The deep mud before the rise holds the soles of my shoes, then releases, holds and releases, making a thick sucking sound with each step, and I know that whoever's inside the farmhouse can hear me. They know I'm here. I'm certain that I'm being watched, but there are curtains on the house at every window, and I'm out in this bright sun, unable to discern anything inside the darkened house.

I tighten my grip on the rifle but I don't point my gun at the house. I want them to know that I'm not stupid—not wandering this floodland unarmed—but also that I'm not a threat to them. Not now anyway. This is a subtle dance, and I'm not sure if I'm sending clear signals.

I look at my gun, then back at the house. Decide not to point it.

I clomp through the bog murk, around to the front, stepping through the long grass growing off the porch. I can hear the wave and click of locusts' wings, see the yellow and brown insects springing arcs away from my feet as I move toward the front door.

I step up onto the wrap-around porch.

Stop.

I'm holding my rifle in my good hand, and I say, "Hello? Is anyone here?"

The porch creaks as I step. I look down at my shoes, covered in mud.

"Hello?" I say again, looking at the windows, closing the distance. "Is anyone here?"

My rifle is loaded, but I don't point it at the door. I still feel okay about this house. Somehow. I don't think I'll have to shoot whoever's living here.

I knock on the door.

Wait.

Nothing happens. No one answers.

I knock again with my left hand. See my missing finger. Make a fist to hide that hand, twisting the fist into the hem of my T-shirt.

I lift the gun to tap the butt of the rifle on the oak door, intending to knock one last time.

But as I reach with the gun, the door opens.

ACKNOWLEDGMENTS

AMERICAN AFTERLIFE IS the first book I've written since my traumatic brain injury (from my collision with an SUV while biking to work). I'll get into that story more with the acknowledgments for book two in this series, since the narrator of that second book has a brain injury, but I will say that I couldn't write for two years. I couldn't work. I couldn't teach. I lost my agent and editor, and most people lost faith in me as a writer. I was unmoored by my accident the way Cielo was unmoored by the earthquake and her own loneliness. Because of that significant drift and loss in my life, I am so grateful to the people who still believed in me and helped this book come to publication even as I struggled.

First, thank you to my oldest writing partner and friend, José Chaves. Without his clear insight, guidance, and critical assessment of my earliest fiction, I would have never become the writer I am today. Each book is a testament to Jose's initial advice and dark sense of humor.

Particular to this story, I am grateful to the people of K-59 and the surrounding pueblos, Mexico, for my experiences there when I was a child, which inspired a lot of this novel's backstory, both light and dark. Standing next to a lettuce field, seeing a dead fieldworker shot in the chest, is one of the strangest images from my childhood. These are the moments that tilt our minds but also help us to become more empathetic, detailed writers in the future.

To the poets and story writers who inspired me while I was creating this novel: Natalie Diaz, Alejandra Pizarnik, Jhumpa Lahiri, Junot Diaz, Lucia Perillo, Mary Oliver, Toni Morrison, Patrick deWitt, and Cormac McCarthy.

And a special thank-you to the author friends who were kind and encouraging as I wrote and revised: Jeff Zentner, Willy Vlautin, Kathleen Glasgow, Anna Grace, Tom Cantwell, David Arnold, Cai Emmons, Dorianne Laux, Mindy McGinnis, and Michael Copperman.

Also a big thanks to incredibly encouraging friends like Hira Shamsuddin, Carlos Felipe Peña, River Donaghey, Greg Dunkin, Rebecca Gourgey, Ben Temple, Luke Mazziotti, Betsie and Caleb Rexius, Horace and Aimee Dodd, Bobbie Willis, Ingrid Bodtker, Corrina Welding, Sonja Jameson, and Jeff Hess.

A special thank-you to UX designer Kristen Burg, who encouraged me and helped me at a time when I felt like my career was over. Your strategies, the website you created for me, and your kind, funny Zoom calls were exactly what I needed right then.

Thank you to Ben "The King" Leroy, my closest ally in the book world and one of my closest friends. For an artist, it is so important to know that you have one person out there who always believes in your work. I don't know how I got so lucky when I met you.

Thank you to Yishai Seidman, who took me on when I was lost. You remained optimistic, encouraged me as we submitted, and worked out the terms for this book when things looked a little bleak.

Thank you to Sara J. Henry, my wonderful editor at Crooked Lane, who helped me to understand the structure of a thriller and who made this book immeasurably better. Your blunt, brilliant editorial style is a perfect match for my writing.

Thank you to the whole team at Crooked Lane: Matt Martz for saying yes, Melissa Rechter for editorial and production help, Madeline Rathle and Dulce Botello for marketing acumen, Kate McManus for skilled intern help, Nicole Lecht for a gorgeous cover that immediately garnered buzz, and a particular thanks to Rebecca Nelson, who seems to do absolutely everything for Crooked Lane authors. Thank you for welcoming me into the house and championing this book.

Also, a special note to Jill Pellarin, copy editor of this book but also the best copy editor I've ever worked with in my eleven-year author career. I was astounded by the diligence of your style sheet. You clearly make books stronger.

Thank you to my climbing partners and adventure friends who helped keep me sane these past three years: Marcos Alamo, Elton Steyding, Phil Morton, Hans Florine, Max Buschini, Taylor Chocek, Elisa Miller, and Brian Naghski; and to my current student leaders in the outdoor program for their collective stoke and senses of humor: Kacy Anderson, Hailey Bertelsen, Acacia Hahn, Jessie Hawes, Whit Schatz, and Sahara Valentine.

Thank you to my siblings, nieces, nephews, and parents, who each gave me different gifts. To my father, for teaching me how to get up early and work on a project every single day, and to my mother, for inspiring me to be an author, reading aloud to me, and making any artist seem like a world-saving hero.

To my J: This is such a complicated and weird time, and I am so grateful to have a partner like you to help navigate these strange experiences. Thank you for always believing that I would write well again. I don't know how you kept the faith, but I am so appreciative.

To my Lluvia, Rainy: Thank you for adventuring with me the last few years. All of our time outside together helped build back my brain, and I'm so grateful for every time I get to rock climb with you. You helped me heal, and your sense of adventure is inspiring to me.

And finally, to my Rue—to whom this book is dedicated, the model for Cielo: these have not been an easy two years for you. Your high school experience should never have been this way. But you are phenomenal, strong, and capable. I am so impressed by who you are and what you are, which is a dragon, always and forever.

With a brain injury, I'm always writing lists yet still forgetting so many things. I'm probably forgetting someone important, and I'm sorry for that. Cielo and I are a little lost right now. We can't predict the future. The floodwaters are still murky.